TO SEE YOU AGAIN

STORIES BY

ALICE ADAMS

To See You Again

TO SEE YOU AGAIN

Stories by
Alice Adams

 Alfred A. Knopf   New York   1982

THIS IS A BORZOI BOOK
PUBLISHED BY ALFRED A. KNOPF, INC.

"An Unscheduled Stop," "At the Beach," "Berkeley
House," "By the Sea," "The Girl Across the Room,"
"Greyhound People," "Lost Luggage," "Snow," and "To
See You Again" were originally published in The New
Yorker.

"The Party-Givers" was originally published in Epoch.

Other stories have been published in The Atlantic
Monthly, Cosmopolitan, Shenandoah, and The Virginia
Quarterly.

Library of Congress Cataloging in Publication Data
Adams, Alice [date]
To see you again. I. Title.
PS3551.D324T6 813'.54 81-15621
ISBN 0-394-52335-0   AACR2

Manufactured in the United States of America
First Edition

For Frances Kiernan,
with love and thanks

Contents

To See You Again

Snow

On a trail high up in the California Sierra, between heavy smooth white snowbanks, four people on cross-country skis form a straggling line. A man and three women: Graham, dark and good-looking, a San Francisco architect, who is originally from Georgia; Carol, his girlfriend, a gray-eyed blonde, a florist; Susannah, daughter of Graham, dark and fat and now living in Venice, California; and, quite a way behind Susannah, tall thin Rose, Susannah's friend and lover. Susannah and Rose both have film-related jobs—Graham has never been quite sure what they do.

Graham and Carol both wear smart cross-country outfits: knickers and Norwegian wool stockings. The younger women are in jeans and heavy sweaters. And actually, despite the bright cold look of so much snow, this April day is warm, and the sky is a lovely spring blue, reflected in distant small lakes, just visible, at intervals.

Graham is by far the best skier of the four, a natural; he does anything athletic easily. He strides and glides along, hardly aware of what he is doing, except for a sense of physical well-being. However, just now he is cursing himself for having dreamed up this weekend, renting an unknown house in Alpine Meadows, near Lake Tahoe, even for bringing these women together. He had hoped for a diversion from a situation that could be tricky, difficult: a visit from Susannah, who was bringing Rose, whom he had previously been told about but had not met. Well, skiing was a diversion, but what in God's name would they all do tonight? Or talk about? And why had he wanted to get them together anyway? He wasn't all that serious about Carol (was he?); why introduce her to his daughter? And why did he have to meet Rose?

Carol is a fair skier, although she doesn't like it much: it takes all her breath. At the moment, with the part of her mind that is not concentrated on skiing, she is thinking that although Graham is smarter than most of the men she knows, talented and successful, and really nice as well, she is tired of going out with men who don't *see* her, don't know who she is. That's partly her fault, she knows; she lies about her age and dyes her hair, and she *never* mentions the daughter in Vallejo, put out for adoption when Carol was fifteen (she would be almost twenty now, almost as old as Graham's girl, this unfriendly fat Susannah). But sometimes Carol would like to say to the men she knows, Look, I'm thirty-five, and in some ways my life has been terrible— being blond and pretty doesn't save you from anything.

But, being more fair-minded than given to self-pity, next Carol thinks, Well, as far as that goes Graham didn't tell me much about his girl, either, and for all I know mine is that way, too. So many of them are, these days.

How can he possibly be so dumb, Susannah is passionately thinking, of her father. And the fact that she has asked that question hundreds of times in her life does not diminish its intensity or the accompanying pain. He doesn't understand anything, she wildly, silently screams. Stupid, straight blondes: a *florist*. *Skiing*. How could he think that I . . . that Rose . . . ?

Then, thinking of Rose in a more immediate way, she remembers that Rose has hardly skied before—just a couple of times in Vermont, where she comes from. In the almost noon sun Susannah stops to wait for Rose, halfheartedly aware of the lakes, just now in view, and the smell of pines, as sweat collects under her heavy breasts, slides down her ribs.

Far behind them all, and terrified of everything, Rose moves along with stiffened desperation. Her ankles, her calves, her thighs, her lower back are all tight with dread. Snow is stuck to the bottoms of her skis, she knows—she can hardly move them—but she doesn't dare stop. She will fall, break something, get lost. And everyone will hate her, even Susannah.

Suddenly, like a gift to a man in his time of need, just ahead of Graham there appears a lovely open glade, to one side of the trail. Two huge heavy trees have fallen there, at right angles to each other; at the far side of the open space runs a brook, darkly glistening over small smooth rocks. High overhead a wind sings through the pines, in the brilliant sunlight.

It is perfect, a perfect picnic place, and it is just now time for lunch. Graham is hungry; he decides that hunger is what has been unsettling him. He gets out of his skis in an instant, and he has just found a smooth, level stump for the knapsack, a natural table, when Carol skis up—out of breath, not looking happy.

But at the sight of that place she instantly smiles. She says, "Oh, how perfect! Graham, it's beautiful." Her gray eyes praise him, and the warmth of her voice. "Even benches to sit on. Graham, what a perfect Southern host you are." She laughs in a pleased, cheered-up way, and bends to unclip her skis. But something is wrong, and they stick. Graham comes over to help. He gets her out easily; he takes her hand and lightly he kisses her mouth, and then they both go over and start removing food from the knapsack, spreading it out.

"Two bottles of wine. Lord, we'll all get plastered." Carol laughs again, as she sets up the tall green bottles in a deep patch of snow.

Graham laughs, too, just then very happy with her, although he is also feeling the familiar apprehension that any approach of his daughter brings on: *will* Susannah like what he has done, will she approve of him, ever? He looks at his watch and he says to Carol, "I wonder if they're okay. Rose is pretty new on skis. I wonder . . ."

But there they are, Susannah and Rose. They have both taken off their skis and are walking along the side of the trail, carrying the skis on their shoulders, Susannah's neatly together, Rose's at a clumsy, difficult angle. There are snowflakes in Susannah's dark-brown hair—hair like Graham's. Rose's hair is light, dirty blond; she is not even pretty, Graham has unkindly thought. At the moment they both look exhausted and miserable.

In a slow, tired way, not speaking, the two girls lean their skis and poles against a tree; they turn toward Graham and Carol, and then, seemingly on a single impulse, they stop and look around. And with a wide smile Susannah says, "Christ, Dad, it's just beautiful. It's great."

Rose looks toward the spread of food. "Oh, roast chicken. That's my favorite thing." These are the first nice words she has said to Graham. (Good manners are not a strong suit of Rose's, he has observed, in an interior, Southern voice.)

He has indeed provided a superior lunch, as well as the

lovely place—his discovery. Besides the chicken, there are cherry tomatoes (called love apples where Graham comes from, in Georgia), cheese (Jack and cheddar), Triscuits and oranges and chocolate. And the nice cold dry white wine. They all eat and drink a lot, and they talk eagerly about how good it all is, how beautiful the place where they are. The sky, the trees, the running brook.

Susannah even asks Carol about her work, in a polite, interested way that Graham has not heard from her for years. "Do you have to get up early and go to the flower mart every morning?" Susannah asks.

"No, but I used to, and really that was more fun— getting out so early, all those nice fresh smells. Now there's a boy I hire to do all that, and I'm pretty busy making arrangements."

"Oh, arrangements," says Rose, disparagingly.

Carol laughs. "Me, too, I hate them. I just try to make them as nice as I can, and the money I get is really good."

Both Rose and Susannah regard Carol in an agreeing, respectful way. For a moment Graham is surprised: these kids respecting money? Then he remembers that this is the Seventies: women are supposed to earn money, it's good for them.

The main thing, though, is what a good time they all have together. Graham even finds Rose looking at him with a small, shy smile. He offers her more wine, which she accepts —another smile as he pours it out for her. And he thinks, Well, of course it's tough on her, too, meeting me. Poor girl, I'm sure she's doing the best she can.

"You all really like it down there in Hollywood?" he asks the two girls, and he notes that his voice is much more Southern than usual; maybe the wine.

"Universal City," Susannah corrects him, but she gives a

serious answer. "I love it. There's this neat woman in the cutting room, and she knows I'm interested, so she lets me come in and look at the rushes, and hear them talk about what has to go. I'm really learning. It's great."

And Rose: "There's so many really exciting people around."

At that moment they both look so young, so enviably involved in their work, so happy, that Graham thinks, Well, really, why not?

Occasionally the wind will move a branch from a nearby tree and some snow will sift down, through sunlight. The sky seems a deeper blue than when they first came to this glade, a pure azure. The brook gurgles more loudly, and the sun is very hot.

And then they are all through with lunch; they have finished off the wine, and it is time to go.

They put on their skis, and they set off again, in the same order in which they began the day.

For no good reason, as he glides along, striding through snow in the early California afternoon, the heat, Graham is suddenly, sharply visited by a painful memory of the childhood of Susannah. He remembers a ferociously hot summer night in Atlanta, when he and his former wife, mother of Susannah, had quarreled all through suppertime, and had finally got Susannah off to bed; she must have been about two. But she kept getting up again, screaming for her bottle, her Teddy bear, a sandwich. Her mother and Graham took turns going in to her, and then finally, about three in the morning, Graham picked her up and smacked her bottom, very hard; he can remember the sting on his hand—and good Christ, what a thing to do to a little baby. No wonder she is as she is; he probably frightened her right then, for good. Not to mention all the other times he got mad and just yelled at her—or his love affairs, the move to San Francisco, the divorce, more love affairs.

If only she were two right now, he desperately thinks, he could change everything; he could give her a stable, loving father. Now he has a nice house on Russian Hill; he is a successful man; he could give her—anything.

Then his mind painfully reverses itself and he thinks, But I was a loving father, most of the time. Susannah's got no real cause to be the way she is. Lots of girls—most girls—come out all right. At that overheated moment he feels that his heart will truly break. It is more than I can stand, he thinks; why do I have to?

Carol's problem is simply a physical one: a headache. But she never has headaches, and this one is especially severe; for the first time she knows exactly what her mother meant by "splitting headache." Is she going to get more and more like her mother as she herself ages? Could she be having an early menopause, beginning with migraines? She could die, the pain is so sharp. She could die, and would anyone care much, really? She's *lonely*.

Susannah is absorbed in the problem of Rose, who keeps falling down. Almost every time Susannah looks back, there is Rose, fallen in the snow. Susannah smiles at her encouragingly, and sometimes she calls back, "You're okay?" She knows that Rose would not like it if she actually skied back to her and helped her up; Rose has that ferocious Vermont Yankee pride, difficult in a fragile frightened woman.

It is breezier now than earlier in the morning, and somewhat cooler. Whenever Susannah stops, stands still and waits for Rose, she is aware of her own wind-chilled sweat, and she worries, thinking of Rose, of wet and cold. Last winter Rose had a terrible, prolonged bout of flu, a racking cough.

Talking over their "relationship," at times Susannah and Rose have (somewhat jokingly) concluded that there certainly are elements of mothering within it; in many ways Susannah takes care of Rose. She is stronger—that is simply true. Now for the first time it occurs to Susannah (wryly, her style is wry) that she is somewhat fatherly with Rose, too: the sometimes stern guardian, the protector. And she thinks, Actually, Graham wasn't all that bad with me; I've been rough on him. Look at the example he set me: I work hard, and I care about my work, the way he does. And he taught me to ski, come to think of it. I should thank him, sometime, somehow, for some of it.

Rose is falling, falling, again and again, and oh Christ, how much she hates it—hates her helplessness, hates the horrible snow, the cold wet. Drinking all that wine at lunchtime, in the pretty glade, the sunlight, she had thought that wine would make her brave; she knows her main problem to be fear—no confidence and hence no balance. But the wine, and the sun, and sheer fatigue have destroyed whatever equilibrium she had, so that all she can do is fall, fall miserably, and each time the snow is colder and it is harder for her to get up.

Therefore, they are all extremely glad when, finally, they are all out of their skis and off the trail and at last back in their house, in Alpine Meadows. It is small—two tiny, juxtaposed bedrooms—but the living room is pleasant: it looks out to steeply wooded, snowy slopes. Even more pleasant at the moment is the fact that the hot-water supply is vast; there is enough for deep baths for everyone, and then they will all have much-needed before-dinner naps.

Carol gets the first bath, and then, in turn, the two younger women. Graham last. All three women have left a tidy room, a clean tub, he happily notices, and the steamy air smells vaguely sweet, of something perfumed, feminine. Luxuriating in his own full, hot tub, he thinks tenderly, in a general way, of women, how warm and sexual they are, more often than not, how frequently intelligent and kind. And then he wonders what he has not quite, ever, put into words before: what is it that women do, women together? What ever could they do that they couldn't do with men, and *why?*

However, these questions are much less urgent and less painful than most of his musings along those lines; he simply wonders.

In their bedroom, disappointingly, Carol is already fast asleep. He has not seen her actually sleeping before; she is always first awake when he stays over at her place. Now she looks so drained, so entirely exhausted, with one hand protectively across her eyes, that he is touched. Carefully, so as not to wake her, he slips in beside her, and in minutes he, too, is sound asleep.

Graham has planned and shopped for their dinner, which he intends to cook. He likes to cook, and does it well, but in his bachelor life he has done it less and less, perhaps because he and most of the women he meets tend to shy off from such domestic encounters. Somehow the implication of cooking *for* anyone has become alarming, more so than making love to them. But tonight Graham happily prepares to make pork chops with milk gravy and mashed potatoes, green peas, an apple-and-nut salad and cherry pie (from a bakery, to be heated). A down-home meal, for his girlfriend, and his daughter, and her friend.

From the kitchen, which is at one end of the living room, he can hear the pleasant sounds of the three women's voices, in amiable conversation, as he blends butter and flour in the pan in which he has browned the chops, and begins to add hot milk. And then he notices a change in the tone of those voices: what was gentle and soft has gone shrill, strident—the sounds of a quarrel. He hates the thought of women fighting; it is almost frightening, and, of course, he is anxious for this particular group to get along, if only for the weekend.

He had meant, at just that moment, to go in and see if anyone wanted another glass of wine; dinner is almost ready. And so, reluctantly he does; he gets into the living room just in time to hear Rose say, in a shakily loud voice, "No one who hasn't actually experienced rape can have the least idea what it's like."

Such a desperately serious sentence could have sounded ludicrous, but it does not. Graham is horrified; he thinks, Ah, poor girl, poor Rose. Jesus, *raped*. It is a crime that he absolutely cannot imagine.

In a calm, conciliatory way, Susannah says to Carol, "You see, Rose actually was raped, when she was very young, and it was terrible for her—"

Surprisingly, Carol reacts almost with anger. "Of course it's terrible, but you kids think you're the only ones things happen to. I got pregnant when I was fifteen, and I had it, a girl, and I put her out for adoption." Seeming to have just now noticed Graham, she addresses him in a low, defiant, scolding voice. "And I'm not thirty. I'm thirty-five."

Graham has no idea, really, of what to do, but he is aware of strong feelings that lead him to Carol. He goes over and puts his arms around her. Behind him he hears the gentle voice of Susannah, who is saying, "Oh Carol, that's terrible. God, that's *awful*."

Carol's large eyes are teary, but in a friendly way she disengages herself from Graham; she even smiles as she says, "Well, I'm sorry, I didn't mean to say that. But you see? You really can't tell what's happened to anyone."

And Susannah: "Oh, you're right, of course you are. . . ."

And Rose: "It's true, we do get arrogant. . . ."

Graham says that he thinks they should eat. The food is hot; they must be hungry. He brings the dinner to them at the table, and he serves out hot food onto the heated plates.

Carol and Rose are talking about the towns they came from: Vallejo, California, and Manchester, Vermont.

"It's thirty miles from San Francisco," Carol says. "And that's all we talked about. The City. How to get there, and what was going on there. Vallejo was just a place we ignored, dirt under our feet."

"All the kids in Manchester wanted to make it to New York," Rose says. "All but me, and I was fixated on Cambridge. Not getting into Radcliffe was terrible for me—it's why I never went to college at all."

"I didn't either," Carol says, with a slight irony that Graham thinks may have been lost on Rose: Carol would not have expected to go to college, probably—it wasn't what high-school kids from Vallejo did. But how does he know this?

"I went to work instead," says Rose, a little priggishly (thinks Graham).

"Me too," Carol says, with a small laugh.

Susannah breaks in. "Dad, this is absolutely the greatest dinner. You're still the best cook I know. It's good I don't have your dinners more often."

"I'm glad you like it. I haven't cooked a lot lately."

And Rose, and Carol: "It's super. It's great."

Warmed by praise, and just then wanting to be nice to Rose (partly because he has to admit to himself that he doesn't much like her), Graham says to her, "Cambridge was where I wanted to go to school, too. The Harvard School of Design. Chicago seemed second-best. But I guess it's all worked out."

"I guess." Rose smiles.

She looks almost pretty at that moment, but not quite; looking at her, Graham thinks again, If it had to be another girl, why her? But he knows this to be unfair, and, as far as that goes, why anyone for anyone, when you come to think of it? Any pairing is basically mysterious.

Partly as a diversion from such unsettling thoughts, and also from real curiosity, he asks Carol, "But was it worth it when you got to the city?"

She laughs, in her low, self-depreciating way. "Oh, *I* thought so. I really liked it. My first job was with a florist on Union Street. It was nice there then, before it got all junked up with body shops and stuff. I had a good time."

Some memory of that era has put a younger, musing look on Carol's face, and Graham wonders if she is thinking of a love affair; jealously he wonders, Who? Who did you know, back then?

"I was working for this really nice older man," says Carol, in a higher than usual voice (as Graham thinks, *Ah*). "He taught me all he could. I was pretty dumb, at first. About marketing, arranging, keeping stuff fresh, all that. He lived by himself. A lonely person, I guess. He was—uh—gay, and then he died, and it turned out he'd left the store to me." For the second time that night tears have come to her eyes. "I was so touched, and it was too late to thank him, or anything." Then, the tears gone, her voice returns to its usual depth as she sums it up, "Well, that's how I got my start in the business world."

These sudden shifts in mood, along with her absolute refusal to see herself as an object of pity, are strongly, newly attractive to Graham; he has the sense of being with an unknown, exciting woman.

And then, in a quick, clairvoyant way, he gets a picture of Carol as a twenty-year-old girl, new in town: tall and a little awkward, working in the florist shop and worrying about her hands, her fingers scratched up from stems and wires; worrying about her darkening blond hair and then, deciding, what the hell, better dye it; worrying about money, and men, and her parents back in Vallejo—and *should* she have put the baby out for adoption? He feels an unfamiliar tenderness for this new Carol.

"You guys are making me feel very boring," says Susannah. "I always wanted to go to Berkeley, and I did, and I wanted to go to L.A. and work in films."

"I think you're just more direct," amends Rose, affectionate admiration in her voice, and in her eyes. "You just know what you're doing. I fall into things."

Susannah laughs. "Well, you do all right, you've got to admit." And, to Graham and Carol: "She's only moved up twice since January. At this rate she'll be casting something in August."

What Graham had earlier named discomfort he now recognizes as envy: Susannah is closer to Rose than she is to him; they are closer to each other than he is to anyone. He says, "Well, Rose, that's really swell. That's *swell*."

Carol glances at Graham for an instant before she says, "Well, I'll bet your father didn't even tell you about his most recent prize." And she tells them about an award from the

A.I.A., which Graham had indeed not mentioned to Susannah, but which had pleased him at the time of its announcement (immoderately, he told himself).

And now Susannah and Rose join Carol in congratulations, saying how terrific, really great.

Dinner is over, and in a rather disorganized way they all clear the table and load the dishwasher.

They go into the living room, where Graham lights the fire, and the three women sit down—or, rather, sprawl—Rose and Susannah at either end of the sofa, Carol in an easy chair. For dinner Carol put on velvet pants and a red silk shirt. In the bright hot firelight her gray eyes shine, and the fine line under her chin, that first age line, is just barely visible. She is very beautiful at that moment—probably more so now than she was fifteen years ago, Graham decides.

Susannah, in clean, faded, too tight Levi's, stretches her legs out stiffly before her. "Oh, I'm really going to feel that skiing in the morning!"

And Carol: "Me too. I haven't had that much exercise forever."

Rose says, "If I could just not fall."

"Oh, you won't; tomorrow you'll see. Tomorrow . . ." says everyone.

They are all exhausted. Silly to stay up late. And so as the fire dies down, Graham covers it and they all four go off to bed, in the two separate rooms.

Outside a strong wind has come up, creaking the walls and rattling windowpanes.

In the middle of the night, in what has become a storm —lashing snow and violent wind—Rose wakes up, terrified.

From the depths of bad dreams, she has no idea where she is, what time it is, what day. With whom she is. She struggles for clues, her wide eyes scouring the dark, her tentative hands reaching out, encountering Susannah's familiar, fleshy back. Everything comes into focus for her; she knows where she is. She breathes out softly, "Oh, thank God it's you," moving closer to her friend.

Greyhound People

As soon as I got on the bus, in the Greyhound station in Sacramento, I had a frightened sense of being in the wrong place. I had asked several people in the line at Gate 6 if this was the express to San Francisco, and they all said yes, but later, reviewing those assenting faces, I saw that in truth they all wore a look of people answering a question they have not entirely understood. Because of my anxiety and fear, I took a seat at the very front of the bus, across from and slightly behind the driver. There nothing very bad could happen to me, I thought.

What did happen, immediately, was that a tall black man, with a big mustache, angry and very handsome, stepped up into the bus and looked at me and said, "That's my seat. You in my seat. I got to have that seat." He was staring me straight in the eye, his flashing black into my scared pale blue.

There was nothing of his on the seat, no way I could have known that it belonged to him, and so that is what I said: "I didn't know it was your seat." But even as I was saying that, muttering, having ceased to meet his eye, I was also getting up and moving backward, to a seat two rows behind him.

Seated, apprehensively watching as the bus filled up, I saw that across the aisle from the black man were two women who seemed to be friends of his. No longer angry, he was sitting in the aisle seat so as to be near them; they were all talking and having a good time, glad to be together.

No one sat beside me, probably because I had put my large briefcase in that seat; it is stiff and forbidding-looking.

I thought again that I must be on the wrong bus, but just as I had that thought the driver got on, a big black man; he looked down the aisle for a second and then swung the door shut. He started up the engine as I wondered, What about tickets? Will they be collected in San Francisco? I had something called a commuter ticket, a book of ten coupons, and that morning, leaving San Francisco, I'd thought the driver took too much of my ticket, two coupons; maybe this was some mysterious repayment? We lurched out of the station and were on our way to San Francisco—or wherever.

Behind me, a child began to shout loud but not quite coherent questions: "Mom is that a river we're crossing? Mom do you see that tree? Mom is this a bus we're riding on?" He was making so much noise and his questions were all so crazy—senseless, really—that I did not see how I could stand it, all the hour and forty minutes to San Francisco, assuming that I was on the right bus, the express.

One of the women in the front seat, the friends of the man who had displaced me, also seemed unable to stand the child, and she began to shout back at him. "You the noisiest traveler I ever heard; in fact you ain't a traveler, you an observer."

"Mom does she mean me? Mom who is that?"

"Yeah, I means you. You the one that's talking."

"Mom who is that lady?" The child sounded more and more excited, and the black woman angrier. It was a terrible dialogue to hear.

And then I saw a very large white woman struggling up the aisle of the bus, toward the black women in the front, whom she at last reached and addressed: "Listen, my son's retarded and that's how he tests reality, asking questions. You mustn't make fun of him like that." She turned and headed back toward her seat, to her noisy retarded son.

The black women muttered to each other, and the boy began to renew his questions. "Mom see that cow?"

And then I heard one of the black women say, very loudly, having the last word: "And I got a daughter wears a hearing aid."

I smiled to myself, although I suppose it wasn't funny, but something about the black defiant voice was so appealing. And, as I dared for a moment to look around the bus, I saw that most of the passengers were black: a puzzle.

The scenery, on which I tried to concentrate, was very beautiful: smooth blond hills, gently rising, and here and there crevasses of shadow; and sometimes a valley with a bright white farmhouse, white fences, green space. And everywhere the dark shapes of live oaks, a black drift of lace against the hills or darkly clustered in the valleys, near the farms.

All this was on our left, the east, as we headed south toward San Francisco (I hoped). To our right, westward, the view was even more glorious: flat green pasturelands stretching out to the glittering bay, bright gold water and blue fingers of land, in the late May afternoon sunshine.

The retarded boy seemed to have taken up a friendly conversation with some people across the aisle from him, although his voice was still very loud. "My grandfather lives in Vallejo," he was saying. "Mom is that the sun over there?"

Just then, the bus turned right, turned off the freeway, and the driver announced, "We're just coming into Vallejo, folks. Next stop is Oakland, and then San Francisco."

I was on the wrong bus. Not on the express. Although this bus, thank God, did go on to San Francisco. But it would be at least half an hour late getting in. My heart sank as I thought, Oh, how angry Hortense will be.

The bus swung through what must have been the back streets of Vallejo. (A question: why are bus stations always in the worst parts of town, or is it that those worst parts grow up around the station?) As our bus ground to a halt, pushed into its slot in a line of other Greyhounds, before anyone else had moved, one of the women in the front seat stood up; she was thin, sharply angular, in a purple dress. She looked wonderful, I thought. "And you, you just shut up!" she said to the boy in the back.

That was her exit line; she flounced off the bus ahead of everyone else, soon followed by her friend and the handsome man who had dislodged me from my seat.

A few people applauded. I did not, although I would have liked to, really.

This was my situation: I was working in San Francisco as a statistician in a government office having to do with unemployment, and that office assigned me to an office in Sacramento for ten weeks. There was very little difference between the offices; they were interchangeable, even to the pale-green coloring of the walls. But that is why I was commuting back and forth to Sacramento.

I was living with Hortense (temporarily, I hoped, although of course it was nice of her to take me in) because

my husband had just divorced me and he wanted our apartment—or he wanted it more than I did, and I am not good at
arguing.

Hortense is older than I am, with grown-up children,
now gone. She seems to like to cook and take care; and when
I started commuting she told me she'd meet me at the bus
station every night, because she worried about the neighborhood, Seventh Street near Market, where the bus station is. I
suppose some people must have assumed that we were a
lesbian couple, even that I had left my husband for Hortense, but that was not true; my husband left me for a beautiful young Japanese nurse (he is in advertising), and it was
not sex or love that kept me and Hortense together but sheer
dependency (mine).

A lot of people got off the bus at Vallejo, including the
pale fat lady and her poor son; as they passed me I saw that
he was clinging closely to his mother, and that the way he
held his neck was odd, not right. I felt bad that in a way I
had sided against him, with the fierce black lady in purple.
But I had to admit that of the two of them it was her I would
rather travel with again.

A lot of new people began to get on the bus, and again
they were mostly black; I guessed that they were going to
Oakland. With so many people it seemed inconsiderate to
take up two seats, even if I could have got away with it, so I
put my briefcase on the floor, at my feet.

And I looked up to find the biggest woman I had ever
seen, heading right for me. Enormous—she must have
weighed three times what I did—and black and very young.

She needed two seats to herself, she really did, and of
course she knew that; she looked around, but almost all the
seats were taken, and so she chose me, because I am rela-

tively thin, I guess. With a sweet apologetic smile, she squeezed in beside me—or, rather, she squeezed me in.

"Ooooh, I am so *big*," she said, in a surprisingly soft small voice. "I must be crushing you almost to death."

"Oh no, I'm fine," I assured her, and we smiled at each other.

"And you so thin," she observed.

As though being thin required an apology, I explained that I was not that way naturally, I was living with an over-weight friend who kept me on fish and salads, mostly.

She laughed. "Well, maybe I should move in with your friend, but it probably wouldn't do me no good."

I laughed, too, and I wondered what she did, what job took her from Oakland to Vallejo.

We talked, and after a while she told me that she worked in Oakland, as well as lived there, not saying at what, but that she was taking a course in Vallejo in the care of special children, which is what she really wanted to do. " 'Special' mean the retards and the crazies," she said, but she laughed in a kindly way, and I thought how good she probably would be with kids.

I told her about the retarded boy who got off the bus at Vallejo, after all those noisy questions.

"No reason you can't tell a retard to quiet down," she said. "They got no call to disturb folks, it don't help them none."

Right away then I felt better; it was okay for me not to have liked all that noise and to have sided with the black woman who told the boy to shut up.

I did like that big young woman, and when we got to Oakland I was sorry to see her go. We both said that we had enjoyed talking to each other; we said we hoped that we would run into each other again, although that seemed very unlikely.

. . .

In San Francisco, Hortense was pacing the station—very worried, she said, and visibly angry.

I explained to her that it was confusing, three buses leaving Sacramento for San Francisco at just the same time, five-thirty. It was very easy to get on the wrong one.

"Well, I suppose you'll catch on after a couple of weeks," she said, clearly without much faith that I ever would.

She was right about one thing, though: the San Francisco bus station, especially at night, is a cold and scary place. People seem to be just hanging out there—frightened-looking young kids, maybe runaways, belligerent-looking drunks and large black men, with swaggering hats, all of whom look mysteriously enraged. The lighting is a terrible white glare, harsh on the dirty floors, illuminating the wrinkles and grime and pouches of fatigue on all the human faces. A cold wind rushes in through the swinging entrance doors. Outside, there are more dangerous-looking loiterers, whom Hortense and I hurried past that night, going along Seventh Street to Market, where she had parked in a yellow zone but had not (thank God) been ticketed.

For dinner we had a big chef's salad, so nutritious and slenderizing, but also so cold that it felt like a punishment. What I really would have liked was a big hot fattening baked potato.

I wondered, How would I look if I put on twenty pounds?

Early mornings at the Greyhound station are not so bad, with only a few drunks and lurching loiterers on the street outside, and it is easy to walk past them very fast, swinging a briefcase. Inside, there are healthy-looking, resolute kids with enormous backpacks, off to conquer the wilderness. And it is easy, of course, to find the right bus, the express to Sacramento; there is only one, leaving every hour on the hour. I almost always got to sit by myself. But somehow the same scenery that you see coming down to San Francisco is very boring viewed from the other direction. Maybe this is an effect of the leveling morning light—I don't know.

One day, though, the bus was more crowded than usual and a young girl asked if she could sit next to me. I said okay, and we started up one of those guarded and desultory conversations that travel dictates. What most struck me about her was her accent; I could tell exactly where she was from —upstate New York. I am from there, too, from Binghamton, although I have taken on some other accents along the way, mainly my husband's—Philadelphia. (I hope I do not get to sound like Hortense, who is from Florida.) Of course I did not ask the girl where she was from—too personal, and I didn't have to—but she told me, unasked, that she worked in an office in Sacramento, which turned out to be in the building next to mine. That seemed ominous to me: a girl coming from exactly where I am from, and heading in my same direction. I did not want her to tell me any more about her life, and she did not.

Near Sacramento, the concrete road dividers have been planted with oleander, overflowing pink and white blossoms that quite conceal oncoming traffic in the other lanes. It is hard to believe that the highway commissioners envisioned such a wild profusion, and somehow it makes me uneasy to see all that bloom, maybe because I read somewhere that oleander is poisonous. Certainly it is unnaturally hardy.

The Sacramento station is more than a little weird, being the jumping-off place for Reno, so to speak. Every morning there are lines for the Reno buses, lines of gamblers, all kinds: big women in bright synthetic fabrics, and seedy old men, drunks, with tired blue eyes and white indoor skin, smoking cigarillos. Gamblers seem to smoke a lot, I noticed. I also noticed that none of them are black.

A large elevated sign lists the departures for South Lake Tahoe and Reno: the Nugget express, which leaves at 3:40 a.m.; the dailies to Harrah's, starting at 9:05 a.m.; and on weekends you can leave for Reno any time between 2:35 a.m. and 11:15 p.m. I find it very hard to imagine going to Reno at any of those times, but then I am not a gambler.

Unfortunately, I again saw that same girl, Miss Upstate New York, the next few times that I took the correct bus, the express at five-thirty to San Francisco. She began to tell me some very boring things about her office—she did not like her boss, he drank—and her boyfriend, who wanted to invest in some condominiums at South Lake Tahoe.

I knew that Hortense would never believe that it was a mistake, and just possibly it was not, but a few nights later I took another wrong bus, really wrong: the local that stops everywhere, at Davis and Dixon and Fairfield, all down the line. Hortense was going to be furious. I began to work on some plausible lies: I got to the station late, this wrong bus left from the gate that the right bus usually leaves from. But then I thought, How ridiculous; and the very fact of Hortense's being there waiting for me began to seem a little silly, both of us being grown up.

Again most of the passengers were black, and I sensed a sort of camaraderie among them. It occurred to me that they were like people who have recently won a war, although I knew that to be not the case, not at all, in terms of their present lives. But with all the stops and starts the trip was very interesting; I would have been having a very good time if it were not for two things: one, I was worried about Hortense; and, two, I did not see again any of those people who were on my first wrong trip—not the very fat black woman or the skinny one in purple, or the handsome man who displaced me from my seat.

Just in front of me were an elderly man and woman, both black, who seemed to be old friends accidentally encountered on this bus. They exchanged information about how they both were, their families, and then the woman said, "Well, the weekend's coming up." "Yep, jes one more day." "Then you can rest." "Say, you ever see a poor man rest?"

Recently I read an interview with a distinguished lady of letters, in which she was asked why she wrote so obsessively about the very poor, the tiredest and saddest poorest people, and that lady, a Southerner, answered, "But I myself am poor people."

That touched me to the quick, somehow. I am too. Hortense is not, I think.

Across the aisle from me I suddenly noticed the most beautiful young man I had ever seen, sound asleep. A golden boy: gold hair and tawny skin, large beautiful hands spread loosely on his knees, long careless legs in soft pale washed-out jeans. I hardly dared look at him; some intensity in my regard might have wakened him, and then on my face he would have seen—not lust, it wasn't that, just a vast and objectless regard for his perfection, as though he were sculptured in bronze, or gold.

I haven't thought much about men, or noticed male beauty, actually, since my husband left, opted out of our marriage—and when I say that he left it sounds sudden, whereas it took a long and painful year.

Looking back, I now see that it began with some tiny wistful remarks, made by him, when he would come across articles in the paper about swingers, swapping, singles bars. "Well, maybe we should try some of that stuff," he would say, with a laugh intended to prove nonseriousness. "A pretty girl like you, you'd do okay," he would add, by which he really meant that he thought he would do okay, as indeed he has—did, does. Then came some more serious remarks to the effect that if I wanted an occasional afternoon with someone else, well, I didn't have to tell him about it, but if I did, well, he would understand. Which was a little silly, since when I was not at my office working I was either doing some household errand or I was at home, available only to him.

The next phase included a lot of half-explained or occasionally overexplained latenesses, and a seemingly chronic at-home fatigue. By then even I had caught on, without thinking too specifically about what he must have been doing, which I could not have stood. Still, I was surprised, and worse than surprised, when he told me that he was "serious" about another woman. The beautiful Japanese nurse.

The golden boy got off at Vallejo, without our exchanging any look. Someone else I won't see again, but who will stay in my mind, probably.

Hortense was furious, her poor fat face red, her voice almost out of control. "One hour—one hour I've been waiting here. Can you imagine my thoughts, in all that time?"

Well, I pretty much could. I felt terrible. I put my hand on her arm in a gesture that I meant as calming, affectionate, but she thrust it off, violently.

That was foolish, I thought, and I hoped no one had

seen her. I said, "Hortense, I'm really very sorry. But it's getting obvious that I have a problem with buses. I mix them up, so maybe you shouldn't come and meet me anymore."

I hadn't known I was going to say that, but, once said, those words made sense, and I went on. "I'll take a taxi. There're always a couple out front."

And just then, as we passed hurriedly through the front doors, out onto the street, there were indeed four taxis stationed, a record number, as though to prove my point. Hortense made a strangled, snorting sound.

We drove home in silence; silently, in her dining room, we ate another chef's salad. It occurred to me to say that since our dinners were almost always cold my being late did not exactly spoil them, but I forbore. We were getting to be like some bad sitcom joke: Hortense and me, the odd couple.

The next morning, as I got in line to buy a new commuter ticket, there was the New York State girl. We exchanged mild greetings, and then she looked at the old ticket which for no reason I was clutching, and she said, "But you've got one ticket left."

And she explained what turned out to be one more system that I had not quite caught on to: the driver takes the whole first page, which is why, that first day, I thought he had taken two coupons. And the back page, although another color, pink, is a coupon, too. So my first ride on the wrong bus to Vallejo and Oakland was free; I had come out ahead, in that way.

Then the girl asked, "Have you thought about a California Pass? They're neat." And she explained that with a California Pass, for just a few dollars more than a commuter ticket, you can go *anywhere in California*. You can't travel on weekends, but who would want to, and you can go anywhere at all—Eureka, La Jolla, Santa Barbara, San Diego; you can spend the weekend there and come back on an early Monday bus. I was fascinated, enthralled by these possibilities. I bought a California Pass.

The Sacramento express was almost empty, so I told the girl that I had some work to do, which was true enough. We sat down in our separate seats and concentrated on our briefcases. I was thinking, of course, in a practical way about moving out from Hortense's. That had to be next—and more generally I was considering the possibilities of California, which just then seemed limitless, enormous.

Actually, the Greyhound system of departure gates for buses to San Francisco is very simple; I had really been aware all along of how it worked. Gate 5 is the express, Gate 6 goes to Vallejo and Oakland before San Francisco and Gate 8 is the all-stop local, Davis, Dixon, everywhere. On my way home, I started to line up at Gate 6, my true favorite route, Vallejo and Oakland, when I realized that it was still very early, only just five, and also that I was extremely hungry. What I would really have liked was what we used to call a frappe in Binghamton, something cold and rich and thick and chocolate. Out here called a milkshake. And then I thought, Well, why not? Is there some law that says I can't weigh more than one-ten?

I went into the station restaurant, and at the counter I ordered a double-scoop milkshake. I took it to a booth, and then, as I was sitting there, savoring my delicious drink, something remarkable happened, which was: the handsome black man who so angrily displaced me on that first trip came up to me and greeted me with a friendly smile. "Say, how you, how're you doing this evening?"

I smiled back and said that I was fine, and he went on

past with his cup of coffee, leaving me a little out of breath. And as I continued to sip and swallow (it tasted marvelous) I wondered: Is it possible that he remembers me from that incident and this is his way of apologizing? Somehow that seemed very unlikely, but it seemed even more unlikely that he was just a friendly sort who went around greeting people. He was not at all like that, I was sure. Even smiling he had a proud, fierce look.

Was it possible that something about me had struck him in just the right way, making him want to say hello?

In any case, I had to read his greeting as a very good sign. Maybe the fat young woman would get on the bus at Vallejo again. Maybe the thin one in purple. And it further occurred to me that traveling all over California on the Greyhound I could meet anyone at all.

The Party-Givers

At the end of a very long and, by normal standards, ghastly San Francisco party, its host, Josiah Dawes, an ex-alcoholic, ex-philosopher, sits on the floor with two women, Hope Dawes and Clover Baskerville, in an almost empty flat on Potrero Hill. The women are propped up on pillows on either side of Josiah, silhouetted against long black naked windows; they both face him and, indirectly, each other. In an idle, exhausted way they are discussing the party, among the inevitable debris, the dirty glasses and plates and ashes, in the still stale air. Josiah liked the party; he smiles to himself at each recounted incident.

Hope, Josiah's small, blond and very rich newlywed wife, during the noisy hours of the party has been wondering if she should kill herself. Her mania for Josiah surpasses love —has, really, nothing to do with love; it is more like an insatiable greed, an addiction or perhaps a religious fervor. She has just begun to wonder whether they moved to San Francisco to be near this other woman, with her silly name— Clover. This is Hope's question: if she killed herself, jumped off one of the bridges, maybe, would Josiah fall in love with

Clover all over again? marry her? or would her death keep them guiltily apart?

Clover, a former lover of Josiah's, of some years back, is a large, dark carelessly beautiful woman, with heavy dark hair, a successfully eccentric taste in clothes. In the intervals between her major love affairs, or marriages, she has minor loves, and spends time with friends, a course that was recommended by Colette, she thinks. This is such an interval, since Josiah who was once a major love is now a friend, and maybe Hope is too; she can't tell yet.

Josiah's very erect posture, as he looks from one woman to the other, and back again, suggests that he is somehow judging between them, or keeping them in balance. He is handsome, in a way, with his drained look of saintliness, his sad pale eyes. His hair and his beard, even his skin and all his clothes, are gray.

Josiah and Hope have just moved to San Francisco and taken this flat; thus the lack of furniture. Also, one of Josiah's somewhat eccentric theories about parties is that people should be uncomfortable, like prisoners; they are more apt to reveal themselves.

This group consisted of some old Berkeley connections of Josiah's, and a few new friends introduced by Clover. For various reasons many people drank too much, which, along with the physical discomfort of sitting on the floor, led to quite a few of the revealing scenes of which Josiah is so fond. One drunk man announced that he would kill his wife if she didn't come along home; in fact he might kill her anyway. A drunk woman accused Clover of lusting after her husband, although Clover was welcome to him if she wanted that slob, said the wife. Another man said that he was gay and proud of it but he was goddamned if he was going to come out of any closet.

Although she laughs, going over all this with Josiah and

Hope, these episodes really made Clover more than a little unhappy, and she is slightly uncomfortable with them both. She senses that something is going on that she does not quite understand. She would much rather be having an overwhelming love affair, and she wonders if she ever will again.

Certain conventions, or rules, have been established for this new three-way friendship. One rule is that all Clover's lovers, past and present, are to be considered hilarious, as fair game for jokes (except of course for Josiah). Their number too is exaggerated. That this picture is not entirely accurate is one of the things that is making Clover uncomfortable, but she enjoys the intimacy of the relationship; the three of them see each other almost every day, and she and Josiah talk for hours on the phone. It almost makes up for the lack of a serious love. Clover has small capacity for being alone, and so for the moment she goes along with the gag; she presents all her lovers as being figures of fun, and herself as being far more promiscuous than she is.

Explicit sexual details are out; they are all far too fastidious for that, especially Josiah, who sets the tone. However, Clover has been unable to resist telling them that Nicholas, the publicist who brought her to this party, and who, being married to someone else, left early—Nicholas shaves his chest. And now, in an exhausted, end-of-party way, they are laughing over Nicholas.

"Think how much more time getting dressed must take him than it does most people," suddenly says Hope, who is a practical person.

At this Josiah and Clover look at each other and burst into near-hysterics. Clover's laugh is deep, a sexy laugh; Josiah's is almost silent, but his whole body shakes with it, his face is convulsed. Hope watches both of them seriously as she thinks, My God, it's like watching them make love, in fact more intimate, really; their laughing is unique.

"Yes," Josiah says, in his calm, still-professorial voice. "A 'shave and a shower' would have an entirely different meaning for poor Nicholas."

Clover laughs again, and then she says, "Oh Lord, I'm so tired. I'm getting old."

"We all are," says Josiah. "Except for Hope, who will always look about ten years old. My pocket-sized wife. Any day I expect to get picked up for child-molesting."

Hope giggles, as she imagines he expects her to, but she wonders: Is that a compliment? Does he like having such a small wife, or does he long to be with big dark Clover again? All he said to her, by way of describing Clover before they met, was "You two certainly don't look much alike. No one can accuse me of being partial to a type," with his ambiguous laugh.

Now Clover, in her loose dark flowered silk, pulls herself to her feet. Hope and Josiah get up too. They all say good night to each other, without touching; somehow either kissing or shaking hands would be all wrong.

And Clover goes home, by herself.

Since Clover and Josiah drank so much when they were in love, when he was an alcoholic and a philosopher, teaching at Berkeley, it is hard for Clover to remember, really, what it was like, what Josiah was like, back then. She just remembers a lot of drinking, with vague intervals of sleep and love, against a backdrop of Berkeley Hills, San Francisco restaurants and bars.

But almost everything that happened between Clover and Josiah is vividly clear to Hope; what Josiah left out her avid imagination readily supplies. On her way to sleep, in the giant bed where she feels a little cold, and lost (Josiah is huddled on the other side), after their party, what Hope sees is: Clover and Josiah propped up in a warm plain double bed, a turmoil of white sheets, the two of them drinking California champagne, and laughing their heads off. Clover: dark and young, even more beautiful than now. And Josiah: beardless, dark hair just graying, his face flushed (not gray) with drink and love and so much laughing, all the time. Or, she sees them on the old ferry, crossing to Oakland; they are standing on the prow, salt wind blowing their hair. They are drinking from a pint bottle of bourbon, they are feeding the sea gulls some peanuts which they have soaked in booze. They are getting the sea gulls drunk—they are laughing, laughing, laughing.

These days Josiah doesn't drink at all, and thanks to Hope's money he doesn't have to work.

How she wishes that he still drank!

It is easy to imagine Clover naked—a Maillol, a Henry Moore.

It is often very hard for Hope to sleep.

Clover supports herself as she always has, in a border-line way, with commercial art. Just now she has a better job than usual, with a gallery, doing promotional brochures, with a more than generous budget and an employer who seems quite civilized, for a welcome change, although he is bald and fat. Gregory Rovensky, a dark Russian-Israeli, an ebullient, enthusiastic type; he sometimes reminds Clover of a balloon, or several balloons, bouncing about in a room. A kindly person, he even tells her that she undercharges, and he ups her fee. "Money is not something for you to be foolishly genteel about," he says. "In a commercial society it's a mistake to undervalue yourself."

This seems sensible advice—and how good it would be if she could earn enough money not to worry! Clover has always lived rather well, and dressed well, on the whole, but the cost in anxiety has been tremendous.

In a grateful way she confides in Gregory some of her unease about her friends, Josiah and Hope. "Sometimes I think I'm not quite catching on. Something is happening that I don't understand," she says.

"It sounds as though you were quite necessary to them," says Gregory.

Clover ponders the wisdom of this, although at first it sounded unreasonable. Surely Hope and Josiah like each other? Hope is crazy about Josiah, Clover feels that—and Josiah has always been diffident, nonexpressive of feelings, she remembers that much.

Clover and Gregory are drinking tea, which Clover too likes Russian-style, very strong and lemony, in Clover's crowded North Beach living room, across town and as far removed in its effect from Josiah's and Hope's still-barren space. Generous Clover is the sort of person whom people like to give things to; her rooms are crowded with presents, paintings and drawings and small sculptures from artists she knows, ferns and straw flowers and records and books, hundreds of books, from years of friends. She is unable to throw things away; she almost never breaks off with a friend, or with a lover, finally.

She works at home. In one corner of the room is a huge slanted table, as littered as is every other space in that apartment. It is hard to imagine how she works there, but she does work, much better and harder than her rather languid manner would suggest. She is *very* good; most of her friends, and Gregory, and a few others among her more generous employers tell her this. For herself, she is not quite sure.

Now both she and Gregory seem to feel that their small conversation about Hope and Josiah is over; perhaps Gregory has said the final word, that they need her, for whatever purposes of their own? In any case, since it is most unlikely that he will ever meet them, Clover sees little point in going on about what at times she feels to be a problem.

Soon Gregory, who has come by to drop off some proofs, takes his leave. In an exaggeratedly "Russian" way, he kisses her hand, a gesture made funnier by both his girth and his baldness.

Alone, with a small sigh, Clover moves toward her bedroom to begin the ritual of bathing and dressing to go out to dinner, with a man whom she does not much care about. At times, many times, she feels that there is something radically wrong with the way she conducts her life, but she does not quite see what to do about it.

Spring can and often does arrive crazily in San Francisco: sometimes in January there are balmy days, blossoming trees and bright green grass. On one such day Clover and Josiah and Hope decide to go on a picnic—or, rather, Clover and Josiah make the plan, on the phone. They will go to a beach that they used to frequent during Berkeley days, near Inverness. And that is what they do; they drive to Inverness, and arrive to find that they have the small beach to themselves. No one else has been so venturesome, in the midst of what is actually winter.

Clover eagerly peels off the sweater and skirt that she has worn over her bathing suit. Like many large women of a certain type—big bones, firm flesh—she looks even better naked than she does in clothes; sometimes clothes make her look constrained. But in the sleek brown bathing suit, a just-darker shade than her skin, she looks naked and wonderful, in the unseasonal hot sun, and she feels terrific.

She and Hope and Josiah spread their blanket on the sand; they eat cracked crab and sourdough French bread and tomatoes, and the two women drink a lot of white wine.

Josiah drinks Calistoga water, which he has just discovered:
quite as good as Perrier, and much cheaper.

Josiah and Hope have both told Clover how great she
looks and Hope takes a lot of snapshots, smiling at Clover
even as she squints behind the lens.

It is a successful day. Clover basks in the sun and in the
intense admiring affection of her friends. She has been wrong
about them: Hope and Josiah are really fond of her, as she is
of them; they are all good friends, and nothing strange or
untoward is going on. She even feels their friendship is something unusual, a triumph of goodwill and sophistication over
more primitive and sometimes stronger emotions. And, curiously, this confirms, at least momentarily, her sometimes-
wavering faith in her own work, her artistic skill: if she is so
much cared for, by such friends, perhaps after all she is a
talented, worthwhile person?

However, it really is January, and by midafternoon the
nearly invisible sun sheds no warmth. This has happened
quite abruptly, or so it seems to Clover, who, suddenly shivering, wraps herself in the heavy old sweater, out at the
elbows, in which she no longer feels beautiful.

"You girls have really put down a lot of wine," observes
Josiah. The "you girls" is a tease; he knows they both dislike
that appellation, but perhaps this afternoon he is also anxious to link them? he wants them to be friends?

As though at his suggestion, Clover begins to feel the
wine, not as an intoxicant but as a weight in her head, a
heavy dull ache.

Collecting possessions, bundling garbage into a bag,
seems to take much longer than it should. The sky has gone
gray at the edges, the sea is gray and cold and they are all
slightly chilled.

However, finally at home, and lounging in her deep

warm scented bath, Clover still thinks of the day and their picnic as a success. It *was* love that she felt from Hope and Josiah, intensely, from both of them.

"Clover is promiscuous for precisely the same reason that I am not," Josiah once remarked to Hope. "Because sex is not important to her." Cold with terror, Hope sees the truth of this, at least in regard to Josiah. He has attachments to women that are *worse* than sexual, from Hope's point of view. She has even thought what a relief it would be to have a simple ordinary husband who chased girls into motel rooms, out of her sight. But no: with Josiah there is always another woman, but Hope has to be there too.

In New York there was Isabel, a lonely cellist, a gaunt dark girl. (They never look like me, Hope has noted; does he secretly hate blondes?) Josiah and Hope were always with Isabel, concerts, plays, the ballet. Hope despairingly thought that Isabel was with them for life; eventually there would be trips to Europe with Isabel, finally hospitals and death with Isabel. She even considered hiring someone to murder Isabel, but she had no idea how you would find such a person. And then she had her inspiration: "Wouldn't it be funny if Isabel married Walter?" she remarked to Josiah, and Josiah (how gratifying!) fell apart laughing; it was the best idea Hope had ever had. And so, insofar as it is possible, Hope and Josiah arranged that marriage, from introductions to flattering confidences ("Isabel said she thought you were exceptionally *sensitive*, Walter") to weekends at Hope's family's house, in Newport—to the gift of a wedding reception. Tall, talented, formerly lonely Isabel, and Walter, a crippled, mildly alcoholic cornetist, out of work. *Very* funny.

Maybe Clover could marry someone?

"Do you think Clover will ever remarry?" Hope asked Josiah.

"Oh, I doubt it. She'll more likely kill herself, in a couple of years. That's what happens when a woman of her sort runs out of affairs."

Hope isn't sure that she can wait for a couple of years.

Then another inspiration reaches Hope. "I wonder," she says to Josiah, in a tellingly idle way. "Do you suppose Clover ever runs into several of her lovers at the same party, some of them with their wives?"

Josiah looks at her for a long moment of speculation, and then he bursts into a laugh of pure delight, which to Hope has the sound of sacred music. "Fantastic," he says. "My dearest Hope, you are invaluable. I will have to keep you forever."

"I think a party sounds terrific," says Clover to Hope, on the phone. "February is such a depressing month, neither one thing nor the other."

"*Really*," Hope agrees.

Clover sighs. "I seem to be freshly out of gentlemen callers. I wonder, should I come alone? Or maybe I'll bring Gregory. I sort of owe him an invitation, or something."

"Whatever. On the other hand, though, maybe not Gregory Bald-Fat. Maybe we'd rather just think about him."

Hanging up, Clover's first emotion is a strong regret that she ever described Gregory to Hope and Josiah, that they have given him that name. She now feels uncomfortably disloyal, and to a man who has been tremendously helpful in her professional life. In fact, although low on lovers, as she puts it to herself, Clover has never worked so well, nor for that matter enjoyed her work so much.

The weather has been dull: gray skies, early mornings and nights of heavy fog, days of moist and heavy air. No real rain, or real cold. Clover can't think what to wear to Hope's and Josiah's party. She thinks, I never know what to wear in February, meaning that she is tired of all the clothes she has worn all winter—meaning, really, that for the moment she is tired of going out.

"Gregory, you know my crazy friends, Hope and Josiah? Well, they're having a party." Clover has decided that she would rather go with Gregory than alone; she plans that with him she will simply appear for a short time.

But, "My dear Clover, I am most sorry. I have a dinner that night, old colleagues, impossible to get out of it," says Gregory. "However, it will be an early evening. I could pick you up at ten, or ten-thirty, and go with you to the party of your friends?"

"Well, I'm afraid not. Dinner, they said. But I'm sorry, Gregory."

"I too, dear Clover."

Another of Josiah's techniques for the discomfort of guests, along with the lack of comfortable furniture, is to serve rather little food and great quantities of cheap wine. This sits well with his innate penuriousness, and it reminds him of his student days at Berkeley, his happiest, even before he met Clover. Tonight he has made what he calls his Berkeley stew, which consists of a few shrimp, some green pepper and a little rice. Also, unlike most alcoholics, who tend to be bored with drunks, Josiah loves to watch them; he meticulously notes each stage of inebriation, from the first slurred syllable to the final lurch toward the bathroom.

Hope also feels that the food served at parties should be minimal, and the drinks very cheap. She always thought her rich parents vulgar in their display of imported foods, vintage wines. Josiah is right: how much better to serve a small simple stew and some California jug wine.

Thus, at the party, people as usual are still hungrily drinking wine after dinner, and some are drunk.

Clover, in a red silk dress (several years old, but she has always liked it), is neither hungry nor drunk. Having worked through most of the day, she forgot about lunch until late afternoon, when she ravenously devoured some cold meat and cheese. By the time she got to the party she was very thirsty, and she had some of Josiah's Calistoga water, which tasted good. It was interesting being the soberest (except for Josiah) person at a party.

The drunkest person there is Nicholas, the only former lover of Clover's (again excepting Josiah) who is present—so much for malevolent plans. Nicholas is satisfactorily drunk, but he has come alone; he and his wife have recently separated.

Clover watches Josiah watching Nicholas, who has risen, with considerable difficulty, from his cushion on the floor, and is lurching in the direction of the bathroom, and Clover thinks what she has not quite dared to put into words before: Josiah is a genuinely mean person—he truly enjoys other people's discomfort.

She wonders if this was always true. She thinks not, but then when she knew him they drank so much that it is hard to remember. Maybe, she thinks, he's mean because he doesn't work anymore—he plays around with people instead? Maybe he used to get drunk to dissolve his meanness?

"I do hope Nicholas hasn't gone to the bathroom to shave," Josiah says, and he and Hope laugh. Possibly they notice that Clover isn't joining in, for then Hope says, "Clover, I hardly know you as a Calistoga drinker."

A mild enough remark, but as Clover looks at Hope she sees in Hope's doll-blue eyes a startling intensity of venom. She wishes I would vanish, go away, would maybe kill myself, thinks Clover.

Someone has put on a record, an old Beatles album. The first song has a lively, attractive beat, and several couples get up from the floor to dance, some drunkenly, but others with real expertise, this being the era of a disco-dancing craze. Clover watches Josiah frown; he doesn't like dancing at parties.

Another song comes on, dreamy, romantic, and more people get up to their feet.

Josiah says to Clover, "But why aren't you dancing, my lady in red? I'm sure if you could rescue Nicholas from the bathroom he'd be delighted." And to Hope he says, "Clover in her day was famous as a dancer."

Clover, who at best has been a mediocre dancer, made awkward by shyness about her height, is genuinely incredulous. "Josiah, how can you say that? We never danced—"

"We didn't? I thought we had." Josiah laughs in a private way, then frowns, looking at Hope. Clover understands that this would be something he has told Hope about her, Clover the wonderful dancer. What else has he said? No wonder Hope hates her.

Nicholas emerges from the bathroom, looking pale and sober. He takes his leave.

The party, then, from every point of view, has been a failure, neither the loud disaster that Hope and Josiah had envisioned, nor, in anyone else's terms, a pleasant party. Although just possibly some of the dancers had a better time than they were supposed to.

And although nothing terrible has happened to Clover, except her unhappy perception of her friends, she is suddenly afflicted with the severest, most terrible cold wave of loneliness, pervasive, penetrating. She almost thinks of chasing after Nicholas, who also looked lonely. The idea of going home alone is quite unbearable, and how can she bear the rest of her life?

Nevertheless, she does go home alone; very soberly she drives across the black night city to her solitary flat on Leavenworth Street.

As she lets herself in and then double-locks the door behind her, the phone begins to ring. She imagines that it must be Josiah, who has sometimes called to go over a party with her—again. And just now not wanting such a conversation, Clover almost does not answer, but then, out of old habit, she does answer, and it is not Josiah but Gregory.

"I do apologize to call so late," he says. "But my party was so borrrring, and I thought perhaps to save the evening with a small brandy with you, that I bring to your house?"

"Oh Gregory, that's the best idea I've heard for months."

Hope and Josiah sit in their scarcely furnished living room; the windows still are bare, everywhere exposing the room and its occupants to the windy black night, and the groaning sound of foghorns from the bay.

"Clover is getting to be less and less of a good party person, don't you think?" asks Hope, in a tentative way.

"She's becoming very tiresome," Josiah says, decisively. "I do hope the poor thing doesn't imagine that not drinking is fashionable."

"About as fashionable as that dress she wore."

They laugh, momentarily pleased with each other.

"Actually I'm afraid she's in pretty bad shape," Josiah pronounces, professorially. "Did you notice the look on her face as she was leaving? However, not being, *au fond*, a charitable person, I can't stand friends in bad shape. Unless, of course, I have put them there."

Yawning and stretching, Josiah gets up, and Hope follows him toward their bed.

No more phone calls to Clover. Hope and Josiah busy themselves with other people; there is always someone new around, if you look, and Hope and Josiah have little other occupation—although, like many idle people, they always sound very busy indeed.

Sometimes, still, they talk about Clover. They hope she isn't *too* badly off, they say to each other, in sepulchral voices.

Or, in an opposite mood, Josiah will cheerily announce, "Well, there's always a great deal to be said for dropping an old friend."

Being out of touch with her, there is no way that they could know that this is one of the happiest seasons of Clover's entire life, this finally arrived-at spring. Too busy and happy to know that she has been dropped (such a confusion often seems to exist between the dropper and the droppee), she sometimes says to Gregory, with whom she is living now, "I suppose I really should call Hope and Josiah?"

"As you will, my darling, but don't think of it as 'should.' Call them when you want to see them, and only then."

She smiles. "That's just the problem: I don't want to see them at all." And then she says, "Gregory, you are the nicest man I've ever known."

He laughs. "Should you say that again I would be in danger of taking you seriously."

One afternoon in late spring, near Memorial Day, Josiah

comes home to tell Hope that he has discovered the most marvelous bookstore down in the Marina. "And the woman who runs it—well, you'll have to see for yourself. She's got to be eighty, if she's a day, and absolutely mad, surely certifiable. She says she's related to both Isadora Duncan *and* Gertrude Stein, can you believe it? It turns out that she lives not far from here, and since tomorrow's a holiday I've asked her over for dinner. *Ça va*, my love?"

Hope, who has been relatively happy in the last few months, more or less alone with Josiah, now feels her heart sink, familiarly, and she thinks, as she has too many times before, of suicide: shouldn't she just leave Josiah alone with his new freak friend?

But then she thinks, Really, why should I bother? I could just go on a nice long trip to Bali, Tahiti, maybe, by myself.

The idea is suddenly terrifically attractive.

By the Sea

Because she looked older than she was, eighteen, and
was very pretty, her two slightly crooked front teeth more
than offset by wheat-blond hair and green eyes, Dylan Ballen-
tyne was allowed to be a waitress at the Cypress Lodge without having been a bus girl first. She hated the work—loathed,
despised it—but it was literally the only job in town, town
being a cluster of houses and a couple of stores on the northern California coast. Dylan also hated the town and the wild,
dramatically desolate landscape of the area, to which she
and her mother had moved at the beginning of the summer,
coming down from San Francisco, where Dylan had been
happy in the sunny Mission District, out of sight of the sea.

Now she moved drearily through days of trays and
dishes, spilled coffee and gelatinous ash-strewn food, fat
cross guests or hyper-friendly ones. She was sustained by her
small paycheck and somewhat more generous tips, and by
her own large fantasies of ultimate rescue, or escape.

The Lodge, an ornately Victorian structure with pin-
nacles and turrets, was on a high bluff two miles south of
town, surrounded by sharply sloping meadows which were

edged with dark-green cypresses and pines, overlooking the turbulent, shark-infested, almost inaccessible sea. (One more disappointment: talking up the move, Dylan's mother, self-named Flower, had invented long beach days and picnics; they would both learn to surf, she had said.)

Breakfast was served at the Lodge from eight till ten-thirty, lunch from eleven-thirty until two, in a long glassed-in porch, the dining room. Supposedly between those two meals the help got a break, half an hour for a sandwich or a cigarette, but more often than not it was about five minutes, what with lingering breakfasters and early, eager lunchers. Dinner was at six, set up at five-thirty, and thus there really was a free hour or sometimes two, in the mid to late afternoon. Dylan usually spent this time in the "library" of the Lodge, a dim, musty room, paneled in fake mahogany. Too tired for books, although her reading habits had delighted English teachers in high school, she leafed through old *House Beautifuls*, *Gourmets* or *Vogues*, avidly drinking in all those ads for the accoutrements of rich and leisurely exotic lives.

Curiously, what she saw and read made her almost happy, for that limited time, like a drug. She could nearly believe that she saw herself in *Vogue*, in a Rolls-Royce ad: a tall thin blond woman (she was thin, if not very tall) in silk and careless fur, one jeweled hand on the fender of a silver car, and in the background a handsome man, dark, wearing a tuxedo.

Then there was dinner. Drinks. Wines. Specifics as to the doneness of steaks or roasts. Complaints. I ordered *medium* rare. Is this crab really *fresh*? And heavy trays. The woman who managed the restaurant saw to it that waitresses and bus girls "shared" that labor, possibly out of some vaguely egalitarian sense that the trays were too heavy for any single group. By eight-thirty or so, Dylan and all the girls would be slow-witted with exhaustion, smiles stiffening on their very young faces, perspiration drying under their arms and down their backs. Then there would come the stentorian voice of the manageress: "*Dylan*, are you awake? You look a thousand miles away."

Actually, in her dreams, Dylan was less than two hundred miles away, in San Francisco.

One fantasy of rescue which Dylan recognized as childish, and unlikely, probably, was that a nice older couple (in their fifties, anyway: Flower was only thirty-eight) would adopt her. At the end of their stay at the Lodge, after several weeks, they would say, "Well, Dylan, we just don't see how we're going to get along without you. Do you think you could possibly . . . ?" There had in fact been several couples who could have filled that bill—older people from San Francisco, or even L.A., San Diego, Scottsdale—who stayed for a few weeks at the Lodge, who liked Dylan and tipped her generously. But so far none of them had been unable to leave without her; they didn't even send her postcards.

Another fantasy, a little more plausible, more grown up, involved a man who would come to the Lodge alone and would fall in love with Dylan and take her away. The man was as indistinct as the one in the Rolls-Royce ads, as vaguely handsome, dark and rich.

In the meantime, the local boys who came around to see the other waitresses tried to talk to Dylan; their hair was too long and their faces splotchily sunburned from cycling and surfing, which were the only two things they did, besides drinking beer. Dylan ignored them, and went on dreaming.

The usual group of guests at the Lodge didn't offer much material for fantasy: youngish, well-off couples who arrived in big new station wagons with several children, new summer clothes and new sports equipment. Apart from these stylish parents, there were always two or three very young couples, perhaps just married or perhaps not, all with the look of not quite being able to afford where they were.

And always some very old people.

There was, actually, one unmarried man (almost divorced) among the guests, and although he was very nice, intelligent, about twenty-eight, he did not look rich, or, for that matter, handsome and dark. Whitney Iverson was a stocky red-blond man with a strawberry birthmark on one side of his neck. Deep-set blue eyes were his best feature. Probably he was not the one to fall in love and rescue Dylan, although he seemed to like her very much. Mr. Iverson, too, spent his late afternoons in the Lodge's library.

Exactly what Mr. Iverson did for a living was not clear; he mentioned the Peace Corps and VISTA, and then he said that he was writing; not novels—articles. His wife was divorcing him and she was making a lot of trouble about money, he said: a blow, he hadn't thought she was like that. (But how could he have enough money for anyone to make trouble about, Dylan wondered.) He had brought down a carload of books. When he wasn't reading in his room, or working on whatever he was writing, he took long, long walks, every day, miles over the meadows, back and forth to what there was of a town. Glimpsing him through a window as she set up tables, Dylan noted his stride, his strong shoulders. Sometimes he climbed down the steep perilous banks to the edge of the sea, to the narrow strip of coarse gray sand that passed for a beach. Perfectly safe, he said, if you checked the tides. Unlike Dylan, he was crazy about this landscape; he found the sea and the stretching hills of grass and rock, the acres of sky, all marvelous; even the billowing fog that threatened all summer he saw as lovely, something amazing.

Sometimes Dylan tried to see the local scenery with Whitney Iverson's eyes, and sometimes, remarkably, this worked. She was able to imagine herself a sojourner in this area, as he was, and then she could succumb to the sharp blue beauty of that wild Pacific, the dark-green, wind-bent feathery cypresses, and the sheer cliffs going down to the water, with their crevices of moss and tiny brilliant wild flowers.

But usually she just looked around in a dull, hating way. Usually she was miserably bored and hopelessly despondent.

They had moved down here to the seaside, to this tiny nothing town, Dylan and Flower, so that Flower could concentrate on making jewelry, which was her profession. Actually, the move was the idea of Zachery, Flower's boyfriend. Flower would make the jewelry and Zach would take it up to San Francisco to sell; someday he might even try L.A. And Zach would bring back new materials for Flower to use—gold and silver and pearls. Flower, who was several months behind in her rent, had agreed to this plan. Also, as Dylan saw it, Flower was totally dominated by Zach, who was big and dark and roughly handsome, and sometimes mean. Dylan further suspected that Zach wanted them out of town, wanted to see less of Flower, and the summer had borne out her theory: instead of his living with them and making occasional forays to the city, as Flower had imagined, it was just the other way around. Zach made occasional visits to them, and the rest of the time, when she wasn't working or trying to work on some earrings or a necklace, Flower sat sipping the harsh, local red wine and reading the used paperbacks that Zach brought down in big cartons along with the jewelry materials—"to keep you out of mischief," he had said.

Flower wore her graying blond hair long, in the non-style of her whole adult life, and she was putting on weight. When she wanted to work she took an upper, another commodity supplied by Zach, but this didn't do much to keep her weight down, just kept her "wired," as she sometimes said. Dylan alternated between impatience and the most tender sympathy for her mother, who was in some ways more like a friend; it was often clear to Dylan that actually she had to be the stronger person, the one in charge. But Flower was so nice, really, a wonderful cook and generous to her friends, and she could be funny. Some of the jewelry she made was beautiful—recently, a necklace of silver and stones that Zach said were real opals. Flower had talent, originality. If she could just dump Zach for good, Dylan thought, and then not replace him with someone worse, as she usually did. Always some mean jerk. If she could just not drink, not take speed.

From the start Flower had been genuinely sympathetic about Dylan's awful job. "Honey, I can hardly stand to think about it," she would say, and her eyes would fill. She had been a waitress several times herself. "You and those heavy trays, and the mess. Look, why don't you just quit? Honestly, we'll get by like we always have. I'll just tell Zach he's got to bring more stuff down, and sell more, too. And you can help me."

This seemed a dangerous plan to Dylan, possibly because it relied on Zach, who Dylan was sure would end up in jail, or worse. She stubbornly stuck with her job, and on her two days off (Mondays and Tuesdays, of all useless days) she stayed in bed a lot, and read, and allowed her mother to "spoil" her, with breakfast trays ("Well, after all, who deserves her own tray more than you do, baby?") and her favorite salads for lunch, with every available fresh vegetable and sometimes shrimp.

When she wasn't talking to her mother or helping out with household chores, Dylan was reading a book that Mr.

Iverson had lent her—*The Eustace Diamonds*, by Trollope. This had come about because one afternoon, meeting him in the library, Dylan had explained the old *Vogues*, the *House Beautifuls* scattered near her lap, saying that she was too tired just then to read, and that she missed television. The winter before, she had loved *The Pallisers*, she said, and, before that, *Upstairs, Downstairs*. Mr. Iverson had recommended *The Eustace Diamonds*. "It's really my favorite of the Palliser novels," he said, and he went to get it for her—running all the way up to his room and back, apparently; he was out of breath as he handed her the book.

But why was he so eager to please her? She knew that she was pretty, but she wasn't all that pretty, in her own estimation; she was highly conscious of the two crooked front teeth, although she had perfected a radiant, slightly false smile that almost hid them.

"I wonder if he could be one of *the* Iversons," Flower mused, informed by Dylan one Monday of the source of her book.

"The Iversons?" In Flower's voice it had sounded like the Pallisers.

"One of the really terrific, old San Francisco families. You know, Huntingtons, Floods, Crockers, Iversons. What does he look like, your Mr. Iverson?"

Dylan found this hard to answer, although usually with Flower she spoke very easily, they were so used to each other. "Well." She hesitated. "He's sort of blond, with nice blue eyes and a small nose. He has this birthmark on his neck, but it's not really noticeable."

Flower laughed. "In that case, he's not a real Iverson. They've all got dark hair and the most aristocratic beaky noses. And none of them could possibly have a birthmark—they'd drown it at birth."

Dylan laughed, too, although she felt an obscure disloyalty to Mr. Iverson.

And, looking at Flower, Dylan thought, as she had before, that Flower *could* change her life, take charge of herself. She was basically strong. But in the next moment Dylan decided, as she also had before, more frequently, that probably Flower wouldn't change; in her brief experience people didn't, or not much. Zach would go to jail and Flower would find somebody worse, and get grayer and fatter. And she, Dylan, had better forget about anything as childish as being adopted by rich old people; she must concentrate on marrying someone who really had *money*. Resolution made her feel suddenly adult.

"Honey," asked Flower, "are you sure you won't have a glass of wine?"

"My mother wonders if you're a real Iverson." Dylan had not quite meant to say this; the sentence spoke itself, leaving her slightly embarrassed, as she sat with Whitney Iverson on a small sofa in the library. It was her afternoon break; she was tired, and she told herself that she didn't know what she was saying.

Mr. Iverson, whose intense blue eyes had been staring into hers, now turned away, so that Dylan was more aware of the mark on his neck than she had been before. Or could it have deepened to a darker mulberry stain?

He said, "Well, I am and I'm not, actually. I think of them as my parents and I grew up with them, in the Atherton house, but actually I'm adopted."

"Really?" Two girls Dylan knew at Mission High had

got pregnant and had given up their babies to be adopted. His real mother, then, could have been an ordinary high-school girl? The idea made her uncomfortable, as though he had suddenly moved closer to her.

"I believe they were very aware of it, my not being really theirs," Whitney Iverson said, again looking away from her. "Especially when I messed up in some way, like choosing Reed, instead of Stanford. Then graduate school . . ."

As he talked on, seeming to search for new words for the feelings engendered in him by his adoptive parents, Dylan felt herself involuntarily retreat. No one had ever talked to her in quite that way, and she was uneasy. She looked through the long leaded windows to the wavering sunlight beyond; she stared at the dust-moted shafts of light in the dingy room where they were.

In fact, for Dylan, Whitney's very niceness was somehow against him; his kindness, his willingness to talk, ran against the rather austere grain of her fantasies.

Apparently sensing what she felt, or some of it, Whitney stopped short, and he laughed in a self-conscious way. "Well, there you have the poor-adopted-kid self-pity trip of the month," he said. " 'Poor,' Christ, they've drowned me in money."

Feeling that this last was not really addressed to her (and thinking of Flower's phrase about the birthmark, "drowned at birth"), Dylan said nothing. She stared at his hands, which were strong and brown, long-fingered, and she suddenly, sharply, wished that he would touch her. Touch, instead of all this awkward talk.

Later, considering that conversation, Dylan found herself moved, in spite of herself. How terrible to feel not only that you did not really belong with your parents but that they were disappointed in you. Whitney Iverson hadn't said anything about it, of course, but they must have minded about the birthmark, along with college and graduate school.

She and Flower were so clearly mother and daughter—obviously, irrevocably so; her green eyes were Flower's, even her crooked front teeth. Also, Flower had always thought she was wonderful. "My daughter Dylan," she would say, in her strongest, proudest voice.

But what had he possibly meant about "drowned in money"? Was he really rich, or had that been a joke? His car was an old VW convertible, and his button-down shirts were frayed, his baggy jackets shabby. Would a rich person drive a car like that, or wear those clothes? Probably not, thought Dylan; on the other hand, he did not seem a man to say that he was rich if he was not.

In any case, Dylan decided that she was giving him too much thought, since she had no real reason to think that he cared about her. Maybe he was an Iverson, and a snob, and did not want anything to do with a waitress. If he had wanted to see her, he could have suggested dinner, a movie or driving down to Santa Cruz on one of her days off. Probably she would have said yes, and on the way home, maybe on a bluff overlooking the sea, he could have parked the car, have turned to her.

So far, Dylan had had little experience of ambiguity; its emerging presence made her both impatient and confused. She did not know what to do or how to think about the contradictions in Whitney Iverson.

Although over the summer Dylan and Whitney had met almost every day in the library, this was never a stated arrangement, and if either of them missed a day, as they each sometimes did, nothing was said. This calculated diffidence seemed to suit them; they were like children who could not quite admit to seeking each other out.

One day, when Dylan had already decided that he would not come, and not caring really—she was too tired to care, what with extra guests and heavier trays—after she had been in the library for almost half an hour, she heard running steps, his, and then Whitney Iverson burst in, quite out of breath. "Oh . . . I'm glad you're still here," he got out, and he sat down heavily beside her. "I had some terrific news." But then on the verge of telling her, he stopped, and laughed, and said, "But I'm afraid it won't sound all that terrific to you."

Unhelpfully she looked at him.

"The *Yale Review*," he said. "They've taken an article I sent them. I'm really pleased."

He had been right, in that the *Yale Review* was meaningless to Dylan, but his sense of triumph was real and visible to her. She *felt* his success, and she thought just then that he looked wonderful.

September, once Labor Day was past, was much clearer and warmer, the sea a more brilliant blue, than during the summer. Under a light, fleece-clouded sky the water shimmered, all diamonds and gold, and the rocky cliffs in full sunlight were as pale as ivory. Even Dylan admitted to herself that it was beautiful; sometimes she felt herself penetrated by that scenery, her consciousness filled with it.

Whitney Iverson was leaving on the fifteenth; he had told Dylan so, naming the day as they sat together in the library. And then he said, "Would it be okay if I called you at home, sometime?"

The truth was, they didn't have a phone. Flower had been in so much trouble with the phone company that she didn't want to get into all that again. And so now Dylan blushed, and lied. "Well, maybe not. My mother's really strict."

He blushed, too, the birthmark darkening. "Well, I'll have to come back to see you," he said. "But will you still be here?"

How could she know, especially since he didn't even name a time when he would come? With a careless lack of tact she answered, "I hope not," and then she laughed.

Very seriously he asked, "Well, could we at least go for a walk or something before I go? I could show you the beach." He gave a small laugh, indicating that the beach was really nothing much to see, and then he said, "Dylan, I've wanted so much to see you, I *care* so much for you—but here, there would have been . . . implications . . . you know . . ."

She didn't know; she refused to understand what he meant, unless he was confirming her old suspicion of snobbery: his not wanting to be seen with a waitress. She frowned slightly, and said, "Of course," and thought that she would not, after all, see him again. So much for Whitney Iverson.

But the next afternoon, during her break, in the brilliant September weather the library looked to her unbearably dingy, and all those magazines were so old. She stepped outside through the door at the end of the porch, and there was Mr. Iverson, just coming out through another door.

He smiled widely, said, "Perfect! We can just make it before the tide."

Wanting to say that she hadn't meant to go for a walk with him—she was just getting some air, and her shoes were wrong, canvas sandals—Dylan said neither of those things, but followed along, across the yellowing grass, toward the bluff.

He led her to a place that she hadn't known was there, a

dip in the headland, from which the beach was only a few yards down, by a not steep, narrow path. Whitney went ahead, first turning back to reach for her hand, which she gave him. Making her way just behind, Dylan was more aware of his touch, of their firmly joined warm hands, than of anything else in the day: the sunlight, the sea, her poorly shod feet.

But as they reached the narrow strip of land, instead of turning to embrace her, although he still held her hand, Whitney cried out, "See? Isn't it fantastic?"

A small wave hit Dylan's left foot, soaking the fabric of her sandal. Unkissed, she stared at the back of his shirt collar, which was more frayed even than his usual shirts, below his slightly too long red-blond hair.

Then he turned to her; he picked up her other hand from her side, gazing intently down into her face. But it was somehow too late. Something within her had turned against him, whether from her wet foot or his worn-out collar, or sheer faulty timing, so that when he said, "You're so lovely, you make me shy," instead of being moved, as she might have been, Dylan thought he sounded silly (a grown man, shy?) and she stepped back a little, away from him.

He could still have kissed her, easily (she later thought), but he did not. Instead, he reached into one of the pockets of his jeans, fishing about, as he said, ". . . for something I wanted you to have."

Had he brought her a present, some small valuable keepsake? Prepared to relent, Dylan then saw that he had not; what he was handing her was a cardboard square, a card, on which were printed his name and telephone number. He said, "I just got these. My mother sent them. She's big on engraving." He grimaced as Dylan thought, Oh, your mother really is an Iverson. "The number's my new bachelor pad," he told her. "It's unlisted. Look, I really wish you'd call me. Any time. Collect. I'll be there." He looked away from her, for a moment out to sea, then down to the sand, where for the first time he seemed to notice her wet foot. "Oh Lord!" he exclaimed. "Will you have to change? I could run you home...."

Not liking the fuss, and not at all liking the attention paid to those particular shoes (cheap, flimsy), somewhat coldly Dylan said no; the guests had thinned out and she was going home anyway as soon as the tables had been set up.

"Then I won't see you?"

She gave him her widest, most falsely shining smile, and turned and started up the path ahead of him. At the top she smiled again, and was about to turn away when Whitney grasped her wrist and said, with a startling, unfamiliar scowl, "*Call* me, you hear? I don't want to lose you."

What Dylan had said about being able to leave after setting up the tables was true; she had been told that she could then go home, which she did. The only problem, of course, was that she would earn less money; it could be a very lean, cold winter. Thinking about money, and, less clearly, about Whitney Iverson, Dylan was not quite ready for the wild-eyed Flower, who greeted her at the door: "We're celebrating. Congratulate me! I've dumped Zach."

But Dylan had heard this before, and she knew the shape of the evening that her mother's announcement presaged: strong triumphant statements along with a festive dinner, more and more wine, then tears. Sinkingly she listened as her mother described that afternoon's visit from Zach, how terrible he was and how firm she, Flower, had been, how final. "And we're celebrating with a really great fish soup," finished Flower, leading Dylan into the kitchen.

The evening did go more or less as Dylan had feared

and imagined that it would. Ladling out the rich fish soup, Flower told Dylan how just plain fed up she was with men, and she repeated a line that she had recently heard and liked: "A woman without a man is like a mushroom without a bicycle."

Dylan did not find this as terrifically funny as Flower did, but she dutifully laughed.

A little later, sopping French bread into the liquid, Flower said, "But maybe it's just the guys I pick? I really seem to have some kind of instinct."

Flower had said that before, and Dylan always, if silently, agreed with her: it was too obvious to repeat. And then, maybe there really weren't any nice men around anymore, at her mother's age? Maybe they all got mean and terrible, the way a lot of women got fat? Dylan thought then of Whitney Iverson, who was only about ten years younger than Flower was; would he, too, eventually become impossible, cruel and unfaithful?

In a way that would have seemed alarmingly telepathic if Dylan had not been used to having her thoughts read by her mother, Flower asked, "What ever happened to your new friend, Mr. Iverson? Was he really one of *them*?"

"I don't know. I guess so," Dylan muttered, wishing that she had never mentioned Whitney to her mother.

Over salad, Flower announced that she was going on a diet. "Tomorrow. First thing. Don't worry, I'll still have the stuff you like around for you, but from now on no more carbohydrates for me."

At least, this time, she didn't cry.

At some hour in the middle of the night, or early morning, Dylan woke up—a thing she rarely did. Her ears and her mind were full of the distant sound of the sea, and she could see it as it had been in the afternoon, vastly glittering, when she had been preoccupied with her wet shoe, with Whitney's not kissing her. And she felt a sudden closeness to him; suddenly she understood what he had not quite said. By "implications" he had meant that the time and place were wrong for them. He was shy and just then not especially happy, what with his divorce and all, but he truly cared about her. If he had felt less he probably would have kissed her, in the careless, meaningless way of a man on vacation kissing a pretty waitress and then going back to his own real life. Whitney was that rarity her mother despaired of finding: a truly nice man. On her way back to sleep Dylan imagined calling him. She could go up to see him on the bus, or he could come down, and they could go out together, nothing to do with the Lodge. Could talk, be alone.

However, Dylan woke up the next morning in quite another mood. She felt wonderful, her own person, needing no one, certainly not a man who had not bothered, really, to claim her. Looking in the mirror, she saw herself as more than pretty, as almost beautiful; it was one of her very good days.

Flower, too, at breakfast seemed cheerful, not hung over. Maybe there was something in the air? Passing buttered English muffins to Dylan, Flower took none, although she loved them. "Tomato juice and eggs and black coffee, from here on in," she said. She did not take any pills.

Later, walking toward the Lodge, Dylan felt lighthearted, energetic. And how beautiful everything was! (Whitney Iverson had been right.) The sloping meadows, the pale clear sky, the chalky cliffs, the diamond-shining sea were all marvelous. She had a strong presentiment of luck; some good fortune would come to her at last.

At the sound of a car behind her she moved out of the way, turning then to look. She had had for a moment the crazy thought that it could be Whitney coming back for her, but of course it was not. It was a new gray Porsche, going slowly, looking for something. Walking a little faster, Dylan began to adjust her smile.

An Unscheduled Stop

Suddenly, on a routine flight between Atlanta and Washington, D.C., a young woman who has been staring intently out of her window bursts into violent tears. No turbulence can have upset her—the air is clear and blue and calm—but in an instant her eyes clench shut, her hands fly up to cover her face and her shoulders convulse in spasms.

She is seated near the front of the plane and the seat next to hers has not been taken. No one is aware of this outburst but the two men across the aisle from her. Because she is good-looking, in a dark, rather stylish way, these men have been observing her since she got on the plane with them in Atlanta; they like the somewhat old-fashioned smooth way her hair is knotted, although, good old Southern boys at heart, they are not so sure about the look on her face, what they could see of it, before she began to cry: wide-eyed and serious, she hardly smiled. One of those women too smart for their own good, they think.

The attention of the men has in fact been divided between the young woman and the landscape below, at which they, like her, have been intently peering: pinewoods,

mostly; some exposed red clay, along winding white high-
ways; a brown river; red fall leaves. Just before the woman
began to cry, one of the men observed to the other, "Say,
aren't we passing over Hilton right about now?"

"Sure looks like it. Yep, I bet you're right."

At that moment the woman's tears begin, and after a
startled minute or two they start to whisper. "Say, whatever's
eating her, do you reckon?" one of them asks.

"Haven't got the foggiest notion; she sure don't look
drunk. Maybe some kind of a drug she took."

The young woman, Claire Williston, who is not on
drugs, or drunk, has been deeply mortified by those tears,
which came on her like a fit, a seizure. Generally she is a
disciplined person; she behaves well, even under emotional
stress. She does not make scenes, does not cry in public, and
rarely cries alone. *Maudlin*, she is censoriously thinking, and,
How could I have done this to myself? How could I take a
flight that would go right over Hilton?

Vague about the specifics of geography, she had simply
not realized what any map could have told her: flying from
Atlanta to Washington of course you go right over Hilton,
the small mid-Southern town where Claire was born and
lived for the years until she went away to school up North.
To which, except for one fatal summer and her father's
funeral, she has not been back for years, and where, as she
sees it, she cannot ever now go back. But here she is, directly
overhead.

At last, gaining some control over the tears, she continues silently to castigate herself: for not having thought
through the implications, geographic and otherwise, of flying
all over the South except to Hilton. It is precisely the sort of
"unconscious" mistake that people who pride themselves on

rationality, on control, are most prone to make, she tells herself; it is how they do themselves in, finally.

In a professional way her own life is indeed rational, is even a moderate success. Based in San Francisco, she is the West Coast editor of a national magazine; she likes the work, and is paid fairly well. (A less successful side of her life, containing the unconscious mistakes of which she accuses herself, has to do with intemperate love affairs, occasional poor judgment as to friends. Flying right over the place you don't want to see or think about.) This is the last leg of a fact-finding trip in which she has thought in an abstract way about "the South," or "the new South," and has not thought about Hilton, or her on the whole painful upbringing there, or the searing love affair which took place on that last summer visit. Now, as a treat, she is on her way to see Susan, an old friend in Washington; she has filled a notebook with observations for the article she will write, but she has reserved some lighter conversational notes for Susan: her fantasy that all the food in New Orleans comes from a single subterranean kitchen with a gigantic black vat of béchamel; her dislike of the self-conscious, daily-manicured prettiness of Charleston; her encounter with the awful loudmouthed racist (*still*) cabdriver in Atlanta: "On Fridays, once they's had they lunch, they's no holding them till midnight, with they singing and they dancing and they razor fights." It was Susan who occupied her thoughts, until the land below began to look so overwhelmingly familiar and she heard the man across from her: "Say, aren't we passing over Hilton?"

At this altitude actual landmarks are impossible to recognize, but as she continues to look down, Claire feels the most powerful pull toward that land, as if there were some special gravity into whose range she has flown. And then a remarkable event occurs; over the loudspeaker comes this announcement: "Well, folks, we're going to be making a little unscheduled stopover right about now. Be landing down at Raleigh-Durham for a little adjustment in the oil-filter system. Won't take no more'n a minute."

Dear God, I do not deserve this, Claire thinks, and at the same time, crazily, she wonders if the plane has been compelled by the same pull that she felt, like an event in science fiction. Dabbing at her face, making a few cosmetic repairs (at which the men across from her sigh with relief: when a woman can tend to her face, she's pretty much all right, they think), she watches as the descending plane approaches the familiar pine-lined, long gray grass field. It bumps down; a few passengers applaud. The plane moves toward the bright beige terminal building.

Passengers get up and move along the aisle, murmuring to each other that they might as well get some air, maybe coffee; the men across from Claire, with a short glance at her, go out with new just-unwrapped cigars in their hands. She remains fixed in her seat; she watches as almost everyone else leaves, and then she turns to the window again. No longer crying, she has just realized that she is deeply afraid to go into the terminal; she might see someone she knows, or once knew. Maybe even Spencer Goddard, that summer's fatal lover, still living in nearby Hilton, presumably with his wife.

She looks toward the pinewoods, the lacing of bright fall leaves, and she thinks of something else that she will say to Susan, describing this last leg of her trip, her South revisited: "Seeing those woods made me actually burst into tears," she will say. "But you know how I always loved the woods down there. When I was a kid there I spent all my time outdoors."

Or maybe she won't tell anyone, ever, about crying in that awful way, at the sight of familiar woods.

.   .   .

The great thing about the woods, from a child's point of view, was that parents almost never came along; the woods were quite safe then, and there was a lot to do: you could dam up streams or build tepees, wade in the creek or swing on the heavy grapevines, or just run—race through dead leaves and overgrown corn furrows, in the smells of pine and dirt and sun.

Later, of course, the woods took on other meanings; they offered romantic shelter and privacy for kissing, touching—whatever forms early love took. Although actually (or so Claire thought) there was always something inherently sexual in that landscape: the lushness of it all, the white overflowing waterfalls and dense green caves of honeysuckle vines—and, in the fall, crimson leaves as bright as blood. The hiding and kissing, those heats and fears of love all came early for Claire, but for many years, all the years of her true childhood, she was busy with dams and Indian huts, with swinging out into the sky, wading and trying not to fall into the creek.

One afternoon, when she must have been five or six, a small dark skinny child, Claire did fall into the creek; she fell right off a log on which she and some other children had all been crossing to the other side—off, splash, into the water. Not hurt, she stood up, soaking wet, her pink dress streaked with brown. The other children, all older than Claire, began to point and laugh at her, and she laughed, too, enjoying all the attention and the drama. "Oh, my mother will kill me!" she cried out as the other kids went on laughing. And then one by one, accidentally on purpose, they all fell in, and stood around in their soaking wet clothes, in the hot, hot sun. It was a wonderful day, until it was time to go home, and then Claire began to get scared. Of course no one would kill her, but they would be very mad. Her mother, Isabel, would look at her and yell, because Claire was so careless, and her father, Bayard, might do almost anything, depending on how drunk he was; he might even yell at her mother for yelling at Claire, and hug Claire, but in a way that hurt. The only safe grown-up person was Lobelia, the maid, but there was no way to make sure of seeing Lobelia first, and Claire approached her parents' large stone hilltop house cold and heavy with fear.

There were five or six cars in the driveway, and then she remembered that they were having a party; good, she could go right into the kitchen, to Lobelia, and with luck they might forget all about her; she could sneak some food up the backstairs to her room, some ham and beaten biscuits, whatever.

But there right in the middle of the kitchen, of all places for her to be, was Claire's mother, with her head of wild red hair that everyone talked about (saying, "Too bad Claire didn't get your hair, Isabel honey"). She was laughing and telling Lobelia something that some new guests had said about her beaten biscuits, so that Lobelia was smiling, very happy. And Isabel had never looked so beautiful, blue eyes and white teeth flashing, wearing a yellow dress, something floating.

Claire's father, Bayard, must have thought she was beautiful, too; coming into the kitchen at just that moment, he stared at Isabel, and then a great smile broke across his red, usually melancholy face, and he went over and kissed her on the neck—a thing that Claire had never seen him do before.

Isabel must also have been surprised. "Well really, Bayard," she said, in her irrevocably Bostonian voice, frowning a little but very pleased.

And no one scolded Claire for her dirty dress, making it a most unusual evening for all of them. Claire took some chicken and biscuits up to her room, with the vague thought that maybe from now on her whole life would be patterned after this extraordinary day: happy hours of attention from the older kids, and smiles and kisses and happy getting-along-well parents at home.

Naturally enough, things did not continue in quite that way. Sometimes the older kids were nice to Claire and sometimes not, and most of the time Isabel and Bayard got along as badly as ever, and they drank, and drank.

And, like many couples whose mainstay is sheer rage, they kept on being married. Flamboyant Isabel had a couple of flagrant affairs (Claire gathered this from local gossip, later); they separated, reconciled; they both threatened suicide and got drunk together, instead.

Later, Claire escaped to a college in New England, where she was for the most part extremely happy: new friends, a turbulent emotional life, with boys—and no parents. She kept vacations at home to a minimum, often visiting New York or New England friends, instead.

And then, having graduated, she further escaped, to San Francisco, to the first of a series of impressive jobs (impressive to her friends; Isabel and Bayard always seemed a little vague as to what it was, exactly, that she did). But, writing letters back and forth, they got along quite well, Claire and her parents. Better than ever.

Which led to one of her more conspicuous errors in judgment: one June, having been told that her parents were going to Greece for a month, on an impulse Claire wrote and asked if (maybe, possibly) she could have—even rent—the house for that period; she was between jobs and had four weeks' vacation coming. She hadn't been home for so long, and she would really like to see them. Getting no answer at all to her letter, she was—well, hurt. And, characteristically, she castigated herself for that silly pain. How could she possibly, after a lifetime of evidence to the contrary, believe that her parents would behave in an ordinary "parental" way, would want to see her and maybe lend her a house?

However, at the very last minute—the week before they were to leave for Greece—Isabel wrote and said of course she could stay in the house; in fact, it would be quite helpful, since the latest maid had just quit; she was only sorry that their timing now worked out so that she and Bayard could not be there when Claire was, not even for a couple of days.

And so Claire rushed about getting tickets, packing—rushed back to Hilton and into love with Spencer Goddard, an impossible man, a local doctor, an allergist, whose wife and children were spending the summer in Vermont. And she fell in love despite several of Claire's private rules: against affairs with men who were married, with doctors and especially with Southern men, to whom she was not usually drawn (an unreliable lot, in regard to women, as she perfectly well knew). She later excused this lapse by concluding that it was not so much Spencer she had fallen in love with as it was the countryside, the land around Hilton. And that was very likely true.

The house itself was a little depressing that summer: floors long unpolished, certain necessary repairs not made to the tiles on the bathroom floors, the pantry shelves. There was even a smashed pane of glass in the sideboard, where the china and glassware were kept. The absence of a maid could explain some of this, or maybe Bayard and Isabel were drinking even more than usual? Claire was not much bothered by the state of the house, however; once she had fallen in love with Spencer Goddard she paid little attention to anything else.

They met at a party that someone gave for Claire the

first week she was back in Hilton (gave out of sheer curiosity, she believed). Spencer was tall and lean, his blond hair almost gray, maybe twenty years older than Claire. Within ten minutes of their meeting he told her that he couldn't keep his eyes off her, that something about her face was haunting—if he never saw her again he would never forget her face. (Claire to Susan, later: "Only a submoron would fall for a man who came on like that.") And the next morning he was at her door with roses, saying that this was the most beautiful day, so far, that summer; wouldn't she come for a walk?

They walked down the white dirt road that led from her house to the woods, and turned off on the path that led to the waterfall and the small meadow of broomstraw, where the children used to build Indian huts.

The waterfall tumbled, still, from a flat ledge of slick black rock, between two densely rooted giant pines, down to an almost perfectly circular pool, dark and deep and always cold. Sometimes there were wild anemones in the crevices between the surrounding rocks, and below the pool the brook ran on through wild tangles of flowering honeysuckle vines—where, naturally enough, Spencer and Claire exchanged their first kiss.

After that day, and that night, Spencer came to her house, the big stone house, for the moment entirely hers, at all hours, several times a day and every night. He couldn't get enough of her, he said. And under such a barrage of apparent adoration, in the familiar June smells of roses and flowering privet and rich earth, the high singing of summer breezes in the pines, Claire began to think that she had, indeed, fallen in love; she had come home in order to find Spencer Goddard.

Actually, San Francisco was his favorite city, Spencer told her; he had often thought he would give anything to live there, and now that he had found her, lovely Claire, whom he could not live without—well, he would have to see. And Claire thought, Well, why not? Men do divorce their wives for younger women, sometimes; it can't be much of a marriage; maybe he will.

She said very little to Spencer along those lines. She said nothing at all until the day he took her to the airport (the airport in which she now sits, in an almost empty plane); on that last morning, sad and sleepless and slightly hung over, she said everything that she had not intended to say; she said that she did not see how she could get through the next few months without him, that if he came to Reno for a divorce she could join him there. And she cried, and for once Spencer said almost nothing at all.

He did not follow her to San Francisco, did not write or call. Once, having come in late from a party at which she had drunk too much wine, Claire called him—to hear him say, in a cold, very wide-awake voice, that she must have the wrong number.

She did hear quite a bit, however, from both Bayard and Isabel. In their version of her summer at home, she had wrecked their house and disgraced them both with her flagrant carryings-on, about which *everyone* was talking.

Almost as angry as she was wounded, Claire wrote back that they seemed to have forgotten that the house was in awful shape when she got there. Was she supposed to have waxed the floors and repaired the tiles and replaced the broken glass in the cabinet? And as for flagrant carryings-on, what about theirs?

A stalemate, no more letters.

And then Bayard died.

Claire went home for the funeral, dreading everything: what would have to be a maudlin, probably drunken reunion with her mother, and the likelihood of some glimpse or word of Spencer Goddard. And she was wrong, all around.

Isabel had stopped drinking entirely and, even more out of character, stopped dyeing her hair. What had been gloriously, if artificially, red was now plain and gray, and Isabel further announced that she was going back to the Catholic Church, from which, she now said, Bayard had stolen her away.

Bayard's funeral, however, was Episcopalian, and also, to Claire's even greater relief, it was not attended by Spencer; she saw and heard nothing of him on that visit.

There followed a period of friendship, or something like it, between Claire and her mother. Claire wrote letters about San Francisco and her job, never mentioning lovers; and Isabel wrote about her new happiness and peace, and her new friends, an order of nuns, cloistered nuns whom she was uniquely privileged to see.

And then quite suddenly Isabel died, and it turned out that she had left the house to the nuns. Which should not have surprised Claire in the least; it was very much an Isabel sort of gesture: attention-getting and absolute. But Claire was surprised, and hurt.

Having been left some money by her father, and being on the whole a fair-minded person, she could not object on material grounds; she could even see the appropriateness of a large stone hilltop house for a cloistered order. It was upsetting, though: the thought of those nuns, whom she envisioned as all clothed in white—white ghosts in all the rooms where Isabel and Bayard had shouted each other down, rooms where, all that summer, Claire and Spencer had violently made love; and the fact of those nuns made the house irrevocably alien, not only not hers but forbidden to her, forever.

. . .

"Well, you do look absolutely great" is the first thing that Susan says to Claire, at Dulles Airport, in Washington. "The trip's been a success?" Trim blond Susan, who does not look great; she looks tired and strained, too pale.

They are in the baggage area, waiting for Claire's suitcase. "Oh yes, on the whole," says Claire. "I learned a lot. I've got a suitcase full of notes." As an afterthought, she adds, "One funny thing—we landed at the Raleigh-Durham airport. An unscheduled stop."

Their eyes meet as Susan asks, "Oh, how did it look?"

"Shabby as ever. You know." Claire looks away for a tiny instant, then turns back to Susan as, smiling, she says, "And I really hated the food in New Orleans. I have this theory . . ." And, still smiling, she tells about the underground kitchen that supplies all the restaurants, and the black vat of béchamel.

Susan laughs, and then Claire asks, "Well, how's Jack?"

Three years ago, Susan was planning to leave Jack, her husband; she even came out to San Francisco, to get away and talk, and to be comforted, presumably. But then she went home and apparently decided not to go through with it. And now she says, "Oh, he's fine. Working too hard. You know."

The two women exchange a reassuring, quick smile, acknowledging that this is not to be a visit for serious conversation; neither of them is up to that, just now, but surely, some other time, they will talk again.

That night Susan and Jack give a party for Claire. Although she has met several of their friends before, people who know that she comes from Hilton, she does not explain, if they ask, how come she went almost all over the South but not to Hilton, and several people do ask that. "I just decided not to, this time," she says.

Nor does she drink too much, or urge anyone, particularly anyone's husband, to be sure to call her when he comes to San Francisco.

Nor, at this party, do Jack and Susan quarrel.

On the way to the airport with Susan, leaving Washington and heading for San Francisco, Claire remembers the story about the cabdriver in Atlanta, which she tells ("Once they's had they lunch . . ."). She and Susan laugh, and then Claire says, "It's curious, the ways in which it will absolutely never change."

"Yes—"

"On the whole I think I prefer the landscape to the people."

Susan laughs again. "Well, that's a good line. You could use it in your piece."

"Well, I just might."

Back in San Francisco, in her small house on the eastern slope of Telegraph Hill, her sanctuary, Claire, who at the moment has no ongoing love affair to disturb and distract her, begins to get to work on her article; she stays home from the office, and for long periods of time she turns off her phone. But not even a good title offers itself. In fact, from the beginning, the trouble that she has with this piece is an unwelcome surprise. Seated at her broad desk, before her window that looks out to the bay, Bay Bridge, Treasure Island and the Oakland hills—to water, boats and birds—in a laborious and quite unfamiliar way she lists possible topics, she tries for a plausible central thesis. At the desk, where she has so often worried and suffered acutely over love affairs, and at the same time managed to work quite hard and well, she now worries and begins to suffer over her work, over what has become an impossible assignment.

After a few such days it does begin to go a little better, but it is sheer labor; at no time does she feel the pleasure that she usually experiences in work, that lively joy in her own competence.

This is all very troubling to Claire, who has prided herself, always, on functioning in a highly professional manner, who has even been somewhat critical of those who do not.

Telegraph Hill is in many ways a small town, or perhaps several small towns; there are neighborhood feuds and passionate loyalties, complex and concentric circles of current and former lovers, husbands and wives, all of whom meet in the local restaurants and bars, the grocery stores and Laundromats along Grant Avenue, Green Street, Vallejo Street, Columbus Avenue. Many people who, like Claire, are for one reason or another alienated from where they grew up feel very much at home on Telegraph Hill.

One of Claire's long-standing, non-lover friends is a man named Dan Breckenridge, an aging, still-handsome bachelor, whose pattern with women is invariable, and unfortunate: a gambit going from heavy pursuit to a few weeks of heady love, quickly followed by elusiveness and distance—to, when he finds it necessary, downright meanness. But as a friend he is perfectly all right; he is amusing and generous and kind. From time to time he makes a semi-serious pass at Claire, a sort of sexual feint in her direction which is easy to head off, although (she has admitted to herself) she does find him attractive. They remain good friends, and their friendship is undoubtedly enhanced by this not-acted-out attraction.

Like many adoptive Californians (he is originally from

Chicago), Dan is enthusiastic about California wine; he has usually just found something new and wonderful, from a small vineyard that no one else has heard of yet.

A week or so after her return from her trip, he invites Claire to dinner and he serves a nice dry Pinot Chardonnay —of which he and Claire both drink too much.

So that when he says, in his decisive Midwestern way, "There must be some reason for that article's hanging you up; I wish you'd really tell me about your trip," she does tell him.

She tells him about the cloying prettiness of Charleston; the more interesting beauty of Savannah; New Orleans food, and the vat of béchamel; the new architecture of Atlanta; the racist cabdriver.

And then she tells about flying from Atlanta to Washington. "I was looking down at the woods, and they looked so familiar," she said, "and then one of the men across from me said it must be Hilton—and, Dan, it was horrible, I burst into tears. I couldn't help it. God, it was awful."

Saying what she has so far said to no one, Claire feels the onset of tears, but this time she is able to control them, almost, as she hears Dan say, "Well, I don't think that's so terrible. Flying right over where you grew up, not expecting it. A lot of people would cry. And you really were exiled from there. Dispossessed."

Looking up at him, Claire sees that he is especially drawn to her at that moment (he likes women who cry?); and his kindness and empathy so move her that she is afraid of losing control. If she begins to cry seriously he will touch her, one thing will lead to another, and the last thing she needs, just then, is an affair with Dan Breckenridge. And so, with all the sobriety that she can muster, she gets up and says she's sorry she's so tired, the dinner was terrific—thanks.

Customarily, although affectionate in a verbal way with

each other, Claire and Dan are not physically so; they almost never touch, and they do not do so now. They do not kiss good night after Dan has walked with her the two blocks from his house to hers, in the cool, very clear starred night. But at her door, he gives her a longer, more serious look than usual.

Can she have fallen in love with Dan? That is what some of the symptoms with which Claire wakes up the following morning suggest: a nervous lassitude, some fear of the oncoming day. However, she gets up and drinks a lot of tea; she concludes that she has a slight hangover; and she tries to get to work.

Around noon Dan telephones. That is not a usual time for him to call, and at first Claire thinks, Oh, I must have sounded terrible last night, and worried him.

He asks how things are going, and she tells him that, curiously enough, they seem to be going a little better. She is getting somewhere, at last, with whatever the problem was.

And then, in an odd, abrupt way, Dan says, "Well, how about tonight? Can we see each other?"

"Uh, sure. I'm not doing anything. Should I cook?"

"No, don't be silly. You're working. I want to take you out. Let's drive to Sausalito, okay?"

"Well, sure."

Claire hangs up, more puzzled than she is pleased. Nervous, apprehensive. She even thinks of calling Susan; she can hear herself saying, "Well honestly, now I've done something really dumb, I think. I've fallen in love with an old friend, Dan Breckenridge, and I think he feels that way too. And he's just my type, mean and selfish and elusive."

And Susan will laugh and say, "Well honestly, that's really too bad."

It is true, though, that she has begun to feel considerably better. After Dan's call she goes into the kitchen and heats up a can of tomato soup, with a lot of Parmesan, for nourishment. And she makes more tea.

Back at her desk, the beautiful bright familiar view is reassuring; this is, after all, where she has chosen to live—at the moment it seems a good choice.

However, instead of finally getting down to work on the serious article that is her assignment, in a dreamlike way Claire sits back in her chair, and she begins, rather, to recall the particularities of her trip. She remembers certain accents, heard on streets, in restaurants, in Atlanta and Charleston, Savannah and New Orleans—and gestures observed, both unique and indigenous to that region. And she sees again the colors of earth and leaves which, at certain times of the year, in a certain place, are absolutely unmistakable.

The Girl Across the Room

Yvonne Soulas, the art historian, is much more beautiful in her late sixties than she was when she was young, and this is strange, because she has had much trouble in her life, including pancreatic cancer, through which she lived when no one expected her to. Neither her doctor nor her husband, Matthew Vann, the musicologist-manufacturer, thought she would make it, such a small, thin woman. Make it she did, however, although she lost much of her hair in the process of treatment. Now, seated with Matthew on the porch of an inn on the northern California coast, her fine, precise features framed in skillfully arranged false white waves, she is a lovely woman. In the cool spring night she is wearing soft pale woolen clothes, a shawl and Italian boots, daintily stitched.

Matthew Vann is also a handsome person, with silky white hair and impressive dark eyes, and he, too, wears elegant clothes. His posture is distinguished. Yvonne has never taken his name, not for feminist reasons but because she thinks the combination is unaesthetic: Yvonne Vann? Matthew looks and is considerably more fragile than Yvonne, although they are about the same age: that is to say, among other things, of an age to wonder which of them will outlive the other. The question is impossible, inadmissible and crucially important. Matthew *is* frailer, but then Yvonne's illness could recur at any time.

They have been married for a little over thirty years, and they live, these days, in San Francisco, having decided that the rigors of New England winters and the overstimulation of Cambridge social life were, in combination, far too much for them. Trips to Europe, also, formerly a source of much pleasure, now seem, really, more strenuous than fun. And so Yvonne and Matthew have taken to exploring certain areas of California, beginning with the near at hand: Yosemite, Lake Tahoe and now this extraordinarily beautiful stretch of coast at Mendocino, where rivers empty into the sea between sheer cliffs of rock.

They are sitting at the far end of the white railed porch that runs the length of the building in which they are lodging. They have had an early dinner, hoping for quiet, and they are tired from a day of exploring the town and the meadows high above the vibrating sea. The other guests are almost all golfing people, since there is a course adjacent to the inn. They are people in late middle age, a little younger than Yvonne and Matthew, mostly overweight, tending to noise and heavy smoking and excessive drink. Not pleasant dinner companions. And Yvonne and Matthew were successful: they finished a quiet dinner of excellent abalone before the boisterous arrival of the golfing group. There was only one other couple in the dining room. That other couple had also been distinctly not a part of the golfing group, and they were as striking, in their way, as Yvonne and Matthew were in theirs. Yvonne had been unable not to stare at them—the girl so young and perfectly controlled in all her gestures, the man much older than the girl, so clearly and happily in love with her. It won't end well, Yvonne had thought.

Everything is fine as they sit now on the porch. This place to which they have come is very beautiful. The walks through wild flowers and the views back to the river mouth, the beaches, the opposite banks of green are all marvelous. Everything is fine, except for a nagging area of trouble that has just lodged itself somewhere near Yvonne's heart. But the trouble is quite irrational, and she is an eminently sensible woman, and so she pushes it aside and begins a conversation with Matthew about something else.

"A thing that I like about being old," she observes to him, at the same time as she reflects that many of their conversations have had just this beginning, "is that you go on trips for their own sake, just to see something. Not expecting the trip to change your life." Not hoping that the man you are with will want to marry you, she is thinking to herself, or that Italy will cure your husband of a girl.

"Ye-e-es," drawls Matthew, in his vague New Hampshire way. But he is a good listener; he very much enjoys her conversation. "Yvonne is the least boring person in the world," he has often said—if not to her, to a great many other people.

"When you're young, you really don't see much beyond yourself," Yvonne muses.

Then, perhaps at having spoken the word "young," thinking of young people, of herself much younger, the trouble increases. It becomes an active heavy pressure on her heart, so that she closes her eyes for a moment. Then she opens them, facing it, admitting to herself: That girl in the dining room reminded me of Susanna, in Cambridge, almost thirty years ago. Not long after we were married, which of course made it worse.

. . .

What happened was this:

In the late Forties, in Cambridge, Yvonne was viewed as a smart, attractive but not really pretty French woman. A widow? Divorced? No one knew for sure. She had heavy dark hair, a husky voice and a way of starting sentences with an "Ah!" that sounded like a tiny bark. Some people were surprised to find her married to Matthew Vann, a glamorous man, admired for having fought in Spain as well as for his great good looks, a man as distinguished as he was rich. Then a beautiful young Radcliffe girl who wanted to become a dancer, and for all anyone knew eventually became one—a golden California girl, Susanna—fell in love with Matthew, and he with her. But Yvonne wouldn't let him go, and so nothing came of it. That was all.

Thus went the story that circulated like a lively winter germ through the areas of Cambridge adjacent to Harvard Square, up and down Brattle Street, Linnaean, Garden Street and Massachusetts Avenue, and finally over to Hillside Place, where Yvonne and Matthew then were living.

But that is not, exactly, how it was. It went more like this:

"You won't believe me, but I think a very young girl has fallen in love with me," Matthew said to Yvonne one night, near the end of their dinner of *lapin au moutarde*, a specialty of Yvonne's which she always thenceforward connected unpleasantly with that night, although she continued to make it from time to time. (Silly not to, really.) Then Matthew laughed, a little awkward, embarrassed. "It does seem unlikely."

"Not at all." Yvonne's tone was light, the words automatic. Her accent was still very French. "You are a most handsome man," she said.

"You might remember her. We met her at the Emorys'. Susanna something, from California. I've kept seeing her in

Widener, and now she says she wants to help me with my research." He laughed, more embarrassed yet.

Yvonne experienced a wave of fury, which she quickly brought under control, breathing regularly and taking a small sip of wine. Of course she remembered the girl: long dark-gold hair and sunny, tawny skin; bad clothes, but not needing good clothes with that long lovely neck; a stiff, rather self-conscious dancer's walk; lovely long hands, beautifully controlled. Anyone would fall in love with her.

In those days, while Yvonne did her own work at the Fogg, Matthew was combining supervision of the factory he had inherited, in Waltham, with the musicologist's career that he had chosen. The research he had mentioned was for his book on Boccherini, for which they would later spend a year in Italy. They had married after a wildly passionate affair, during which Yvonne had managed to wrest Matthew away from poor Flossie, his alcoholic first wife, now long since dead in Tennessee.

And, thinking over the problem of Susanna, one thing that Yvonne said silently to her rival was: You can't have him; I've already been through too much for Matthew. Also, in her exceptionally clearheaded way, Yvonne *knew* Matthew, in a way that violent love can sometimes preclude. She knew that he would not take Susanna to bed unless he had decided to break with Yvonne—this out of a strong and somewhat aberrant New England sense of honor, and also out of sexual shyness, unusual in so handsome, so sensual a man. Yvonne herself had had to resort to a kind of seduction by force. But a young, proud girl could not know of such tactics.

Yvonne was right. Matthew did not have an affair with Susanna; he probably never saw her outside of Widener, except for an intense cup of coffee at Hayes-Bickford, where they were noticed together. However, Matthew suffered se-

verely, and that was how Yvonne treated him—like someone
with a serious disease. She was affectionate and solicitous,
and very slightly distant, as though his illness were something that she didn't want to catch.

One March evening, after a bright, harsh day of inter-
mittent sun, rain and wind, Matthew came home for dinner a
little late, with a look on his face of total and anguished
exhaustion. Handing him his gin—they were in the kitchen;
she had been tasting her good lamb stew, a *navarin*—Yvonne
thought, Ah, the girl has broken it off, or has given him an
ultimatum; such a mistake. She thought, I hope I won't have
to hear about it.

All Matthew said during dinner was "The Boccherini
project is sort of getting me down. My ideas don't come together."

"Poor darling," she said carefully, alertly watching his
face.

"I should spend more time at the factory."

"Well, why don't you?"

As they settled in the living room for coffee, Yvonne saw
that his face had relaxed a little. Perhaps now he would want
to talk to her? She said, "There's a Fred Astaire revival at the
U.T. tonight. I know you don't like them, but would you
mind if I go? Ah, dear, it's almost time."

Not saying: You unspeakable fool, how dare you put me
through all this? Are you really worth it?

Alone in the crowded balcony of the University Theatre,
as on the screen Fred and Ginger sang to each other about
how lovely a day it was to be caught in the rain, Yvonne
thought, for a moment, that she would after all go home and
tell Matthew to go to his girl, Susanna. She would release
him, with as little guilt as possible, since she was indeed fond
of Matthew. *Je tiens à Matthew.*

Tenir à. I hold to Matthew, Yvonne thought then. And

she also thought, No, it would not work out well at all. Matthew is much too vulnerable for a girl like that. He is better off with me.

Of course she was right, as Matthew himself must have come to realize, and over the summer he seemed to recover from his affliction. Yvonne saw his recovery, but she also understood that she had been seriously wounded by that episode, coming as it did so early in their life together. Afterward she was able to think more sensibly, Well, much better early than later on, when he could have felt more free.

That fall they left for Italy, where, curiously, neither of them had been before—Yvonne because her Anglophile parents had always taken her to the Devon coast on holidays, or sometimes to Scotland, Matthew because with drunken Flossie any travel was impossible.

They settled in a small hotel in Rome, in a large romantically alcoved room that overlooked the Borghese Gardens. They went on trips: north to Orvieto, Todi, Spoleto, Gubbio; south to Salerno, Positano, Ravello. They were dazed, dizzy with pleasure at the landscape, the vistas of olive orchards, of pines and flowers and stones, the ancient buildings, the paintings and statuary. The food and wine. They shared a mania for pasta.

A perfect trip, except that from time to time Yvonne was jolted sharply by a thought of that girl, Susanna. And, looking at Matthew, she wondered if he, too, thought of her—with sadness, regret? The question hurt.

She would have to ask Matthew, and deliberately she chose a moment of pure happiness. They were seated on a vine-covered terrace, at Orvieto, across the square from the gorgeously striped cathedral, drinking cool white wine, having made love early that morning, when Yvonne asked, "Do you ever wonder what happened to that girl, Susanna?"

Genuine puzzlement appeared on Matthew's distinguished face, and then he said, "I almost never think of her. I don't have time."

Knowing Matthew, Yvonne was sure that he spoke the truth, and she wryly thought, I undoubtedly think more often of that girl, that episode, than Matthew does.

And so she, too, stopped thinking of Susanna—or almost, except for an occasional reminder.

Leaving Rome, they traveled up to Florence, then Venice, Innsbruck, and Vienna.

That was the first of a succession of great trips.

Yvonne and Matthew remained, for the most part, very happy with each other, and over the years their sexual life declined only slightly. Then, in her late fifties, Yvonne became terribly sick, at first undiagnosably so. Surgery was indicated. On being told the probable nature of her illness—she had insisted on that—Yvonne remarked to her doctor, one of the chief surgeons at Massachusetts General, "Well, my chances are not exactly marvelous, then, are they?"

He looked embarrassed, and gazed in the direction of the Charles, just visible from his high office window. "No, not marvelous," he admitted.

After surgery, oppressively drugged, Yvonne was mainly aware of pain, which surged in heavy waves toward her, almost overwhelming her, and very gradually receding. She was aware, too, of being handled a great deal, not always gently, of needles inserted, and tubes, of strong hands manipulating her small body.

Sometimes, half conscious, she would wonder if she was dreaming. But at least she knew that she was alive: dead people don't wonder about anything, she was sure of that.

The first face that she was aware of was her surgeon's: humorless, stern, seeming always to be saying, No, not marvelous. Then there was the face of a black nurse, kind and sad, a gentle, mourning face. At last she saw Matthew, so gaunt and stricken that she knew she had to live. It was that simple: dying was something she could not do to Matthew.

"She's got to be the strongest woman I've ever seen, basically," the dubious surgeon remarked later on to Matthew, who by then could beamingly agree.

Chemotherapy worked; it took most of her hair but fortunately did not make her sick. Yvonne very gradually regained strength, and some health, and with a great effort she put back on a few of the many lost pounds. Matthew learned to make a superior fettuccine, and he served it to her often.

After her illness and surgery, they did not make love anymore; they just did not. Yvonne missed it, in a dim sad way, but on the other hand she could sometimes smile at the very idea of such a ludicrous human activity, to which she herself had once devoted so much time. She was on the whole amused and a little skeptical of accounts of very sexually active seventy- and eighty-year-olds: why did they bother, really?

While she was recuperating, Yvonne finished a study of Marie Laurencin that she had been working on for years, and her book had considerable acclaim, even reasonably good sales. Matthew did not finish his Boccherini study, but from time to time he published articles in places like the *Hudson Review*, the *Harvard Magazine*.

A year ago, they left Cambridge and moved to the pleasant flat on Green Street, in San Francisco.

. . .

Now, on the porch in Mendocino, thinking of the girl across the room at dinner, and remembering Susanna, all that pain, Yvonne has a vivid insight as to how it would have been if she had abandoned Matthew to Susanna all those years ago. Matthew would, of course, have married the girl —that is how he is—and they would have been quite happy for a while. He would have gazed dotingly upon her in restaurants, like the man in the dining room, with his Susanna. And then somehow it would all have gone bad, with a sad old age for Matthew, the girl bored and irritable, Matthew worn out, not understanding anything.

But what of herself? What would have happened to her? The strange part is that Yvonne has never inquired into this before. Now, with perfect logic, she suddenly, jarringly sees just what would have happened: for a while, considerable unhappiness for her, a slow recovery. And then she would have been quite herself again, maybe a little improved. She would have remarried—amazing, she can almost see him! He is no one she knows, but a man much younger than herself, very dark. In fact, he is French; they have many intimate things in common. He might be a painter. He is very unlike Matthew. Would she still have had her great illness? She is not sure; her vision ends with that man, her marriage to him.

Something in her expression, probably, has made Matthew ask a question never asked between them, a question, in fact, for adolescent lovers: "What were you thinking about, just now?"

And he is given, by Yvonne, the requisite response: "I was thinking, my darling, of you. At least in part."

The air on the porch is perceptibly chillier than when they first came out from dinner. Time to go in, and yet they are both reluctant to move: it is so beautiful where they are. In the distance, gray-white lines of foam cross the sea, be-

neath a calm pale evening sky; closer to hand are the surrounding, sheltering pines and cypresses.

Then, from whatever uncharacteristic moment of strong
emotion, Matthew says another thing that he has not said
before. "I was thinking," he says, "that without you I would
not have had much of a life at all."

Does he mean if they had never met? Or does he mean if
he had left her for that girl, for fair Susanna? Or if she had
died? It is impossible to ask, and so Yvonne frowns, unseen,
in the gathering dusk—both at the ambiguity and at the
surprise of it. And she, too, says something new: "Ah, Matthew, what an absolute fool you are." But she has said it
lightly, and she adds, "You would have got along perfectly
well without me." She knows that out of her true fondness
for Matthew she has lied, and that it is still necessary for her
to survive him.

Lost Luggage

I can only explain my genuine lack of concern, when I first realized that my suitcase was missing, not coming up with the others off the plane, by saying that at that moment I was in a mood of more than usual self-approval; you could call it pride, or maybe hubris, even: I had just managed to enjoy a vacation alone—to come out unscathed, anyway—at a Mexican resort where I had often gone with my recently dead husband, a trip warned against by my children and well-meaning friends, of course. But it had been all right; I was glad that I had gone there. My other source of pride was sillier but forgivable, I think; it was simply that I was looking very well. I was tan, and the warm, gentle green Mexican water had been kind to my hair. I was brown and silver, like a weathering country house, and I did not mind the thought of myself as aging wood.

In any case, I watched the procession of luggage as it erupted from the maw of the baggage area in the San Francisco terminal, up from the Toltec Airlines plane that I had just got off; I watched each piece as it was claimed and lifted off the treadmill and taken away. With no sinking of my heart (that came much later), I waited until all the other bags were gone, as the empty treadmill moved in its creaking circle, and I realized that that was it: no more bags. An official-looking person confirmed that view: my suitcase was somewhere else, or lost, or irreparably smashed. And I was not at all upset.

I had not been so foolish as to take anything valuable (had I indeed owned anything of that sort of value) to a somewhat ratty resort, on a Mexican beach, and I even thought, Oh, good, now I won't have to wash out that robe with the suntan-lotion stains.

A pretty black girl in the uniform of the airline gave me a form to fill out, describing the suitcase, and giving my name, Janet Stone Halloran, my address and phone. She gave me a claim number, and she said, "You'll be given twenty-five dollars for makeup and drugs, you know, for tonight."

Good, is what I thought again. Very good. I can take a cab home and buy some toothpaste, a brush, astringent, cream. For various reasons, mostly having to do with pride and with my new role as a single woman, I had spent too much money in Mexico, paid for too many rounds of margaritas, so I was quite conscious of even small sums of money. I assumed then that a check for twenty-five would come to me automatically, probably tomorrow.

The truth is that I was quite broke; I needed to get a job as soon as possible, Walter not having believed in insurance, but I wasn't dealing with that problem yet. I had dealt as best I could with Walter's death, I had successfully gone to Mexico. I would think about money and jobs tomorrow; I would go out looking while I still was tan.

Actually, and this did not make his death any easier, Walter and I had not liked each other much lately. We had married young, for love (well, sex, really); in our day that is what you did when strongly attracted. And as the physical intensity calmed down, diminished, all our other energies seemed to go in opposite directions. A familiar story, I guess, but that made it no easier to bear.

Like many lonely women, I became bookish, an obsessive reader, my favorites being long Victorian novels. (Once, reading *The Egoist*—Meredith's best, I thought—I started to recommend it to Walter, such a wonderfully funny book. But then I recognized that Walter would not think it was funny at all.)

Walter's major passion, his obsession, turned out to be cars: even after professionally he went from selling Fords to selling life insurance, he was constantly buying, selling, trading, trading in cars. We must have averaged four or five cars a year, and last year, the year he died, we went through seven. And always terrifically fancy ones; I now have a 1935 Franklin, in mint condition, up for sale. I hated to be unsympathetic, but I found all this car business scary, something we couldn't afford, and I sometimes said as much. But Walter, a fast-talking red-haired Irishman, a looker, a flirt, was not much of a listener, or not to me. He would frown distractedly, and go on with his dreams of cars.

None of which helped when he died. Along with natural grief and shock, I felt guilty as hell: why couldn't I have been nicer about a relatively harmless habit? He could have been "sleeping around," as we used to say; well, maybe he was doing that, too. In any case, his death was a dreadful—an appalling—event.

None of our friends knew how little money Walter and I had (no doubt misled by all those fancy cars), any more than they knew how little we liked each other. Neither fact had been something that I could ever speak of, or maybe I had long ago got used to not saying those things—a New England habit of reserve. And there was a connection between those conditions: if we had had money, especially if I had had a little of my own—that enviable condition—we could have split up; but no, we had children very early on (red-haired, all of them, of course), four children who seemed to stay young forever as we aged. Now they were all away at school, except our oldest daughter, who was married, and when I say that I had no money I mean that I had barely enough to keep them there, and not enough to live on much longer by myself. Probably we would all have to go to work. I didn't think it would hurt us much; more New England Puritanism, I guess.

And my choice of the Mexican beach had been connected with both of those unmentionable facts, lack of money and not getting along with Walter. It was extremely cheap, and it was where Walter and I had got along least well. I always loved it; he hated it there, and went along as a concession to my poor taste, if grudgingly. For one thing, there were no tennis courts within miles, and Walt was an impassioned tennis buff. (He died on the courts, in fact, after what I was told was a magnificent overhead smash. A good death, in that way, I guess you could call it.)

To a degree, naturally enough, my friends and children were right; it was lonely being there without even an unloved, quarrelsome Walter. And, as widows will, or anyone will just after a serious love affair, for a while I found it hard to remember anything but the good times between us, the early years when we both had jobs with conflicting schedules, his selling Fords, mine doing research for some lawyers; and so whenever we were even briefly at home together we would make love, as instantly and happily as mating birds.

Also, as I sat alone on my terrace, watching one of those incredible tropical sunsets, the whole sky covered with bright rags of clouds, I would feel really frightened, and not unreasonably so. There was not exactly a superabundance of jobs around, and suppose I couldn't find one, or not for years? I was well trained, I'd had occasional research jobs along the way, helping out with family money, and I knew a lot of people; still, I was quite a few years over twenty-five, or even thirty. What would I do? (I know, nowhere near the poverty level; but still a cause for concern, I thought.)

At other times, however, down there in the balmy breezes, I would experience an exhilarating sense of adventure. I knew myself to be a strong woman: surely I could turn my life around? I was not really dependent on a middle-class support system, on certain styles of dress and entertaining, on "safe" neighborhoods. I could even, I imagined, find a big house to share with some other working women, about my age—not exactly a commune but a cooperative venture. Such prospects excited and to a degree sustained me.

And there was always the extreme beauty of the place itself, the big horseshoe cove of lovely water, with its white, white beach and rocky promontories at either edge. The green tropical growth that rose from the outer edge of sand into hills. And the clear enormous sky, its brilliant blue, then gaudy sunsets, and, later, billions of stars. Not to mention the flowers spilling over everywhere—the profusion of bougainvillea, of every shade of pink and orange. I could feel it all seeping into me, with the stillness, the peace.

Fortunately, in a way, the last time Walt and I were in Mexico was by far our worst. Nothing dramatic or specific— just a miasma of incommunicable depression that settled on us both. What exactly was on Walt's mind I have no idea, just boredom and restlessness, perhaps—or he could have been having a "relationship" in San Francisco (I always at least half suspected that he was), with someone whom he missed. I myself was depressed at the changes that I saw in us, and in our bodies. Our slowing middle-aged flesh seemed to parody its former eager, quick incarnation, and I looked at the other couples, many considerably older than we were, who had come down to the tropics to warm their hardening bones—timorous people looking outward rather than toward each other, their flesh no longer joined. And I thought, Is that where we are going, Walt and I? Is the rest of our life together, if we stay together, to be such a process of attrition?

And so, in that sense, being there without Walt was better; I could remember the good days quite as easily as the bad—in fact, more easily; I was no longer daily, hourly reminded by his presence that we no longer loved or even much liked each other. In a dignified way I could be sad about him, even. He had enjoyed his life, his tennis and skiing, parties, drinking, and, for the most part, he had enjoyed and liked our children. It was grossly unfair that he should be cut off from all that, so relatively young.

At the beach, then, I thought my own thoughts, and swam a lot, and read, and I let the gentle beauty of the place drift through my mind. And I observed, rather than actively participating in, what social life there was.

I saw a woman who, like myself, seemed to be traveling alone; some years older than I was, she could easily have been a widow also, or maybe divorced. And she was talking too much. I would see her with groups on the beach, or at the bar, talking and talking. I had earlier noticed such an impulse in myself; as though to compensate for Walter's lack, to say enough for us both, I had developed a new tendency to garrulousness. And now, in a distant, sympathetic way, I wanted to say to this woman, Please don't, you don't have to make up for being alone, in that way.

I further observed a young man, also alone, but seemingly having attached himself to a group of older people. He was not really as young as he felt that he was. He would be very good with old ladies, except for a certain kind of old lady (the kind I plan to be), who will suddenly wonder why she is paying for all his drinks, and will decide that he is not quite worth it. I watched as, each time someone in the group was due to sign for drinks, that aging boy would be engaged in animated conversation somewhere else —as, still unobserved by him, the smiles around him congealed and froze.

Which is one reason that whenever I fell in with a group at the bar I made a point of buying more than my share of drinks.

I looked, and thought, and observed, and I wrote down a great deal in a daybook that I had begun to keep, begun just after Walter died. Two friends had suggested this, women who did not know each other. A coincidence, possibly, but enough to make me listen—although I later concluded that they were both influenced by the fact that I write letters much more often than I telephone.

Also, like so many women of my generation (and I would hope some men and younger women, too), I had been powerfully moved by Doris Lessing's *The Golden Notebook*. Not that I saw much connection between myself and her heroine, Anna (or with Lessing herself); still, for weeks and then months after Walter died, I made myself write everything down, like Anna in the Blue Notebook section, trying to understand.

And it did help, quite a lot. I could see a certain progress from the rage and despair of the first entries, the nightmare scene at the funeral parlor. I had not wanted to "view" Walter; I was talked into it—shamed into it, really— by my oldest daughter, the married one, and by, of course, the funeral-parlor person. How wonderful he looks, they both murmured, though in a questioning way; he looks asleep. Having spent many hours looking at Walter asleep— he always slept well, whereas I had occasional insomnia—I thought he did not look asleep; he looked dead, very dead, dead for good. I hated myself for breaking down and crying noisily in that place.

Well, all that was vividly in my notebook, and then there were some better days recorded, and a few more bad ones. Kind friends, insensitive friends, intuitive strangers.

It was encouraging on those bad days to look back to worse ones, earlier on, and when I actually felt well, restored to my old self, competent and strong—with what pride I recorded that sense.

It was not until I was in the taxi, heading home from the airport, and thinking with foolish pleasure about my check for twenty-five dollars, that I realized that my notebook was in the missing suitcase, along with the stained robe and the other things I didn't much care about. And in that moment of understanding that my notebook could be gone forever, I did not see how I could go on with my life. Everything within me sank. It was as though my respirator, whatever essential machine had kept me breathing, was cruelly removed. This is worse than Walter's death, I crazily thought, and then amended (I revised, as I had learned to do with crazy thoughts) so that in my mind it now read, I can deal with this less well than I did with Walter's death.

Arrived at my door, I paid for the taxi with several of my last vacation dollars, and I let myself into my small (though now too large) "safe" flat.

There was a pile of letters on the floor which, since I had no bag to unpack, I immediately sat down to read. And there, among the bills and circulars, the demands, were three letters which, had I been in a more normal mood, might have made me happy: two of them from two of my scattered children, both simply nice, kind and friendly—sounding like the sort of people I would have wanted them to turn out to be—and the third from a lawyer for whom I had once worked, offering sensible job-getting advice and strong encouragement. As I say, had it not been for my missing bag and my lost notebook, it would have been a good homecoming.

I lay awake planning phone calls.

Toltec Airlines, as it turned out the following morning, did not have its own Lost and Found (a bad sign right there, I thought); its losses and finds were reported to another airline, Griffith International. I described my bag to a cheerfully inattentive girl: a cheap make, I said, black vinyl, with a safety pin in the zipper. Yes, it was clearly marked with my name and address.

Had I reported its loss?

Yes, of course. Last night.

Well, most bags eventually turn up, she said, and I must believe that they were just as eager to return my bag to me as I was to get it.

I could not possibly believe that, I told her severely; it was simply untrue. And then, as though it were an afterthought, I asked about the twenty-five-dollar compensation check.

Oh, that's only for people just stopping over, she said.

Oh.

She suggested that I might want to call the night person at Toltec Airlines; he comes on every night at six, she said, and she gave me a number.

The man's name was Dick Parker—a too simple, forgettable name, but I managed to keep it in my mind all day; in fact I thought of nothing else.

He turned out to be both less interested and less optimistic than the morning girl. Well, sometimes bags did get stolen, he said. Nothing the airlines could do, thefts happen.

Even old shabby bags like mine?

Older, shabbier ones got ripped off. For all the thieves knew, there were diamonds inside, he picturesquely said.

After a long pause, during which I tried to digest his gloomy and irrefutable logic, I asked about compensation.

The airline pays three hundred dollars after two weeks, he said.

Oh.

The young woman who answered the Lost and Found number the next morning sounded Mexican, I thought, which I found irrationally cheering, as though national pride would encourage more strenuous efforts on her part. I again described my bag, and again she went off to look. Only later did it occur to me that she might—she *should* have had that description already filed.

No, she announced on her return; my bag was not there, I should immediately call Mr. Playa, Pablo Playa, who was in charge of Toltec Airlines, and she gave me a number.

This was encouraging—someone in charge—and I was charmed by the name Pablo Playa. The numbers that I dialed, however, felt familiar; just as Mr. Playa answered, I realized that it was the number of Dick Parker: Pablo Playa was the daytime Dick Parker.

But he had a mellifluous Latin voice, Pablo Playa did, and his tone was the most, if not the only, sympathetic official voice that I had heard. Of *course* I was upset, he said, and *everything* would be done to find my bag. I must believe him, the bag would be returned to me within days. And also, at the very worst, the airline paid five hundred dollars for lost bags, within fifteen days.

For a few minutes I felt vastly cheered—my automatic response to warmth and charm, to promises—and then, with a characteristic reversal, certain grim and obvious truths appeared, to rebuke my foolish optimism. First, none of those people knew what the others were doing; there was no one in charge. Second, there was no fixed policy about compensation. Third, there was no concentrated or even directed effort to retrieve my bag.

That night I again called Dick Parker, who instantly confirmed all those suspicions. How long had it been since I lost my bag, he wanted to know.

It was not I who had lost the bag, I reminded him; it was *them*. And maybe they should coordinate their files, as well as their efforts.

Thank you for telling me how to do my job, he said, in a furious way.

I think we both hung up at the same moment.

Over the long haul of my life, I have noticed that even the most upsetting things get better with the simple passage of time; even deaths become less painful. But it was not so with my missing bag; it was, in many ways, like the aftermath of a robbery. Once, Walter and I had been burglarized, and for weeks I kept discovering more things that were not there: a set of silver grapefruit spoons, some pretty cocktail napkins, all the Beethoven quartets (a tasteful ripper-offer, that one was). And now, having thought everything but my notebook valueless, I began to remember a nice old pink cotton shirt, inexplicably becoming; some big white beads (cheap, from Cost Plus, but where would I find them again).

Far worse was my deranged sense of being crippled without my notebook, my notes; and my awareness that it made no sense was not much help. I considered, and discarded, the obvious theory that this was a substitute mourning for Walter, that it was actually Walter whom I could not live without; that explanation simply did not grip me in the way that a true insight invariably does. I also asked myself if the lost notebook was an excuse for postponing other tasks at hand, like scrubbing the open kitchen shelves. Looking for a job.

The next day, as though to refute that thought, I did scrub the shelves. I've read somewhere that all women have a least favorite household task, and that is mine: the irritation of putting those little spice jars and bottles somewhere else, displacing the adorable little keepsakes, spilling the cleaning stuff on the floor. Et cetera.

And then, like a reward, it came to me, something that probably anyone else would have thought of days before: I would go out and buy another notebook, I would write down all that I could remember from the former entries and then I would start in again. Obviously, I had become addicted to writing things down; that was the core of my problem.

A wonderful idea, a solution—but in the stationery store I hesitated. The lost notebook, whose duplicate was right there on the shelf before me, had been rather expensive, seven dollars, now up to eight-fifty. (I could measure the time since Walter's death by the rate of inflation, I thought.) Maybe I would get the old notebook back? In that mood, I compromised on a much smaller, though matching, book; its spine was also stamped RECORD, and it cost two-fifty.

I took it home, and eagerly, right away, I began to

record the newest chapter in my life, which I headed, of course, Lost Luggage.

By rights my suitcase should then have been returned—my reward for maturity and strength—and I superstitiously believed that it actually would be. It had been missing now for five full days. And, still expecting that it would reappear, I concentrated on writing. I stopped calling the Toltec people and, instead, I called my travel agent and told her of those troubles; she would take care of everything, she said.

I had imagined that I might try, as a sort of exercise, to record some of what I had felt and had written in my original book about the days and months just after Walter's death, but I did not. I wrote about the colors of Mexico, still lively and brilliant in my mind, and from there I moved farther back, much farther, to some childhood colors: the calm blue-black depths of a New Hampshire lake in summer; gray winter slush on Tremont Street, in Boston. I had no purpose, really; I only knew that the hour or so I spent writing every day was a happy time for me. I finished that notebook and I bought another small one, and probably I will keep on buying them. And, without really noticing it as something remarkable, I began to feel a great deal better.

Fate, as I should have recognized by now, tends to reward happiness rather than virtue: having to a large extent cheered up, in the same week I acquired both a paying guest and a good part-time job. The guest was a younger friend, Daisy, with whom I had worked on a couple of political campaigns; she had split with her most recent lover, and she wondered if maybe—now that—I would like to rent her a room. Well, knowing Daisy, it would not be for long, but she was entertaining, and kind, and reliable, in her way. And if this was not the cooperative venture I'd earlier dreamed of, it could be a step in that direction.

The job was with the lawyer for whom I'd worked before—a little less work than I needed, but, like the room arrangement, it seemed a strong step forward.

And, a month or so after that, I received, through my travel agent, a check for $343.79, from Toltec Airlines—a figure that I will never understand, but it paid a couple of bills.

I don't think much anymore about my lost notebook, or of those sad early days that it recorded, although I do occasionally wonder if Dick Parker, the night man at Toltec, could possibly have been right—if some misguided thief could have believed that I carried diamonds or cocaine in that shabby old bag, and found, instead, some well-worn summer clothes and the unhappy jottings of a very confused, a searching, woman.

I don't plan to go back to that particular Mexican resort; I believe that it has served its purpose in my life. But it has occurred to me that the next time I go on any trip, one of these new notebooks will fit easily into a carryon bag, and that even if the book were to be lost, the loss would be minimal.

Berkeley House

Although Charlotte O'Mara lived in San Francisco, and her third and final stepmother, Blanche, in Berkeley, just across the bay, they traditionally communicated by postcard, an aversion to the telephone being one of the few things they had in common. Thus it was by way of a crowded card from Blanche that Charlotte first heard that the Berkeley house in which she had grown up was being sold.

That night, at dinner with her lover, Lyman Clay, a bookseller from Portland, Maine, a tall towheaded young man, Charlotte drank too much wine, and she cried out to Lyman, "You don't know how much I loved that house!"

Since theirs was a relatively recent friendship, a couple of months old, Charlotte had not, so far, talked much, if at all, about her parents, both now dead. And she had said nothing about the house other than that it was in the Berkeley hills. And so, although kind and intelligent, intuitive, Lyman was understandably puzzled at the extremity of her reaction. "It was a really great house?" he asked.

"No, actually it was pretty peculiar. Adobe, all sprawled

out. It's just that—just that I always lived there," she told him hopelessly.

The next day, along with some gratitude for Lyman's kindness, and a slight hangover, Charlotte had an embarrassed sense of falseness. "Love" was too simple a word for her feelings about that house. She had reacted to its sale with rage and anguish, with an acute and wild sense of loss that she could not, for the moment, fathom, any more than she could get rid of the pain.

Charlotte was a painter, and in that precarious way she made her living—although that year, the year of the sale of the house, she had a very good fellowship. She thought she knew a lot about joy and grief, about broke and flush, failure and relative success. Still, she was surprised at the violence of her feelings about the house, about Blanche's selling it. Waking at three in the morning, she thought of crossing the Bay Bridge from Potrero Hill, where in their separate flats both she and Lyman lived, and going over to Grizzly Peak Boulevard, in Berkeley, where the house was. And burning it down. If I can't have it no one will, she wildly thought, at that most vulnerable predawn hour.

And she had no right to any of those emotions, any more than she had any "legal" right to the house. After all, her father, Ian O'Mara, had left the house to Blanche, his fourth wife, "to make her feel more secure." He had told Charlotte this in the same letter in which he first told about his will. But at that time Charlotte was living in Paris, studying, happily broke, and she hardly paid attention to what he said. She could not then focus on anything as distant and unlikely as her father's death.

She was aware, though, in a distant way, that Blanche, a fading tall blond Southern belle from Savannah, had not found much security in Berkeley, with those threatening academic people, or with Ian, who was inveterately mean to women: mean to Charlotte's mother, who had died young, and miserable; mean to his next, long-wooed wife, Pinky; and mean to Avis, the third. Mean to Blanche, often not speaking to her for days. In a way, leaving the house to Blanche was one of Ian's kinder gestures, although not exactly kind in regard to Charlotte.

Later, back from Paris and living in New York, very broke, nowhere near making it, Charlotte had remembered Ian's letter, and with uncharacteristic bravado—she was generally, and with good reason, quite frightened of her father—she wrote to him and said, "What exactly did you mean about leaving Blanche the house? Don't I get any of it?" And Ian, a smooth talker, wrote back reassuringly, "Of course Blanche will leave it to you. You'll get it all, eventually." But he did not say that in his will, and, what with taxes and repairs, the place probably was too much for Blanche, who was getting on. No surprise that she would have to sell the place, except that Charlotte was surprised; she was horrified.

A week or so after the postcard came, after Charlotte had begun to lie awake thinking always of the house, she had lunch with her friend Margery, an architect. Charlotte had formed the habit of telling Margery much, although never all, of what was on her mind. That day she talked for a while to Margery about Lyman, saying that it bothered her that he was five years younger, although why should that be a problem? She did not say that she really liked him enough to scare her, a little.

And then she tried to say what she felt about the house. She spoke, however, without much hope of comfort or understanding; she believed that because of her profession

Margery would have a rather anatomical view of houses. To Margery, a house would be a shell for living in, designed and built in a certain way, in a certain state of repair.

Charlotte said, and she felt her breath tighten as she spoke, "It's crazy, the very idea of that house's being sold makes me feel dislodged. Deracinated." She tried to laugh, and coughed.

Margery laughed, too, and then she said, "Well, once I felt pretty much that way, when the house in Illinois that I grew up in was being sold. And then I thought, What's wrong with me? I spent the worst years of my life in that house, I was miserable there."

"Oh, Margery," Charlotte cried out. "It was horrible. My mother dying, and then Ian fighting with Pinky, and then Avis. Not speaking to Blanche."

Home from lunch, in her studio, from which on clear days she could see the Berkeley hills, Charlotte thought back to all the misery and unhappiness of the Grizzly Peak house. And maybe now, remembering, she would be all right?

But she was not all right. Lyman had gone to a convention of booksellers in Los Angeles, and that night, instead of sleeping, Charlotte argued ragingly with Ian, who had been dead for five years: "Why didn't you say in your will that I was supposed to have the house? What made you trust Blanche? You know she doesn't like me, none of them have. Why didn't you think of me when you made your will?"

And to Blanche: "If you're so broke why don't you go to work, for a change? You could try interior decoration, or real estate. I've always supported myself, one way or another, and if you think I liked being a waitress at Zim's . . ."

She got up in the morning scratchy-eyed, heavy in the head and heart, with no mind for work. She did work, though, on a stylized landscape, its tidiness possibly being a counter to the confusion in her mind: a great flat yellow stretch of fields, hills nearly the same color and a paler-yellow sky.

One of the things that Charlotte did not tell Margery—and she hated to think what a shrink would make of this—was about her dreams: almost always, all her life, they had taken place in that pale adobe hilltop house, with its sprawling wings, in its high grove of redwood and eucalyptus trees. Even in Paris, or New York, in her dream life, there she would be. This struck her as unbearably sentimental, not to mention infantile. Nevertheless, it was true.

For a time, then, Charlotte managed to get her worrying about the house down to ten or fifteen minutes a day; during those minutes she would still rave and rage, first at Ian, then at Blanche, but afterward she would get to work. She was working well, on that yellow landscape.

Also, she was getting along happily with Lyman Clay—surprisingly, since most of her love affairs had been marked by turbulence. Lyman was in fact such a gentle man, sensitive and keenly appreciative of her painting, and of her, that at times Charlotte wondered if he could be gay; no evidence pointed in that direction, it was just a way that living in San Francisco in those end-of-the-Seventies years could make you think. She very much liked his unmanageable white-blond hair, his flat Maine voice and his Yankee wit.

A couple of weeks after getting the first postcard, in a mood of relative peace Charlotte decided that, in a simple and honest way, she would tell Blanche that she was indeed upset about her selling the house but that she now almost understood. She could almost stand it. After all, Blanche had been nicer than her two other stepmothers; once she had taken the trouble to polish and pack and deliver some old wineglasses of Charlotte's mother's (just in time, Charlotte was sure, to keep Ian from breaking them). But Charlotte forgot, as she thought of writing to Blanche, Blanche's deep suspicion of anything Charlotte did or said. Suspicion, Charlotte had to admit, not entirely unfounded. "I've tried to love Charlotte," Blanche had remarked one time to Ian, who reported this to Charlotte, in a concurring way—the effort of loving her being too much for anyone, it would seem.

And so, in answer to her postcard, Charlotte got back a long typed letter from Blanche, mainly to the effect that Charlotte had no legal right to the house. As if Charlotte didn't know her father's will by heart.

Even in her postcards, Blanche spoke what Charlotte thought of as "Southern," by which she meant the content as well as the accent. It was always necessary for Charlotte to shove aside a lot of words to get at what Blanche meant. That letter, translated, meant: Your father didn't care about you at all, he only cared for me. Which Charlotte had heard and even concluded on her own. Still, it hurt to have it pointed out.

In other, lighter moods, Charlotte could almost think of Blanche as funny; she was much a master, or mistress, of the velvet barb—as when she once remarked to Charlotte, "And I've always thought you were so pretty, even if no one else ever did." Well, Charlotte had never thought of herself as especially pretty—except maybe for a few minutes, sometimes. She no more needed to have that pointed out than she needed to be reminded of her father's non-caring. Still, the way Blanche got it across was fairly funny, Charlotte guessed.

Because Charlotte had been only six when her mother died, her memories of Eugenia, though clear, were brief, truncated. Eugenia had played the recorder, and she had gone to all the chamber-music concerts that came to Berkeley—a lot of concerts. Her erudition in both musical and literary areas was legendary. To this day she was talked about. She had had many friends in the academic community —professors, musicians, literary types, who no doubt disliked noisy, self-made Ian, as he probably disliked them back, and disliked Eugenia's friendships with them, and finally disliked Eugenia. And turned to beautiful, rich Pinky.

What Charlotte remembered best was lying in bed, her wing of the house juxtaposed to her mother's solitary wing, and hearing Eugenia weeping, weeping—hours of tears. Those terrible sounds were what Charlotte instantly, audibly remembered when her friend Margery said how miserable she had been in her parents' house. Eugenia's tears, her thick and heavy unhappiness had made the child Charlotte sick and heavy with unhappiness as Eugenia lay there crying over Ian—Ian the handsome, the unkind, the menace to women.

Given Ian, then, it is hardly surprising that Charlotte should have had her share of troubles with men. And maybe more. It sometimes seemed that way to Charlotte. She had been known to fall madly in love with the most impossible men—but a lot of women did that. What Charlotte also did, and what seemed even more dangerous, was: on the rare occasions when she was involved with a nice man, she would somehow induce him to behave in a cruel way. Or, even if she did not really succeed in that enterprise, she would somehow, nevertheless, begin to see the nice man as cruel.

The next Blanche postcard announced that since the house was for sale, and she was thinking of moving to Santa Barbara, she was putting the furniture in storage; if there was anything Charlotte wanted, would she please come over and get it right away, at least before next Tuesday. Well, "next Tuesday" was the day after Charlotte got the card, and for that and several other reasons she decided not to take Blanche up on her offer.

Other considerations being: if there was anything Charlotte really wanted, Blanche would come up with a strong justification for not giving it to her. That had been established when Ian died and the carved Spanish bench that Charlotte asked for turned out to have already been promised to a distant cousin.

"I just never would have known you wanted that little old bench," rambled Blanche, in her explanatory postcard. "You never once sat on it when you came here to visit, and I just knew it was too teeny and old-fashioned to be anything you'd ever want."

Of course I never sat there, not since I was a child, but I liked to look at it, it's so graceful and pretty—is what Charlotte despaired of trying to say to Blanche. Except for the bench, which would have been nice, furniture was actually the last thing Charlotte needed, her apartment being already crowded with canvases. Finally, and maybe most important, she could truly not bear the thought of going to the house, and going over all those remaining things, those silver and mahogany souvenirs of her past. With Blanche. Any more than she could bear the house's being sold.

"It isn't so much the money that's involved," Charlotte had said to Margery when telling her of the house, "but it hurt my feelings, being disinherited." She had meant what she said, but as she listened to the echo of her words she heard an unexpected sanctimoniousness in them, a falseness, really. It was certainly true that her feelings had been hurt, badly hurt, but it was also true that she minded about the money. Her livelihood was precarious; certainly she could have used the proceeds from the sale of a large house.

"How much do you think she'll get for the house?" asked Margery, who had never seen it, Charlotte not being given to taking friends over to meet Blanche.

"I haven't any idea. I don't know about real estate," Charlotte said. "It's a big house, though. Sort of spread out."

"Well, anything in the Berkeley hills is worth at least two hundred grand," said Margery, who did know about those things.

Two hundred thousand dollars. With even half that, decently invested, Charlotte figured that she could live for the rest of her life. Not worry about selling paintings. Just paint.

But, in a way, the realization that something as concrete as money figured in her pain was comforting; it made her feel less blackly doomed—less crazy.

Margery mused, "It would be interesting to know what she'll get for it."

"I can't exactly ask her, though."

"Maybe I could find out."

. . .

As though things in her life were not difficult enough at that moment, Lyman Clay began to push Charlotte toward getting married. Or that is how Charlotte felt: pushed.

Typically, he presented his ideas in a literary way, over a dinner at his place. A dinner that he had cooked. And Lyman's cooking was another source of amazement and slight suspicion for Charlotte.

"A marriage is like the imposition of form on feeling in poetry," Lyman said. "Or in painting, for heaven's sake."

With a sharp leap of her heart, Charlotte saw what he meant; she felt it, but she was too disturbed—about the house, about Blanche, about Ian—to think in a serious way about what Lyman was suggesting.

And gloomily she foresaw that she and Lyman would eventually come to a parting over this issue, since he was clearly serious in what he said. A year or so later, when Lyman had married someone else (lots of women really want to marry, she knew, and Lyman was exceptionally nice), she, Charlotte, would wish that she were with him; then she would mourn for Lyman, as she had for various other departed men.

It was at Lyman's that Margery reached her—not wanting to wait to call Charlotte in the morning. She had to tell her the news.

"I can't believe this," said Margery over the phone. "The place is going for a hundred thousand. Honestly, Char, it must be a wreck."

Not grasping the sum of money, her mind instead wandering back to the actual house (a wreck?), Charlotte only said, "Well, it didn't use to be."

"Who ever would have thought that a hundred thousand could come to look like a bargain?" said Margery.

Vaguely offended at the word "bargain" being attached to her house, Charlotte murmured, "Not I."

. . .

An odd lapse, or confusion, of memory had been disturbing Charlotte, along with her other troubles, ever since first hearing from Blanche about the house: simply, she could not remember whether a giant pine that had been near the side porch had been cut down or not. In her earliest memories it was there; as a small child she had played with dolls and Dinky toys among its roots. And she could remember it when, as an older girl, she had sat there on the porch, making out with some boy. But then: had there been talk about cutting it down? Had Ian said it had to go, that it menaced the roof, or the porch? Possessed of an unusually active visual imagination, Charlotte could see the waving heavy-boughed pine, and she could also see its stump, raw and flat and new—or was she seeing the stump from another tree, somewhere else?

Without waiting to show it to Lyman or to Margery—to anyone—Charlotte took the yellow landscape to her gallery, a new one, in Embarcadero Center, and it was sold the next day, for more money than Charlotte could believe: enough to live on for five or six months, she thought.

To celebrate, and because, marriage or not, he was an extremely nice man, Charlotte took Lyman out to dinner, inviting him to a new French place, all polished brass and big mirrors and white linen, which they had sometimes walked past.

Exactly the kind of occasion that should be fun and won't be, Charlotte thought as she dressed, putting on an unaccustomed skirt and silk shirt and high sandals. Lyman will make some dumb scene about not letting me pay, and we won't have anything to talk about except the food, which will not be good.

The restaurant was attractive. And as they sat down, Lyman in a coat and tie, straw hair under control, Charlotte thought, Well, we do make a fairly handsome couple.

Easily, Lyman told the waiter to put the wine on a separate check, he would take care of that.

"*Mais bien sûr, Monsieur.*"

As Charlotte thought, Well, so far so good.

The food, too, was good, but then after a while something in the tone of the restaurant, maybe, began to make them unfamiliar to themselves. Charlotte heard Lyman talking in a new and stilted way—indeed, discussing the food— and she began to think, I was right.

Mainly for something new to say, she asked, "How come you never talk about Portland?" more complainingly than she had meant to. "Did you like it, growing up there?"

He grinned, showing white, white teeth. "Well, I really did," he said. "It's still small enough to be comprehensible, sort of. There are even some cobbled streets left. And we lived out on Cape Elizabeth, right on the Atlantic."

He went on and on about Portland—the coast, the beaches, the rocks—and Charlotte could see it all vividly as he spoke.

But why was this conversation making her so sad? And then she knew: she was hearing the nostalgia in Lyman's voice; his missing the place he came from was making her miss her own place, her house.

She also took Margery out, for lunch, for further celebration.

"I honestly think I must be going crazy," Charlotte said. "Lyman could not be a nicer person; he's kind and smart, and being five years younger than I am is not important, really. But I keep making trouble. If I had better sense I could be perfectly happy with Lyman. I sometimes am."

Margery laughed. "If you had better sense you might not be a painter."

"Well, I guess."

Margery raised her wineglass in a toast, and then she asked, "What ever will you do with all that money?"

Charlotte frowned, her hands gestured helplessness. "I don't know, it's been worrying me. I should do something—sensible."

"What about our buying the Berkeley house?"

"*What?*"

"Your house in Berkeley. I have some money saved up ... and I could ... and you could ... we could ... rent ... invest ... property values."

Margery made the appointment and got the key from the real-estate agent—all the negotiations would have to be in her name, obviously—and on a bright October afternoon she and Charlotte drove over to Berkeley: two prospective buyers of an empty house.

They drove up Marin, and up and up, and then turned right on Grizzly Peak, at which point the sheer familiarity of everything she saw accelerated and heated the flow of Charlotte's blood: how she *knew* all those particular turns of the road, those steep sudden views of the bay. And then there it was, in a clump of tall waving eucalyptus: her house. Sand-colored adobe bricks and a red tiled roof, a narrow wooden porch stuck out to one side like an ill-advised whim, long one-storied wings seeming to wander off behind. Perhaps because of the five years' lapse since she had been there, or maybe because she was seeing it with Margery, Charlotte thought,

What a nutty-looking house, it's crazy. But that was an affectionate thought; the house could have been an eccentric relative. In fact, it reminded her considerably of Ian: uncontrolled, given over to impulse. (An adobe house in the Berkeley hills had been itself an eccentric impulse, or a sentimental one: Ian and her mother had spent their honeymoon in Mexico.)

When Margery had parked the car, they got out and walked toward it, toward Charlotte's house. All the vines and shrubbery had increased considerably in the five years since her last visit; a green growth of wisteria almost covered the porch.

Like a thief, an accomplice in crime, Charlotte followed Margery up to the front door, which, with the real-estate agent's key, Margery opened, and they walked into an absolutely empty, echoing house.

But why was Charlotte so frightened? She could have been an actual intruder, even a thief, so violent was her apprehension as they walked from room to room, both of them on tiptoe. And along with this fear came a total disorientation: was this small stained room the one that had always been called the guest room but where Ian slept from one wife to another? And was this smaller room her own, in which she had lain and listened to Eugenia's weeping? Shivering, to Margery she whispered, "It all looks so small."

"Rooms do, without any furniture. Honestly, they weren't kidding about its being in bad shape."

"I'm going back outside," whispered Charlotte.

Outside was more familiar: the sweeping view of the bay—the water and sky, the darker skyline. The shrubs and trees and vines were all in their proper place, except for the big pine, which indeed was missing. Nor was there any stump where Charlotte thought the tree had been. Instead, in that spot Blanche (it must have been Blanche) had put in a bed of geraniums, her favorites; in the intense October sunlight they gave off a dusty, slightly rancid smell.

Margery came out at last, and together she and Charlotte walked around the house, Margery stopping to peer down at foundations, to mutter about dry rot.

Once back in the car, seemingly having put dry rot out of her mind, Margery began to talk animatedly about possible reconstruction of the house: "It really has marvelous potential; it needs a lot of work, but I could . . . knock out walls . . . open up . . . a deck."

By this time they were on the bridge, crossing the shining water far below—that day an interesting slate blue, a color that wet stones sometimes are.

"Well, so what do you think?" asked Margery.

"I don't know. I guess it really doesn't seem my kind of thing," Charlotte said, with a certain effort.

"But I thought you wanted—I thought it would help." Although clearly intending kindness, sympathy, Margery sounded very slightly huffy: her professional imagination was being rebuffed.

Margery would get over her huffiness in time, Charlotte thought. And while Charlotte could not entirely "get over" her pain at the loss of what she continued to think of as her house, it would perhaps become bearable, little more than an occasional sharp twinge.

She began a new painting, this time all shades of blue, from slate to brightest azure.

When, a few weeks later, a postcard came from Blanche, in Santa Barbara, showing lots of palms and flowers, and announcing that she was going to marry the most wonderful (underlined) man with a lovely house on the ocean, near the Biltmore Hotel, Charlotte stuck the card in a box with letters that she meant to answer soon.

It was a few months after that, near Christmastime, that, waking with Lyman in his wide, eccentrically carved oak bed—their most recent decision had been to make no decision, no firm plans about legalities or moving in—in a wondering voice Charlotte said, "You know, it's curious, I don't dream that I live in Berkeley anymore. My dreams don't take place in that house."

"I didn't know they ever did," Lyman said.

A Wonderful Woman

Feeling sixteen, although in fact just a few months short of sixty, Felicia Lord checks into the San Francisco hotel at which her lover is to meet her the following day. Felicia is tall and thin, with the intense, somewhat startled look of a survivor—a recent widow, mother of five, a ceramicist who prefers to call herself a potter. A stylish gray-blonde. Mr. Voort, she is told, will be given the room next to hers when he arrives. Smiling to herself, she then follows the ancient, wizened bellboy into an antique elevator cage; once inside, as they creakingly ascend, he turns and smiles up at her, as though he knows what she is about. She herself is less sure.

The room to which he leads her is a suite, really: big, shabby-cozy living room, discreetly adjoining bedroom, large old-fashioned bath, on the top floor of this old San Francisco hotel, itself a survivor of the earthquake and fire, in an outlying neighborhood. All in all, she instantly decides, it is the perfect place for meeting Martin, for being with him, in the bright blue dazzling weather, this sudden May.

San Francisco itself, connected as it is with Felicia's own history, has seemed a possibly dangerous choice: the scene of her early, unlikely premarital "romance" with Charles, her now dead husband; then the scene of holiday visits from Connecticut with the children, treat zoo visits and cable-car rides, Chinese restaurants; scene of a passionate ill-advised love affair, and a subsequent abortion—all that also took place in San Francisco, but years ago, in other hotels, other neighborhoods.

Why then, having tipped the grinning bellboy and begun to unpack, silk shirts on hangers, silk tissue-papered nightgowns and underthings in drawers, does she feel such a dizzying lurch of apprehension? It is too intense in its impact to be just a traveler's nerves, jet lag. Felicia is suddenly quite weak; she sits down in an easy chair next to a window to absorb the view, to think sensibly about her situation, or try to. She sees a crazy variety of rooftops: mansard, Victorian curls, old weathered shingles and bright new slate. Blue water, paler sky, green hills. No help.

It is being in love with Martin, she thinks, being "in love," and the newness of Martin Voort. I've never known a farming sailor before, and she smiles, because the words don't describe Martin, really, although he owns some cranberry bogs, near Cape Cod, and he builds boats. Charles was a painter, but he was rich (Martin is not rich) and most of his friends were business people. Martin is entirely new to her.

And at my age, thinks Felicia, and she smiles again, a smile which feels tremulous on her mouth.

"Wonderful" is the word that people generally have used about Felicia. She was wonderful with Charles, whose painting never came to much, although he owned a couple of galleries, who drank a lot. Wonderful with all those kids, who were a little wild, always breaking arms or heads.

Her lover—a Mexican Communist, and like Charles a

painter, but a much better painter than Charles—Felipe thought she looked wonderful, with her high-boned face, strong hands and her long, strong voluptuous body. She was wonderful about the abortion, and wonderful too when he went back to his wife.

Felicia was wonderful when Charles died, perfectly controlled and kind to everyone.

Wonderful is not how Felicia sees herself at all; she feels that she has always acted out of simple—or sometimes less simple—necessity.

Once married to Charles, and having seen the lonely, hollow space behind his thin but brilliant surface of good looks, graceful manners, skill at games—it was then impossible to leave him; and he couldn't have stood it. And when the children had terrible coughs, or possible concussions, she took good care of them, sometimes staying up all night, simply because she wanted them well, and soon.

During the unanesthetized abortion, she figured out that you don't scream, because that would surely make the pain much worse, when it is already so bad that it must be happening to someone else, and also because the doctor, a Brazilian chiropractor in the Mission District, is hissing, "Don't make noise." And when your lover defects, saying that he is going back, after all, to his wife in Guadalajara, you don't scream about that either; what good would it do? You go back to your husband, and to the clay pots that you truly love, round and fat or delicately slender.

When your husband dies, as gracefully as he lived, after a too strenuous game of tennis, you take care of everything and everyone, and you behave well, for your own sake as well as for everyone else's.

Then you go to visit an old friend, in Duxbury, and you meet a large wild red-haired, blue-eyed man, a "sailor-farmer," and you fall madly in love, and you agree to meet him for a holiday, in May, in San Francisco, because he has some boats to see there.

She is scared. Sitting there, in the wide sunny window, Felicia trembles, thinking of Martin, the lovely city, themselves, for a long first time. But supposing she isn't "wonderful" anymore? Suppose it all fails, flesh fails, hearts fail, and everything comes crashing down upon their heads, like an avalanche, or an earthquake?

She thinks, I will have to go out for a walk.

Returned from a short tour of the neighborhood, which affords quick beautiful views of the shining bay, and an amazing variety of architecture, Felicia feels herself restored; she is almost her own person again, except for a curious weakness in her legs, and the faintest throb of blood behind one temple, both of which she ascribes to fatigue. She stands there for a moment on the sidewalk, in the sunlight, and then she re-enters the hotel. She is about to walk past the desk when the bellboy, still stationed there, waves something in her direction. A yellow envelope—a telegram.

She thanks him and takes it with her into the elevator, waiting to open it until she is back in her room. It will be from Martin, to welcome her there. Already she knows the character of his gestures: he hates the phone; in fact, so far they have never talked on the telephone, but she has received at least a dozen telegrams from Martin, whose instructions must always include: "Deliver, do not phone." After the party at which they met he wired, from Boston to Duxbury: HAVE DINNER WITH ME WILL PICK YOU UP AT SEVEN MARTIN VOORT. Later ones were either jokes or messages of love—or both: from the start they had laughed a lot.

This telegram says: DARLING CRAZY DELAY FEW DAYS LATE ALL LOVE.

The weakness that earlier Felicia had felt in her legs

makes them now suddenly buckle; she falls across the bed, and all the blood in both temples pounds as she thinks: I can't stand it, I really can't. This is the one thing that is too much for me.

But what do you do if you can't stand something, and you don't scream, after all?

Maybe you just go to bed, as though you were sick?

She undresses, puts on a pretty nightgown and gets into bed, where, like a person with a dangerously high fever, she begins to shake. Her arms crossed over her breast, she clutches both elbows; she presses her ankles together. The tremors gradually subside, and finally, mercifully, she falls asleep, and into dreams. But her sleep is fitful, thin, and from time to time she half wakes from it, never at first sure where she is, nor what year of her life this is.

A long time ago, in the early Forties, during Lieutenant (USN) Charles Lord's first leave, he and Felicia Thacher, whom he had invited out to see him, literally danced all night, at all the best hotels in town—as Felicia wondered: Why me? How come Charles picked me for this leave? She had known him since childhood; he was one of her brother's best friends. Had someone else turned him down? She had somewhat the same reactions when he asked her to marry him, over a breakfast glass of champagne, in the Garden Court of the Palace Hotel. Why me? she wondered, and she wondered too at why she was saying yes. She said yes, dreamily, to his urgent eyes, his debonair smile, light voice, in that room full of war-time glamor, uniforms and flowers, partings and poignant brief reunions. Yes, Charles, yes, let's do get married, all right, soon.

A dream of a courtship, and then a dream groom, handsome Charles. And tall, strong-boned, strong-willed Felicia Thacher Lord.

Ironically, since she had so many, Felicia was not especially fond of babies; a highly verbal person, she was nervous with human creatures who couldn't talk, who screamed out their ambiguous demands, who seemed to have no sense and who often smelled terrible. She did not see herself as at all a good mother, knowing how cross and frightened she felt with little children. Good luck (Charles's money) had provided her with helpful nurses all along to relieve her of the children, and the children of her, as she saw it. Further luck made them all turn out all right, on the whole. But thank God she was done with all that. Now she liked all the children very much; she regarded them with great fondness, and some distance.

Her husband, Charles, loved Felicia's pregnancies (well, obviously he did), and all those births, his progeny. He spoke admiringly of how Felicia accomplished all that, her quick deliveries, perfect babies. She began to suspect that Charles had known, in the way that one's unconscious mind knows everything, that this would be the case; he had married her to be the mother of his children.

"I have the perfect situation for a painter, absolutely perfect," Charles once somewhat drunkenly declared. "Big house, perfect studio, money for travel, money to keep the kids away at school. A wonderful kind strong wife. Christ, I even own two galleries. *Perfect.* I begin to see that the only thing lacking is talent," and he gave a terrible laugh.

How could you leave a man in such despair?

Waking slowly, her head still swollen with sleep, from the tone of the light Felicia guesses that it must be about midafternoon. Eventually she will have to order something to eat, tea or boiled eggs, something sustaining.

Then, with a flash of pain, Martin comes into her mind, and she begins to think.

She simply doesn't know him, that's half the problem, "know" in this instance meaning able to predict the behavior of, really, to trust. Maybe he went to another party and met another available lady, maybe someone rather young, young-fleshed and never sick or tired? (She knows that this could be true, but still it doesn't sound quite right, as little as she knows him.)

But what does FEW DAYS mean to Martin? To some people a week would be a few days. CRAZY DELAY is deliberately ambiguous. Either of those phrases could mean anything at all.

Sinkingly, despairingly, she tells herself that it is sick to have fantasies about the rest of your life that revolve around a man you have only known for a couple of months.

Perfectly possibly he won't come to San Francisco at all, she thinks, and then: I hate this city.

When the bellboy comes in with her supper tray, Felicia realizes for the first time that he is a dwarf; odd that she didn't see that before. His grin now looks malign, contemptuous, even, as though he recognizes her for what she now is: an abandoned woman, of more than a certain age.

As he leaves she shivers, wishing she had brought along a "sensible" robe, practical clothes, instead of all this mocking silk and lace. Looking quickly into the mirror, and then away, she thinks, I look like an old circus monkey.

She sleeps through the night. One day gone, out of whatever "few days" are.

When she calls to order breakfast the next morning, the manager (manageress: a woman with a strong, harsh Midwestern accent) suggests firmly that a doctor should be called. She knows of one.

Refusing that suggestion, as firmly, politely as she can, Felicia knows that she reacted to hostility rather than to concern. The manageress is afraid that Felicia will get really sick and die; what a mess to have on their hands, an unknown dead old woman.

But Felicia too is a little afraid.

Come to think of it, Felicia says to herself, half-waking at what must be the middle of the afternoon, I once spent some time in another San Francisco hotel, waiting for Felipe, in another part of town. After the abortion.

She and Felipe met when he had a show at one of Charles's galleries; they had, at first tipsily, fallen into bed, in Felipe's motel (Charles had "gone to sleep") after the reception; then soberly, both passionately serious, they fell in love. Felipe's paintings were touring the country, Felipe with them, and from time to time, in various cities, Felicia followed him. Her excuse to Charles was a survey of possible markets for her pots, and visits to other potters, which, conscientiously, she also accomplished.

Felipe was as macho as he was radical, and he loved her in his own macho way, violently, with all his dangerous strength. She must leave Charles, Charles must never touch her again, he said. (Well, Charles drank so much that that was hardly an issue.) She must come with him to Paris, to a new life. All her children were by then either grown or off in schools—why not?

When they learned that she was pregnant he desperately wanted their child, he said, but agreed that a child was not possible for them. And he remembered the Brazilian chiropractor that he had heard about, from relatives in San Francisco.

The doctor seemingly did a good job, for Felicia suffered no later ill effects. Felipe was kind and tender with her; he said that her courage had moved him terribly. Felicia felt that her courage, if you wanted to call it that, had somewhat unnerved him; he was a little afraid of her now.

However, they celebrated being together in San Francisco, where Felipe had not been before. He loved the beautiful city, and they toasted each other, and their mutual passion, with Mexican beer or red wine, in their Lombard Street motel. Then one afternoon Felipe went off alone to visit a family of his relatives, in San Jose, and Felicia waited for him. He returned to her very late, and in tears: a grown man, broad-backed, terrifically strong, with springing thick black hair and powerful arms, crying out to her, "I cannot—I cannot go on with you, with our life. They have told me of my wife, all day she cries, and at night she screams and wakes the children. I must go to her."

Well, of course you must, said Felicia, in effect. If she's screaming that's where you belong. And she thought, Well, so much for my Latin love affair.

And she went home.

And now she thinks, Martin at least will not come to me in tears.

Martin Voort. At the end of her week in Duxbury, her visit to the old school friend, Martin, whom in one way or another she had seen every day, asked her to marry him, as soon as possible. "Oh, I know we're both over the hill," he said, and then exploded in a laugh, as she did too. "But suppose we're freaks who live to be a hundred? We might as well have fun on the way. I like you a lot. I want to be with you."

Felicia laughed again. She was secretly pleased that he hadn't said she was wonderful, but she thought he was a little crazy.

He followed her home with telegrams: WHEN OH WHEN WILL YOU MARRY ME and ARRIVING IN YOUR TOWN THIS FRIDAY PREPARE.

And now, suppose she never sees him again? For the first time in many months (actually, since Charles died) Felicia begins to cry, at the possible loss of such a rare, eccentric and infinitely valuable man.

But in the midst of her sorrow at that terrible possibility, the permanent lack of Martin—who could be very sick, could have had a stroke: at his age, their age, that is entirely possible—though grieving, Felicia realizes that she can stand it, after all, as she has stood other losses, other sorrows in her life. She can live without Martin.

She realizes too that she herself has just been genuinely ill, somewhat frighteningly so; what she had was a real fever, from whatever cause. Perhaps she should have seen a doctor.

However, the very thought of a doctor, a doctor's office, is enough to make her well, she dislikes them so; all those years of children, children's illnesses and accidents, made her terribly tired of medical treatment. Instead she will get dressed and go out for dinner, by herself.

And that is what she does. In her best clothes she takes a cab to what has always been her favorite San Francisco restaurant, Sam's. It is quite early, the place uncrowded. Felicia is given a pleasant side table, and the venerable waiters are kind to her. The seafood is marvelous. Felicia drinks a half-bottle of wine with her dinner and she thinks: Oh, so this is what it will be like. Well, it's really not so bad.

Returned to the hotel, however, once inside her room she experiences an acute pang of disappointment, and she understands that she had half consciously expected Martin to be there; Martin was to be her reward for realizing that she could live without him, for being "sensible," for bravely going out to dinner by herself.

She goes quickly to bed, feeling weak and childish, and approving neither her weakness nor her childishness, not at all.

Sometime in the middle of the night she awakes from a sound sleep, and from a vivid dream; someone, a man, has knocked on the door of her room, this room. She answers, and he comes in and they embrace, and she is wildly glad to see him. But who is he? She can't tell: is it her husband,

Charles, or one of her sons? Felipe? Is it Martin? It could even be a man she doesn't know. But, fully awake, as she considers the dream she is saddened by it, and it is quite a while before she sleeps again.

The next morning, though, she is all right: refreshed, herself again. Even, in the mirror, her face is all right. I look like what I am, she thinks: a strong healthy older woman. She dresses and goes downstairs to breakfast, beginning to plan her day. Both the bellboy and the manager smile in a relieved way as she passes the desk, and she smiles back, amiably.

She will see as much of San Francisco as possible today, and arrange to leave tomorrow. Why wait around? This morning she will take a cab to Union Square, and walk from there along Grant Avenue, Chinatown, to North Beach, where she will have lunch. Then back to the hotel for a nap, then a walk, and dinner out—maybe Sam's again.

She follows that plan, or most of it. On Union Square, she goes into a couple of stores, where she looks at some crazily overpriced clothes, and buys one beautiful gauzy Indian scarf, for a daughter's coming birthday. Then down to Grant Avenue, to walk among the smells of Chinese food, the incense, on to North Beach, to a small Italian counter restaurant, where she has linguine with clam sauce, and a glass of red wine.

In the cab, going back to the hotel, she knows that she is too tired, has "overdone," but it was worth it. She has enjoyed the city, after all.

An hour or so later, from a deep, deep sleep she is awakened by a knocking on her door, just as in her dream, the night before.

Groggily she calls out, "Who is it?" She is not even sure that the sound has been real; so easily this could be another dream.

A man's impatient, irritated voice answers, "It's *me*, of course."

Me? She is still half asleep; she doesn't know who he is. However, his tone has made her obedient, and she gets out of bed, pulling her pale robe about her, and goes to the door. And there is a tall, red-haired man, with bright blue eyes, whom of course she knows, was expecting—who embraces her violently. "Ah, Martin," she breathes, when she can.

It is Martin, and she is awake.

The only unfamiliar thing about his face, she notes, when she can see him, is that a tooth is missing from his smile; there is a small gap that he covers with his hand as soon as she has noticed. And he says, "It broke right off! Right off a bridge. And my dentist said I'd have to wait a week. How could I send you a telegram about a goddam dentist? Anyway, I couldn't wait a week to see you."

They laugh (although there are tears somewhere near Felicia's eyes), and then they embrace again.

And at last they are sitting down on the easy chairs near the window, next to the view, and they are quietly talking together, making plans for the rest of that day and night.

Legends

Partly because she was so very plain, large and cumbersome, like her name, at first I liked Candida Heffelfinger better than any interviewer who had come around for years. Tall, almost gaunt, she had a big white pockmarked face, lank brown hair and beautiful dark eyes—have you ever noticed how many otherwise ugly women have lovely eyes? Also, she had that special, unassuming niceness that plain women often have; I should know, it was years before I dared to be as mean and recalcitrant, as harsh-mannered as I had always wanted to be.

I liked her as soon as I saw her awkwardly getting out of the red Toyota that she must have rented at the Raleigh-Durham Airport, and start up the pine-strewn path to my (Ran's) house. And I liked her although I knew that she would want to talk about my legendary love affair, about Ran, rather than about my work, the sculpture. I was used to that; it interested everyone, our "love," and besides, what can you say about structures almost twenty feet high, some weighing thousands of pounds?

In a welcoming way, and also as a surprise—I would not be the ogress that almost anyone in New York would have warned her about—I went to the door to greet her.

"Miss Phelps?" she puffed out. "Jane Phelps?"

Well, who in hell else would I be? But I said yes, and asked her to come in, and what would she like to drink?

In her dowdy-expensive gray flannel suit she followed me into the living room, and said that she drank bourbon-and-water.

I made the drinks, and we both settled down in that high-ceilinged, glassed-in living room; we stared out at the fading November sunset, against the black lace network of trees. We smoked our cigarettes, and drank, and we made friendly small talk about her flight, the drive from the airport to Hilton. This house, its view.

I not only liked Ms. Heffelfinger; I felt that I knew a lot about her. With that name, and that flat, unaccented voice, she would be Midwestern, as I am, from somewhere in Minnesota, or Wisconsin. I imagined a rural childhood for her, and I saw her as the eldest in a family of brothers, whose care would often fall to her. Then adolescence—well, we all know about the adolescent years of ugly girls: the furtive sexual encounters with boys who later don't speak to you in the halls at school, who invite small fluffy blondes to their parties. Then college, at a state university, where the social failure would be somewhat balanced by academic triumph, and maybe even a passingly satisfactory affair with a young instructor, although more likely an aging professor, paunchy and grimly married. Next the New York experience, the good job and the lonely love affairs: married men or alcoholics, or both, or worse.

You might ask why such an unattractive girl would be chosen in that way at all, but only if you had never heard the old saying that ugly women as lovers are fantastic. I remember the first time I heard that voiced, by a short, very truculent and quite untalented painter. I was entirely outraged, as though one of my most intimate secrets had been spoken aloud, for of course it is often true: a beautiful woman would expect to be made love to, we expect to make love.

Ms. Heffelfinger and I said what we could about the town—very old pre-Civil War—and the house, Ran's house, which was built in the Twenties—and then considered very innovative, all that glass—with prize money from his first symphony. (Ran was once a famous composer.)

Perhaps by way of changing our direction, I asked her if she minded living alone in New York—and I was totally unprepared for her answer.

"Well, actually we don't live in the city," she said. "We live in a small town in northern New Jersey. It's very unchic, but it's great for the kids, they love it."

We? Kids? Perhaps unfairly I felt that I had been deceived, or at least misled. I tried to keep surprise and suspicion from my face but they must have shown (everything does), for she laughed and said, "I know, I don't look married, or much like a mother, but maybe that's just as well?" And then she said, "Well, we might as well start? It's okay to turn on the tape?"

I said yes as I noted what nice teeth she had, just then exhibited in her first smile. I thought too that I had better be on my guard, more than usually so.

Now the sky beyond all that naked glass was entirely black, and you would have thought that everything outside was stilled, unless you knew—as I, a night walker, knew—that in those depths of woods small leaves yet stirred, and tiny birds were settling for the night. Ms. Heffelfinger turned on her recorder, and she began to say what I had known that she would say: a small speech to the effect that she knew very little in a general way about sculpture, "although I am really moved by it, more so than any other visual form." (Was that true?)

I said I understood, and I gave the snort that over the years I had perfected. "Actually no one knows a damn thing about my work but me, and sometimes I'm not at all sure that I do," I told her.

She smiled, again those nice teeth, our smoke circled up to the arched, beamed ceiling, and then she made her second predictable speech; everyone said it, in one form or another. "Of course you realize that the main interest, prurient though it may be, is in your relationship with Randolph Caldwell."

I smiled, showing my tolerant indifference to prurience, to vulgar curiosity. "Of course, the legendary love affair," I said.

"By now I'm quite an expert on the legend," Ms. Heffelfinger assured me, looking off into a distance that might have contained her notes. "You came to Hilton not long after Lucinda Caldwell died, is that right? Mr. Caldwell at that time was still in mourning for his wife?"

"In his way. Yes. Mourning." I had never met Lucinda, of course, but I too, in my way, had sometimes mourned for her.

And while I had strayed off in that direction, poor Lucinda's, Ms. Heffelfinger slowly inserted her knife into my heart.

"One thing I don't quite understand," she said, beginning gently, so that I hardly felt it. Then, "About Gloria Bingham." *In.* "Just when was it that she first came here, and met Randolph Caldwell?"

All the books and articles, if they mention her at all, other than as a footnote, make it perfectly clear that Gloria

Bingham was a totally unimportant figure in Ran's life, a girl who came after Lucinda, and before me, his major love. But I was unable just then to parrot the legend to Ms. Heffelfinger—or even, had I wanted to, to tell her that it was a bloody lie. I began to cough, passionately, as though I were trying to cough up my heart, that sudden cold stone in my chest.

Candida Heffelfinger looked alarmed, of course. She got up—for a moment I thought she meant to hit me on the back; fortunately she decided not to. She looked wildly about, and at last discovered the bar. She went over and brought me a glass of water, so helpful.

By then I could thank her, weakly. "But I really don't think I can talk anymore just now. I'll call you tomorrow," I told her. "You're staying at the inn?" In fact, I was not at all sure that I would call her—*why?*

She said yes, fine, and got up to go. I did not rise, I barely could have. I gave her a limp old lady's hand to shake, and I watched as she walked down the hall to the door, then turned to wave. Her suit was now rumpled, as though that brief encounter with me had messed up her clothes, as well as her good intentions.

It was the maid's night off, and so I decided not to bother with dinner. I made myself another drink, and then another, and later I had some cheese for nourishment. I watched the stars come out among the blackened pine and oak boughs, and then a waning moon come up, and I thought about life, and truth, and lies, as an old drunk person is very apt to do.

The true story, my—"our"—story, began a long time ago, in the Thirties, my own late twenties, when I came to Hilton to begin an instructorship in the art department. I

rented a tiny house, a cabin, on the road leading up to the
Caldwell house, in the deepest, leafiest, most romantic
Southern woods. And on that white road I first saw, driving
fast in a snappy open car, a handsome man in early middle
age, with thick gray hair, dark eyes and a bright red plaid
wool shirt. Randolph Caldwell, the composer, I was told
when I asked Dr. James, the head of the art department,
about my conspicuous neighbor. (This was just after Lucinda Caldwell had died, and no one then had ever heard of
Gloria Bingham. So you may conclude, Ms. Heffelfinger, that
it was I, not Gloria, who formed the unimportant link, who
came between Lucinda and Gloria.)

And later it was Dr. James who introduced me to Ran,
in the A. & P., at the vegetable counter.

"I'm delighted to meet a near neighbor," he said as he
took my hand, but his eyes glazed over in the automatic way
of a man meeting a not pretty woman, a look I knew.

"I've admired your car," I told him, half-lying, and hoping that he would not imagine I knew anything whatsoever
about cars.

But his voice and his eyes were beautiful. I loved him.

Actually I loved the whole town, the crazily hetero-
geneous architecture of the campus: cracked yellow plaster
on its oldest buildings, with their ferociously clinging red
Virginia creeper; and the newer brick additions, with their
corny Corinthian pillars, which now, several generations
later, look almost authentic. I loved my cabin in the woods,
on a slope of poplars, looking out to early fall dusks, almost
unpopulated hills of black, like a sea, the darkness stippled
here and there with straight blue lines of smoke from other
cabins, country people, mostly Negroes. The town and its
surrounding hills, its woods, were exotic to me; I might have

just arrived in Scotland, or East Africa. And, given my age and general inclinations, that excitement had to find a focus, a sexual object. I had to fall in love, and there was Ran, so handsome and seemingly unavailable, a man of the age I was used to choosing.

The next day I managed to be on the road just before he came by. I thought, even hoped, that he would wave in a friendly way, but he was much too Southern to let a lady walk; he stopped, and elaborately opened the door for me, and smiled, and instantly launched into a complicated monologue about the weather.

I soon worked out his schedule so that I could always be in his path. I would linger there in the smell of pines and leaves and dust and sunlight until I heard the sound of his car, and then I would move on briskly, until he should see me and stop. If he had passed me by, just waving, in a hurry, I would probably have died, my heart stricken and stilled then and there, and with a not pretty girl's dark imagination I always thought that would happen, but it never did—or never until he had Gloria with him in the car, and then they would both smile and wave, and hurry on.

Until Gloria, he would stop and open the door and I would clumsily get in; I was so dizzy, so wild with love, or lust, whatever, that I could hardly look at him. I am sure that he never noticed then, although much later, after we were lovers, of a sort, he claimed that he had always noticed everything about me. A typical Southern man's lie.

Now when I try to remember what we talked about, on those short important drives, I come up with nothing. The weather, the passage of time, the changing seasons. But that particular fall, I do remember, was extraordinarily beautiful, with vibrant, brilliant leaves against a vivid sky; it was more than worthy of our notice.

One problem in the way of talk was Ran's quite impenetrable accent. You think of a Southern accent as being slow, and lazy; Ran spoke more quickly than anyone I had ever known, and he constantly smoked—all those quick light Southern words arrived filtered through all that smoke. Half the time I hadn't the slightest idea what he was talking about, but I was excited by his voice, as I was by everything about him, his hair and his sad dark eyes, his cigarettes, his hunting shirts, his shabby tweeds, his snappy car. At worst, you could call it a crush.

Once in those early days he said to me, and this came out more distinctly than most of his sentences: "Lucinda never liked it here, you know. A Boston girl. She always said the woods down here were too *cluttered* for her taste," and he gestured with an elegant large white hand in the direction of the piny woods through which we passed, with their bright leaves, thick undergrowth.

For me just that luxuriance, that overplentitude of bush and wild grass and weed, was beautiful, was vaguely sexual. Still, I responded to her word, "cluttered," with the odd emphasis that Ran had given it; he had almost made me hear her Boston voice. I liked Lucinda's precision, and I felt a curious linkage with her, my dead rival.

Much later, during one of our more terrible drunken fights, Ran cried out, "You might as well be Lucinda, I can't stand it," and I countered, "You're just so stupid, you think all women are alike."

Still, he had a point; though I hadn't known her I sensed an affinity with Lucinda, as strong as my total antipathy to Gloria.

In early December of that year, that winter in Hilton, it suddenly snowed; one morning I woke to a white silent world, deep soft drifts everywhere, the road outside my house deeply buried in snow, the boughs of trees heavily ladened. Just after my second cup of coffee the telephone rang, and my heart leapt up, for I knew it could only be Ran.

"*Well,*" he said, and I could hear the quick inhalation of smoke. "It looks like we both will be 'hoofing it' this morning. Nor man nor beast could budge my car. How would it suit you if I knocked at your door in fifteen minutes or so?"

That would be the best thing in the world, I did not say. "I'll be ready, that's swell" is what I said.

Half an hour later he knocked at my door—the house that he had never seen inside. "Well, I can see you're very cozy here." He then asked, "It doesn't bother you, living all alone?"

"Oh no, I love it, the privacy," I lied.

"I don't love it," he announced, with a look almost of pain. I quickly regretted having sounded so silly and glib, but I could not say, as I wanted to, Please let me move into your house with you. I'll pay rent, or cook and sew, clean up, make love to you. Anything.

We exchanged a small smile, and set off through the snow.

We were becoming friends, and we continued in that process, over the winter. Occasionally we diverged from talking about the weather, noting changes in the colors and shapes of trees, leaves and underbrush, the early coming of spring in the woods that surrounded our lives, and Ran would talk about Lucinda, sadly, regretfully. I became, in a limited way, his comforter. In my life I have noticed that after a time of deep sorrow the greatest comfort may come from a person you do not know well, nor much care about. (God knows, Ran did not care much about me at that time, and you may even conclude, Ms. Heffelfinger, that he never did.) When Ran died I was comforted, a little, by a silly and very ambitious young art critic, in Westport, Connecticut, whom I did not like. Anyway, our most nearly intimate conversations were about Lucinda, her taste for Victorian novels and Elizabethan songs, her dislike of almost all Southern women. He never said what she died of, not then, and I assumed sheer misery.

I did not see Ran at the parties that I sometimes went to, graduate student, poor instructor parties. And for the most part I avoided them myself, those forlorn attempts at conviviality. I worked hard preparing for my classes, I was available for conferences with students and I had begun in a secret way to do some work of my own with wood, small sculptures. There was so much wood around, cheaply available, and I was fascinated by the variety of grains, of possible shapes. Also, my obsession with Ran took up considerable time, those daydreaming, fantasizing hours.

But late one night, in early April, I did see Ran at a party, at Dr. James's. I saw him across a very smoky room, looking handsome and sad and slightly drunk, and alone. I quickly divested myself of the philosophy instructor who was about to ask if he could take me home, and in my rush toward Ran I bumped into a sharp-cornered table, which happily he could not observe. I slowed down as I got to him, and assumed an expression of mixed surprise and pleasure, the latter at least being genuine. "*Well,*" I said, and it occurred to me that I had begun to sound like him. "Fancy meeting you here."

He said, "Well, fancy," and we both laughed again.

In my left hand was an empty glass that I had forgotten, but Ran noticed at once, with his Southern-hospitable-drunk instincts. "Well," he said, "you need more than a sweetening; you've got to have a real drink."

I did not—neither of us needed a drink—but of course I smiled, pleased and grateful, and I accepted a long dark glass of bourbon, barely iced. Our first drink together, and dear God, I hate to think how many others followed.

We began to talk, and in a quick excited way Ran told me about a trip that he was taking; he was leaving for Atlanta the next day, where a newly formed orchestra was to perform an early work of his. (The sad truth, as I had learned from local gossip, was that by now all Ran's work was "early"; for many years he had produced nothing new, beyond a short suite of songs, dedicated to Lucinda and often performed by the music department's chorus.) That night he looked, for the first time since I had known him, really happy, and, to me, most dazzlingly attractive. (A puzzle: did Ran ever know how handsome he was? Hard to miss, his good looks, but for such a deeply Presbyterian-Puritan it would have seemed a wicked thought. He certainly never dressed like a consciously handsome man.)

At last he said what I had been waiting to hear since I first spotted him across the room. He said, "Well now, don't you think it's high time we made our escape from here? I've got to get up and pack, and I wouldn't want to deprive a young woman of her necessary rest."

(I realize that Ran sounds silly, quoted literally, even pompous. I can only say that in his rich Southern voice, in the lightness and variety of tone, the actual effect was enchanting; certainly I was enchanted, and so was almost everyone who knew him.)

For years I have reviewed that spring night: driving home with Ran, in the scents of honeysuckle and wisteria, in his manic speeding open car. And in my mind I try to give that night a different ending, not its humiliating true one, and quite often I succeed, only thinking of flowers and scents of night. For even in a horticultural way, my memory of that whole April seems unlikely, but there it is: I remember that for several weeks all the flowers in bloom were white, dogwood and spirea, white Japanese quince, white roses, every-where luminous blossoms.

We raced down the highway, and then Ran turned off on the white dirt road, our road, leading to both our houses. We drove fast between the arching pines, the scented tall bent cedars, raced past my house, as I had somehow known or hoped we would. And suddenly there we were in a broad graveled parking area, just down from a hugely looming house, all its areas of glass reflecting shadows, the fabled house that I had so far never visited.

"Well," said Ran, in his characteristic tone that made everything almost, not quite, a joke. "I seem to have come a little too far—I seem to have taken you out of your way."

I laughed lightheartedly, excitedly, imagining that now we would go inside for the obligatory nightcap that neither of us needed, and that then we would go to bed, like grown-ups.

But no. Ran reached toward me, and at his touch I moved closer, and we kissed, passionately. And that is ex-actly how we spent the next hour or so, in kissing, like steamy adolescents, although I was close to thirty and Ran must have been almost fifty, or so. We writhed against each other, both violently aroused. Once or twice I reached for him in an explicit way—well, that's how plain girls are, ag-gressively sexual—and each time he stayed my hand.

(This amuses you, Ms. Heffelfinger? You find it hard to credit? In that case, it's clear that you've never tangled with a small-town, Southern white Protestant, a Presbyterian conscience.)

At last, in a moment of relative disengagement, Ran looked at his watch and exclaimed, "Good Lord, it's hours past a decent time for bed. You must forgive me, I'll take you right along home."

Still imagining that we were going to sleep together, as it were, I started to suggest that we stay at his house instead, my bed was so hard and narrow. Thank God I did not say that, but only smiled. I was worried about my face, which I knew at best to be unpretty, which must by now look ravaged, smeared, terrible.

Ran started his car, turned around in the driveway and headed toward my house, and for that short distance I was as happy as I have ever been, anticipating our long night hours together. He stopped the car, I in my eagerness hurrying out before he could be his usual chivalrous self and come around for me. Together we walked up to my door, and there, with a chaste kiss on my forehead, Ran murmured good night.

I was as horrified as I was surprised, as stricken, as frustrated. And although I may have been too upset to know what I was doing, I'm afraid I did know; in any case, I then forced a passionate kiss upon his unwilling mouth, I forced my whole body up against his as I said, "Come in with me, I want you."

"Well, my dear, I'm sure that would be delightful"—as though I had invited him in for cocoa—"but the fact is, it's just terribly late, and so I will have to bid you adieu."

He got away; he even waved as he got into his car and drove off, as I simply stood there.

Well, at least I didn't run up the road after him, and pound on his door, shouting; that would have been even worse to remember, and if I had been a little older, or a little more drunk, that is precisely what I would have done, what every instinct wanted me to do. It is in fact just what some years later I did do, after one of our nights of drunken fighting, tears and threats, departures. That night, I only went into my house and went to bed, where all my crying failed to soothe my rage and pain, where I could not sleep.

. . .

I did not see Ran for a couple of weeks after that, first because he was in Atlanta, and then, when I knew he must be back, because I avoided the time when I knew he would be driving by. However, one day either I had miscalculated or he had sought me out, for there he was, racing up from behind a few minutes after I had left my house, stopping, reaching to open the door for me.

He began talking his head off—I might have known that the next time I saw Ran he would distance me with conversation. "Well, my dear girl, I don't believe I've seen you since my recent sojourn in Atlanta." Et cetera, on and on about Atlanta: the heat, the ugliness of the local architecture, the too many parties—"Too much bourbon would be stating the case more accurately, I fear." The stupid hostesses who would not take no for an answer. "One of them even managed to wangle an invitation to come up here," he told me. "Can you imagine such a thing?"

This is the first I heard of Gloria Bingham, and I might have guessed then from Ran's excited tone exactly how it would all work out; I might also have guessed that Gloria was small and stupid-smart, in that special Southern way, and that she was beautiful. My total opposite, my natural enemy.

Gloria was "petite," dark-haired; a more just God, I thought, would have given her small dark eyes to match, but no, her eyes were exceptionally large and blue, unfairly brilliant. And her voice was remarkably low, for such a little person. "I'm so very glad to meet you; Ran's talked so much about his artistic neighbor," she told me, the first time we met. She managed, in the special way she pronounced "artistic," to combine awe with insult, a famous Southern-lady trick, at which Gloria was especially adept.

By the beginning of that summer two things were clear to me: first, that Gloria and Ran were embarked on a serious love affair, she would be coming up for lots of visits, if not to stay; and second, that I could not stand it, I really couldn't. I couldn't stand knowing that she was there, just up the road, with Ran, and I alone with my ugly, rampant fantasies—nor when they drove by, both waving, friendly and happy. Nor was it bearable to feel her presence in Ran's mind, the few times I saw him alone after the advent of Gloria.

Out of sheer desperation I did what I had sworn never to do: I telephoned my banker-father, in Milwaukee, and said that I had to have some money for a year in Italy. We had quarreled badly ten years back, when I had first mentioned art school, so that now he was so startled at hearing from me at all, and maybe even a little pleased, stonehearted bastard that he was, that he gave in after almost perfunctory resistance—just a few mutterings about my extravagance, which we both knew to be trumped up; I had always been the soul of thrift. There were also a few stern warnings about the dangers of Italy under Mussolini, about which he was not very well informed either.

Next I went to Dr. James; I asked for and was granted a year's leave of absence.

In early July I sailed for Genoa, on a cheap, rather small Greek freighter, during the course of which voyage I had an affair with a Greek sailor, who was very handsome, and I thought about Ran, obsessively.

In Italy I reverted to my old bad habit of affairs with married men, dark fat middle-aged Italians who spent pious afternoons in the museums, on the prowl for silly American girls; but these affairs were less lonely than their American counterparts; Italian men had more free time, their wives at home being more docile, less questioning. Among other things I learned to say "I love you" in Italian: *Ti voglio bene*, I wish you well. I thought considerably about the difference between that sentiment and what I felt for Ran, whom God knows I did not wish well—I often wished him dead—or, better still, painfully dying. I was obsessed with him in an ugly, violent way that seemed to preclude other softer, gentler feelings.

The most significant experience of my Italian year, by far, was that there for the first time I saw real Michelangelos, and it was as though I had never seen sculpture before. Later I said this to Ran, and he told me about the first time he heard a Beethoven symphony performed: he was very young, of course, and it was inevitably the Fifth, but he remembered thinking, Ah, so that's what music is. In the Bargello, in Florence, I was tremendously moved by the great unfinished marbles, the huge figures just emerging from the stone, and later, at the monumental sculptures in Rome, in the Vatican, I felt the most extraordinary excitement, exhilaration.

I had not in Hilton made any friendships that would warrant a correspondence; therefore, on the boat that took me back from Genoa to New York, a voyage on which I had no affairs with sailors, I did not know what to expect on my return. The strongest possibility was that by now Ran and Gloria would be married, given the extremely conventional habits of everyone involved. While I faintly hoped that they would have decided to live in Atlanta—maybe Gloria would have a family house down there, a "showplace"—I was also braced for their proximity in Hilton; I even thought that occasional views of Ran, yoked to such a fatuous woman, might diminish him in my mind; I might recover from my crazed preoccupation, my ugly lust.

But no. On my first afternoon in Hilton, back in my small house in the woods, the tender bright green June trees that were leafed out all over the landscape, Dr. James informed me on the telephone, other business being out of the way, that a terrible misfortune had befallen my neighbor Randolph Caldwell: Ran had been engaged to marry Gloria Bingham, their wedding had been imminent; indeed it was on a shopping trip to New York for wedding and honeymoon clothes that Gloria had met a younger, much richer man, with whom she had run off out West. Phoenix, Tucson, some place like that. Poor Ran was in bad shape; he was said to be drinking too much, up there in his big glass house, all alone. Maybe, once I got settled, in a neighborly way I could call on him? I could tell him about my year in Italy? Ran had been there on his wedding trip with Lucinda, and later on a concert tour; he loved to talk about Italy, Dr. James assured me.

Hanging up, I digested this outrageous suggestion, a neighborly call from me, as best I could, along with the news of Gloria's defection. I found myself violently agitated, pacing about, unable to unpack, unable to do anything but smoke a lot of cigarettes and stare at nothing.

At last, in a mood of what-the-hell, or, what-have-I-got-to-lose, I did exactly what Dr. James had suggested: I went to the telephone and I dialed the number that I had memorized two years ago, which I still knew, although I had never used it before.

"This is Jane Phelps," I said in a clear strong voice, quite startling to my ears: who would have thought I could manage it? "I've just got back from Italy, and I thought—"

"Well, my dear Jane," he crashed into my sentence, as

though he had been waiting to hear from me. "What an entirely delightful surprise, how quite wonderful to hear from you! And Italy, ah, how I would love to hear of your stay there, all of it. I don't suppose you could possibly—"

He was asking me up to his house for a bite of supper, as he put it, and I was saying yes. Yes, yes.

As we approached his door, Ran having gallantly driven down to pick me up at five-thirty—"Well, we might as well start with the cocktail hour, don't you agree?"—Ran seemed to have forgotten that I had never been to his house before, and I saw no reason to mention it. He did mumble as we entered that he was afraid it was a little messy, the "girl" got in his way; she hadn't been there for a while. I then walked into a huge room, the room that is now my own, to a scene of the most incredible squalor: spilled drinks and spilling-over ashtrays, scattered newspapers, magazines, unopened letters, face-down books. Dust rabbits at the edges of the rugs. Long grime-streaked windows that looked out to the lovely leaves, the hills, the gentle June twilight.

It was obviously the dwelling place of a person too miserable to function in a normal way, incapable of emptying an ashtray, of reading, finishing anything, probably of eating, and I wondered about the bite of supper. But mainly I was stricken with waves of pity for Ran, perhaps my first kindly emotion in his direction, which did nothing to diminish my other feelings. I sat down in a cleared space on a sofa as Ran went off for drinks. I knew that I would do well not even to think about the kitchen.

Sorrow, what he had recently been through, even too much bourbon had not made Ran less attractive; if anything, he looked better, leaner and sadder, his dark eyes larger and his hair, I thought, a shade more white. That night he was wearing, as I will (evidently) always remember, an old plaid wool shirt, probably from L. L. Bean, his favorite store.

We sat for a long time, there in the deepening dusk; from time to time Ran would get up and go and "sweeten" our drinks, not turning on any lights. And we talked, as Dr. James had more or less instructed, about Italy. Ran was upset that I had only gone to Florence and Rome; he didn't count Genoa. "But Siena," he said. "Bergamo. And Todi, Gubbio, Spoleto. Ravello! You can't believe the views of hills of olives. But after all you are so young, you can go many times to Italy." At that last I thought I heard a small quaver in his voice, but I could have been wrong. In truth I was barely listening; I was only looking at him, wanting to touch him, to be touched. And I was a little afraid: I knew that I could not stand another evening that ended as our last evening of intimacy had ended; this time I would behave very badly indeed.

Another fear was that he would get drunk and pass out: I didn't yet know that Ran was the stay-up-all-night sort of drinker.

He had been sitting on an armchair near my perch on the sofa. Coming back with what must have been our fifth or sixth drinks, he then sat down instead on the sofa, on another cleared space near mine, with only a pile of letters, bills, whatever, stacked between us. It was I who finally reached across, reached for Ran, but at least he was responsive; as though he had been waiting for just that gesture, and maybe in a way he had been, he grasped and kissed me, and at last, in the fumbling way of adolescents in a darkened room, on a cluttered family sofa, we managed to make love. And when Ran cried out, "Oh, my darling," although I partly knew that he did not mean me, my heart leapt gratefully anyway.

And that was the beginning of our legendary love affair, the great love of Jane Phelps and Randolph Caldwell. From then on we saw each other almost every day, one way or another, as the seasons changed around our separate houses on that road, in the deep beautiful woods. Wisely enough, we never even considered moving in together; after a night of love one or the other of us would return to his or her own dwelling. We both knew that we needed those hours apart, sometimes simply to gather more energy for love, at other, too frequent times to refuel a quarrel, to lick our wounds.

After the lush green summer, of honeysuckle, roses, wisteria everywhere, came an autumn landscape of the most brilliant leaves, crimson and gold against a blue, blue sky, in the brighter, colder air. Then winter, sometimes snow, or more often just cold, the woods full of thin crisp leaves, and the smell of wood smoke from the Negro cabins, far down the hill. As much as with Ran, I fell in love with that landscape, his countryside. Permanently.

One great shared pleasure, discovered early between us, was in talking about our work. It was the deep, extraordinary excitement between two people whose pursuits are quite separate, but whose dedication to these activities is similar, two people who can thus find areas of the most passionate affinity. These conversations occurred infrequently; like most "creative" people, neither of us was often moved to talk in that vein, but when we did it was entirely wonderful, talk that even now gives me the greatest joy to remember.

But a sad fact about these conversations, of course, was that for Ran it was all in the past; he was talking about how he used to feel, what he once had done. Whereas I had just begun to work in a serious way; I worked furiously, excited about what I was producing, what I dreamed of making in the future. In those early days I was just moving from small carved wooden sculptures to larger figures, and in my mind were even larger constructions, the sort of shapes that I eventually achieved.

What demons, then, drove us so frequently to ugly rages, unspeakable recriminations? We would goad each other on, until Ran would say that no, he did not love me at all, he never had, I did not know what real love was. Or I would go on and on about my great and numerous Italian lovers, exaggerating wildly, until Ran would get up and lurch toward me, and slap my face—this happened more than once, and then I would hit him back, of course.

Too much drink was certainly a cause of trouble between us, that endless succession of bourbons-and-water, but booze was not a necessary cause, I wouldn't think. Surely there must be at least a few blowsy alcoholic couples who get along affectionately, slurring their words of love?

No, with us there were at least two basic and seemingly irreparable causes of conflict, deep-rooted, unavailable to rational thought, or control.

To blame Ran first: one of our troubles was his basic mistrust-suspicion of sex, especially good sex, and ours was mostly excellent—hard to explain, but there it was, great sex. Although he never would have admitted it, being such a sophisticated man, a distinguished composer, Ran really believed all those Protestant-Puritan myths, especially strong in small-town Southern men, I think. He believed that sex weakened your intellectual processes: "Well, my dear, I fear that I must bid you an early adieu; I have to get a great deal done in the morning," he would say, over my impassioned protests, my threats, and this was not something that we could ever talk about. He believed too that nice women, good women, didn't really like sex; my evident sensual relish made me suspect, was probably proof of a bad character.

The other problem, maybe worse, was mine: my own unshakable, implacable self-dislike. Its causes no longer interest me; it was just a fact, like being tall. And we all know how it is with such people: anyone who claims to love us is either lying or soft in the head, inferior; at various times I accused Ran of both conditions, but mostly of lying. Even when he assured me, as he often did, that the happiest moments in his life had been with me, that he had never truly cared so much for any woman, and for so long, I was always sure that his heart and mind were still vividly inhabited by Gloria. I believed that even in our most tender moments he thought of her, and that to me he was simply being polite, saying what he felt the situation called for.

(But is it possible, Ms. Heffelfinger, that I was wrong, that I was indeed much loved by Ran? A heady thought: I can hardly take it in.)

The next phase of our "relationship" was mostly occupied with Ran's illness, and it was mostly terrible.

He had always coughed a lot, ever since I had known him, hardly surprising in such a perpetual smoker, although at the time I smoked as much as he and rarely coughed. We even joked sometimes about his smoker's hack, since he seemed to cough most violently in bed. Then, in a gradual way, we both noticed that the cough was getting worse, and worse and worse. He would be taken with terrible paroxysms, fits, during which he would seem to be trying to cough up his very lungs; he would clutch his arms together, his face an awful red, and wet with sweat.

I began to have secret fears of TB, then still relatively common, or of lung cancer, less prevalent, and not much known. At last I was so frightened that I dared his rage; I knew he would feel an imputation of illness as an accusation (one more!) but I said to him, "Ran, darling, that cough of yours is getting out of hand. You've got to get it seen to."

He answered so mildly that I was more alarmed than ever. "I know," he said. "I'm going up to Johns Hopkins next week."

My first thought, which I managed not to say, was: But I have to go to New York next week, I can't go with you. (I had begun, in the long course of my association with Ran, to enjoy some success, from a show in the small gallery of the Hilton art department, to several pieces in a statewide show, in the capital city, then moving north to a show in Washington, D.C. And then New York, Madison Avenue. The Whitney.)

I did say, "You'll give me a call? I'll be in New York. The Brevoort."

"Okay, if you're going to be such a silly bitch about it."

"Yes, I am, you dumb bastard."

That was how we often spoke to each other, affection concealed in abuse. I think Ran may even have felt rather daring, calling a woman a bitch right to her face, and God knows he often meant it.

Most of that trip to New York I spent on the phone, leaving messages as to my whereabouts: if Mr. Caldwell called I would be having a drink at the Plaza, in the Oak Room; I would be with Betty Parsons; I was back in the hotel, having dinner on the terrace, by myself.

By now we were in the early Forties. Ran and I had been together for almost ten years, and the country was at war. New York, that bright October, was full of uniforms, arrivals and departures. Since the Brevoort was fairly expensive most of the uniforms there were officers', lots of brass and braid, ribbons and stars. I had just got rid of a very drunk colonel, who was insisting that he join me—how dare I have dinner alone, didn't I know there was a war on?—when there, where the colonel had been, was Ran, very dashing, very happy, almost drunk.

He kissed me lavishly, which was unusual: he disliked a public display. He sat down across from me, and he spoke the great news: "I thought I should tell you in person that I am a certified healthy man. Those gentlemen, with their innumerable tests, which were not at all pleasant—they all failed to turn up a single evil diagnosis. I have no infections, no malignancies."

Well. We celebrated with champagne and lobsters, and more champagne for breakfast. I took Ran around to some galleries, and he was very proud of me, I think. Later we met some old music friends of his for drinks, on Patchen Place, and more friends for dinner, at Luchow's. We had never had such a good time: how wonderful, Ran was not seriously sick.

What we both ignored, or failed for quite a while to see as significant, was that he was still coughing, badly.

Back in Hilton nothing else had changed much either. We drank and quarreled and talked as much as ever. I think we made love a little less, by then.

Sometime the following spring Ran announced that he had been offered a teaching job in the music department in Tucson, the University of Arizona. "Although I confess that the word 'emeritus' rather gives me pause," he said.

He rambled on, but I wasn't listening at all; I was thinking *Gloria.* Gloria had moved out to Phoenix or Tucson, to me almost the same place. Out West. Of course she must be Ran's true direction. That night we had one of our bad quarrels, about something else—naturally.

. . .

I went out to visit him in October, which was not one of our best times together.

For one thing, the place itself was so strange that it made us seem alien even to each other. Surrounded by the bizarre, inimical desert, the flat, palm-lined, unnaturally sunny town, Ran's apartment had the look of a motel: stucco, one-storied, part of a complex built around a large, much too blue swimming pool, in which it was never quite warm enough to swim.

Motels have always seemed somehow sexual to me, and I was unable to rid myself of fantasies involving Ran and Gloria: had she visited him there, did she maybe come for visits frequently? All morning, every day, when Ran was off teaching his classes, I would ransack his apartment (though tidily, a cautious spy), every cranny and corner, drawer and wastebasket, his desk, even the linen closet, in a search for Gloria, any trace of her—a quest that was as compulsive as it was humiliating, degrading. And it was also fruitless, yielding up nothing but a crick in my back, a broken fingernail and dust.

At night we went out and ate Mexican food and drank too much Mexican beer, and, out of character for us, we neither quarreled nor talked very much. I was afraid—in fact, I knew—that if we did talk much of it would lead to a fight, and any conversation might summon Gloria. And Ran had, seemingly, almost no energy. He coughed a lot, and we almost never made love.

(But then tonight, Ms. Heffelfinger, as I remembered that time, from such a long distance, and I recalled my desperate need to *know* about Gloria, I came to an odd conclusion: I thought, How strange of me to care, when really it didn't matter. What was the difference, finally, whether or not Gloria spent an afternoon or a weekend with Ran, within those garish stucco walls. Even whether or not they made love. I could almost hope they had; I could almost, if belatedly, halfheartedly, wish for a little almost final happiness for Ran. But not too much, and I was still consoled by the fixed idea that Gloria would have been uninteresting in bed.)

When he came back to Hilton, at the beginning of the following summer, I knew that Ran must be very sick indeed —his speech was so radically altered. Whereas before he had said everything so elaborately, with such a smoke screen of complicated verbiage, now he spoke very simply and directly, as though he had not much time or breath remaining. Which in fact he did not: he had what we now know as emphysema, he was dying of it.

That summer we spent most evenings in Ran's huge high glassed-in living room, watching fireflies and the lengthening shadows, among the barely stirring summer leaves, the flowering shrubbery.

"Sometimes I can't remember when you first came here," Ran said one night. "Was it before or after Lucinda killed herself?"

"Just after," I told him as I digested what I had only half known, or heard as rumor before, what he thought I already knew—Lucinda's suicide. And I sadly wished that he had been able to say this before; it might have eased some pain for him, I thought. And I thought about Lucinda, her long novels and small madrigals, her dislike of the "cluttered" landscape, and I cursed her for adding to a deeply guilty man's store of guilt. In the long run, really, Gloria had done him a lot less harm.

"I guess by now I think you've always been around," he said, with a new half-smile, so that my heart lurched with an aching, unfamiliar tenderness for him.

On another evening of that summer Ran told me that he was going to sell his house. "It's too big," he said. "Taxes. So many rooms. Maids. The windows." He had a new and alarming habit of quick breaths between almost each word, and deep difficult breaths between sentences. Now, after such a labored pause, he added, "I'm tired of it."

"You lying bastard." Fear made me rough; it was at about this time that I began to adopt my stance of gruffness, to perfect my just-not-rude snort. "You wouldn't know what to do without this house," I told him, and then I laughed. "But if you really want to sell it, I'll buy it from you."

That night was as close as we had come to quarreling for some time, but in the course of those hours we worked out a highly original real-estate deal, whereby I would buy Ran's house, but I would not take possession of it until I had paid for over half of it, by which time we both knew that Ran would be dead.

And that, Ms. Heffelfinger, in brief, is how it went. I bought Ran's house, and soon afterward, early that fall, he died, and I moved in. I sorted and labeled and stored away all his papers, his manuscripts, his library, as though it had all been infinitely valuable, which, to me, it was. (He had kept no letters from Gloria, which was both gratifying and frustrating.)

·   ·   ·

After so much heavy thought, and so much to drink, I should have awakened the next day in a state of hung-over exhaustion—a state that my poor guilty Presbyterian Ran used to describe as being "richly deserved." But I did not feel terrible, not at all. I got up and made myself a healthy breakfast, and then I telephoned the inn, for Candida Heffelfinger.

She came over promptly, in answer to my invitation (a summons, it must have sounded like), and she looked as I had imagined that she would: contrite and tired, and rumpled. Unlike me, she could not have slept well.

She told me that she had been walking around the town, and how much she liked it, and I agreed. Then we both admired, again, the bright fall view from my windows.

And then she said, "I've been thinking—and I hope this won't sound presumptuous, but would you mind if I shifted the focus of our talk a little? I mean, so many people have written about the legendary love affair."

This was irritating: she was saying to me exactly what I had meant to say to her.

I snorted. "I suppose you mean to take another tack, and zero in on our fights?"

"Oh no, of course not. I wouldn't—"

"In point of fact," I told her, "the written accounts are remarkably close to the truth. I was in Italy, and Gloria Bingham visited here for a while, and then she left. Ran and I both had our flings, but no one else mattered much to either of us."

Candida seemed to find that statement both moving and final, as I did myself. She was silent for a while, and then she said, "I really meant about your work. It's interesting, your beginning with those small figures. The gain in scope."

"It undoubtedly had something to do with my physical size," I told her, very dry.

"I can understand that," she said. Well, I believed that

she could, indeed; we are about the same height. Big ladies.

"What really happened," I then told her, "was in Italy, for the first time, I saw real Michelangelos. In the Bargello, and in the Vatican, St. Peter's—"

We talked for several hours, and I saw that I had been right all along about Candida; my instincts still were fine. She was very nice indeed, and smart. I liked her. Our talk went on all morning, and into the afternoon.

I had a marvelous time.

Related Histories

In the late Forties, just after the Second World War, a large party—in fact, a dance—took place in a small castle in Central Europe. It was late August, a very black, hot still night. In the castle's million-windowed central hall, American music, on records, issued from a Victrola. Glasses and pitchers of pale watery wine were set out on a long table. An elderly man in a shabby white coat poured out the wine and changed or turned over the records—indifferently, since he did not speak English and disliked the music.

Couples, some in costume, most in some variety of festive or at least dressed-up attire, danced out on the floor; other people stood about in clusters, in animated or sometimes serious conversation. The next day, everyone there would be leaving the castle, the American professors, instructors, American wives and all the European students, for this had been an experiment in international education, and the six weeks were just over.

One person, the very distinguished Professor Howard Stein, an elegant Bostonian, brilliant, of a high, exacerbated consciousness, was neither dancing nor talking to anyone. He was listening to the saccharine, meretricious music—longing for Mozart, for a soaring of Bach—and thinking that the experiment, the seminar, had been a failure. With deep embarrassment, and perfect clarity—his fate—he recalled the speech that he himself gave on the first afternoon of the conference, in a small clearing, among romantic statuary, beside the castle's lake. They had all come to this place, he had said and now could hear himself saying, from widely divergent histories, geographies, in some cases opposing ideologies, but they were all now united in staunch and sober anti-Fascism, were all opposed to the forces of darkness recently defeated.

Wild applause and cries of approval, in various languages, greeted those remarks, and later, fervent handshakes from moist-eyed colleagues, fellow teachers at the eminent Midwestern university that had sent them all there.

And what he had said turned out to be, quite simply and horribly, *not true.* Many of the German and Austrian students, and one of the Italians, a skinny young woman, had gradually and sometimes inadvertently revealed themselves as Nazi-Fascists still. During the second week of the seminar, the Danish students, a splendidly blond and handsome group, had left in a body, having recognized one of the Germans as a former professor who had been forced to leave Denmark because of Nazi sympathies. (The German left too, a day later, with a face-saving story of illness.) At a poetry reading a German student loudly remarked that Heine was not a German, he was Jewish. And a supposedly "reconstructed" Austrian, who had spent time in a POW camp in Texas and had been horrified at the Southern treatment of Negroes, announced, when asked, that he saw no relationship between that treatment of a "race" and what had gone on in Germany. That same Austrian and the Italian woman were later overheard (by Howard Stein) in a shared reference to "our Navy."

The question about the treatment of races had been put to the Austrian by Howard's least favorite wife of an instructor, one of his own former students; an unbearably serious young woman, too thin, with hyperintense brown eyes, who was just then dancing past with an authentic anti-Fascist, a young Italian who was known to have fought with the partisans.

Diana McBride, the young American wife not liked by Howard Stein, would surely have agreed with him, however, about the seminar. In fact, earlier in the evening she had said to the university dean who organized the whole thing, in her half-tentative, half-bold way, "Wouldn't it have been better to have it in a more friendly country, like France?"

"You should not make that suggestion unless you are prepared to act on it, to perform the work of removal," she was told, with considerable force, by the dean. Of necessity, he believed that the seminar had been a great success.

Silenced by power, although uncomfortably aware of the illogic of what he had said, Diana felt that everything she had done, all summer, had been wrong. To begin with, their very presence at the seminar, hers and her husband's, was suspect. The other instructors were chosen for academic distinction, whereas Braxton McBride was asked in the hope that his father, rich old William McBride, would contribute substantially to the project. Instead, Mr. McBride's contribution was as penurious as were most of his gestures, and there Braxton was, already announced as an instructor. Hideously embarrassing: Diana felt it much more than Braxton did. He behaved as he always had, like a plump rich spoiled only child, taking interest in and appreciation of himself for granted. Not bothering to please anyone.

Diana, in many ways her husband's opposite, took very

little for granted, and sometimes she tried too hard to please; it was this latter quality which had gone so wrong with Howard Stein on one of the first days of the seminar. They were coming home from a group excursion to a neighboring, larger and grander castle, and by accident, surely, Diana and Howard sat down next to each other in the long open truck, the transportation for that day's excursion. Wildly casting about for something to say to the distinguished critic, her former professor, Diana seized upon the passing scenery: a gentle landscape of woods and meadows. "It looks rather like New England, don't you think?" she observed (unavoidably tight-voiced, and stilted). Dr. Stein turned fully on her; he glared as what she took to be tears of rage filled his eyes. "Most emphatically not," he said, and he turned around to begin a conversation with a knot of Spanish students (Loyalists) on his other side. Confronted with his narrow back and the black, patrician shape of his skull, Diana felt tears sting her own eyes.

Howard Stein had a reputation for not liking wives, even for being rude to them; still, Diana was sorely aware of it.

However, the afternoon before the dance, a good thing happened to Diana: in the neighboring town, in a small shop, she found a pretty dress which fit her perfectly, a dark silk, embroidered with small flowers. It was a little peasanty, a costume, but perfect for the farewell dance. And since for six weeks there had been nothing to spend money on but ice cream at the local PX, she had plenty of traveler's checks.

Generally, Diana did not like the way she looked, but that night, in that dress, she felt transformed. It fit her so smoothly, seeming to shape her thin body; its sheen added color to her face and eyes.

And then that nice boy, Vittorio, asked her to dance.

. . .

Out on the porch, Stanley Morris, from Brooklyn, a young, enthusiastic and most promising instructor, was vigorously embracing a young Estonian girl, and at the same time deciding that he would, after all, marry the dark, graceful, intelligent and clearly rich girl whom he had met on the boat coming over.

With her natural elegance, Vassar, Phi Beta, she would be a terrific asset wherever Stanley went; even at Harvard, his wild and not unfounded hope, she would fit right in. And she was sexy, too; those nights on the boat were wonderful.

The Estonian girl, a small round blonde, was terribly attracted to that handsome American; she couldn't help squirming against his hands. But some still cool part of her mind was thinking that she didn't trust him, quite. He had told her that he had no girlfriend, and that after the seminar he would come up to visit her, in the small town in Brittany where her family now lived, but somehow she didn't believe him, and she managed to push his hand away.

It was an extremely hot night, still; an almost full pale moon, earlier a slight illumination, now had set. The lake was flat, unmoving, and no breeze stirred in the surrounding shrubbery, the concealing pines.

Tired of watching the dancers, and there was no one around he wanted to talk to—he was tired of everyone there —Howard Stein decided to go out for a breath of air. He opened the wide door to the porch, and as he passed them, he dimly recognized Stanley Morris amorously engaged with the slutty-looking Estonian girl. Howard gave a slight twitch of disgust; he felt infinitely alone.

And with the most terrible sadness, as he walked out toward the lake, he remembered another, much happier summer of his life, twenty years back, when as a young man he had taken a hiking tour through some of the Loire Valley, the Dordogne, with Kenneth Carlisle, his great friend, now dead for several years. It was quite possible, tortured Howard had forced himself to admit, that he had been in love with Kenneth; certainly those were his strongest feelings, ever, about another human being. However, Kenneth, who later married, could never have suspected anything of the sort; they were, quite simply, perfect friends, perfectly happy together. And there had been nothing of that nature in Howard's later life, nothing at all.

Passing the grove, with its silly statuary, where he made that awful sentimental speech, Howard realized that he was close to tears.

He would have to do something, get a grip on himself, somehow. This fall he would start a new book; maybe at last the one on Melville.

And tomorrow he would force himself to make a final visit to the Jewish DP camp just down the road from the castle. This hastily and poorly thrown together camp, housing some four hundred displaced Jews who were waiting to go to Israel, had been, for Howard, an aching problem. First, Stanley Morris, good-looking, warm and ebulliently sympathetic to those people, went over there to pay a sort of investigatory call. He returned to the castle with wrenching stories of how he had been received: with such dignity and grace, such appreciation. He was served tea; those people were overjoyed to find a cultivated American who spoke Yiddish—they were terrific people, Stanley said. Compassionate and concerned, and feeling strong kinship with those displaced Jews, Howard overcame his own shy reluctance to go anywhere; the next time Stanley visited the camp, Howard went along. (Howard did not speak Yiddish; for generations no one in his family had.) And Howard too was deeply moved by just what Stanley had described: the dignity, the courage, the gratitude for distinguished visits. One of the men had been a classics professor in Munich; another, a Polish physicist.

However, after that Stanley announced that he had been too disturbed ever to return; it tore him apart, he said, alluding to relatives lost in the Holocaust. Believing that in all conscience he must respect Stanley's feelings, Howard returned to the camp for several visits alone. In his academic German he had to explain Stanley's absence: extreme busyness, he said. He felt apologetic about not knowing Yiddish; in fact, he felt himself to be a poor substitute for Stanley.

But tomorrow he would visit them once more, to say goodbye.

One reason that Diana McBride felt badly about Howard Stein's evident distaste for her was that he was the greatest teacher in her experience. She had taken two courses from him as an undergraduate, one on Donne and the Metaphysical poets, another an American literature survey. She had not read Donne before, nor any of those poets, and she was powerfully affected both by the marvelous poetry and by Howard Stein's concise and brilliant lectures. She would leave the lecture hall in a sort of daze, illuminated, stirred, still in her mind hearing that crisp and elegant voice, those sharp Bostonian vowels.

And his lectures at the seminar had been wonderful; he spoke on Melville, Whitman, Wallace Stevens, William Carlos Williams.

To the Italian boy, as they slowly danced, she said, "Dr. Stein's lectures were terrific, weren't they?"

"I think that he is a great man," said Vittorio Garibaldi.

Vittorio was a slender, fair-complected northern Italian from Padua. There was the faintest physical resemblance between him and Diana; both were light, slight people—a kinship of which they themselves were unaware, being so entirely unfamiliar to each other, but which they may have sensed as a sort of affinity.

Diana was aware of feeling less shy with Vittorio than she usually was, even dancing better. She felt light on her feet as they whirled to "Tuxedo Junction," and a little light-headed, almost silly; possibly from the wine? But she hadn't had that much.

The record stopped and she and Vittorio looked at each other, and for no reason at all they laughed.

"Is that young girl, young McBride's wife, partly Italian?" an eminent historian asked an eminent economist; both were American professors.

"I haven't a clue. I don't know her, actually."

"Funny, she and that Italian boy look rather alike."

The economist peered in the direction indicated. The idea of a conversation about an instructor's wife bored him a great deal, but then so had the one they were just having, about prices in Paris before the war. "If you ask me they both look drunk," he decisively said.

"My country is—how do you say?—a complete mess," Vittorio seriously told Diana, during a long pause between records. "So torn in pieces, so everywhere divided. People with not homes. And the political parties, everybody fighting. Communists fighting Socialists, fighting Christian Democrats, fighting Monarchists. So much to do. I have to find some place in all that. Some work."

"Which is your party?" asked Diana, with timid but intense interest.

"It is called the Action Party. Mainly former partisans.

But it is so small, it will be absorbed by some larger, stronger party, either Socialists or Communists."

His high seriousness was stirring to Diana; he seemed to take a useful life for granted; work to be done meant that he must do it. She tried to think of her own country, the States, in that way, and she then sighed with helplessness; undoubtedly there too were things to be done, but she would not know how to start, having so far never thought in those terms.

Very gently Vittorio asked her, "And you, what of your life?"

The truth was that for the moment Diana planned to follow the course currently prescribed for wives of graduate students. She would get a job and help support her husband until he got his doctorate (William McBride did not hand out a lot of money, not believing in "spoiling" his son, unaware that he already had); then, according to this pattern, the husband with the Ph.D. could get a job and the wife could start having babies.

So far, this is what Diana had vaguely imagined would happen, but suddenly, seeing it from the center of Europe, as she stood so close to Vittorio Garibaldi, she was unable to commit herself to such a plan, unable even to say it. Instead she told him what was half a lie. With a little laugh she said, "Actually, I've thought of going to law school." It was true that once she had thought about law school, but that was quite a few years ago, as a freshman in college, an enthusiastic innocent, long before meeting Braxton, years before this marriage.

Naturally, Vittorio took her at her word. "That is marvelous," he told her, with great warmth, a wide white smile. "You will be a wonderful lawyer, I know that."

And then he said, "I have never seen brown eyes to have so much gold in them as yours do."

Vittorio was a highly serious young man; gold-brown

eyes cannot have been all that drew him to Diana, and he was powerfully drawn. He must have sensed a potentiality in her of which no one else was then aware, not her husband, nor her former professor Howard Stein, nor, surely, Diana herself. Vittorio thought she would be a good lawyer, would even attain some greatness.

Stanley Morris, aware that he had been caught at that ignominious activity, that adolescent wrestling with a vulgar little girl from nowhere, irrationally but quite humanly directed his rage toward her.

"You stupid little tease," he whispered into her ear, the ear that a moment ago was listening to his endearments, his amorous persuasions. "You're nothing but a waste of my time." He sat up and began to rearrange his disordered clothes.

The Estonian girl began to cry, as softly as a kitten.

In total disgust, for he now thought the whole summer had been a waste of time, not getting him anywhere, Stanley went back into the hall, where the dance was still going on.

If he could find Howard Stein and engage him in serious conversation, thus reassuring Howard that he, Stanley, was a worthwhile person, the evening could not be counted as a total loss. But Howard did not seem to be around.

"Honey—" That nasal sound announced the plump presence of Braxton McBride, her young husband, at Diana's elbow. Her just-soaring spirits dropped as she turned around.

"Honey, I think I'm getting a sort of a headache. I'd better go on to bed. No, you stay, I'll be all right."

According to the previous rules of their relationship,

Diana was then supposed to express strong sympathy and concern: Braxton had frequent terrible headaches. And of course she should accompany him to bed. But tonight she did not do this. She said, "Well, okay. Sleep is probably the best thing. I'll be along later."

Braxton was surprised, but there was not much he could say. With a martyred look he kissed her left cheek. He said good night and left.

The party seemed to be winding down. The wine was not strong enough for any long-range effect, and by now they had run out of it. And the good fellowship engendered by general awareness that this was the last night was running out too.

A conversation between the organizing, success-oriented dean and a visiting anthropologist came apart when the anthropologist described the seminar as "a bizarre but predictable group situation."

The dean scowled as the anthropologist tried to explain. "I mean, all the groups acted within their assigned national characters. The Danes were noble, high-minded, the Austrians untrustworthy, the Spaniards dark and mysterious. The Italians were sexually active, the Americans foolishly ignorant and the Germans pigs."

This did not work. The dean was thinking: Christ, these generalizing, bigoted remarks from an anthropologist? And that sentence could be read on his face.

"Of course I am generalizing," said the anthropologist.

They parted in mutual distrust, dislike.

Various people went off to their beds.

No one was any longer playing records, the old man having gone to his bed in a narrow room just off the kitchen.

And, strangely, the still night was hotter than ever.

. . .

One of the "mysterious" dark Spaniards, an intelligent and kindly fellow, walked out onto the porch for a taste of air, and there he came upon the Estonian girl, still crying. For several weeks he had been looking at her with a sort of lustful affection, and so he sat down beside her and did the obvious thing, which was to take her in his arms and stroke her hair.

She soon calmed down, and in a gentle way they talked, in French—whispering, because it was so late and dark. It turned out that by the most wonderful coincidence, the two of them would be attending the Sorbonne that fall. They would see each other again very soon—in Paris!

Quite suddenly visited by despair—it was over, their evening—Diana said, very soft-voiced, to Vittorio, "I guess I ought to go now. To bed."

"No, you must not."

Taking her hand, he led her strongly out through the door, across the porch and into the hot black still night, past the clearing where, among the ghostly statuary, Howard Stein had made his hopeful commencing speech.

After the clearing there was a small forest of pines that ran along the lake, and within that forest there was a ring of small thick trees, forming a cave. Into the cave Vittorio led Diana. Where, kissing, embracing each other, they slowly removed their clothes.

At a certain point he said to her, sighingly, "Ah, you are so *thin*."

And suddenly, for Diana, who had always felt scrawny, inadequate, "thin" was the most beautiful word in the world. *Thin.*

Years later she would sometimes hear that word said in a certain way, and she would be pierced through with remembering Vittorio, his voice and those dark hours that ended sometime close to dawn.

Since all those events took place so long ago, more than thirty years, it is possible now to know how things turned out, what happened to everyone.

To begin with the worst: Howard Stein committed suicide, an overdose of pills, in the early Fifties. In various intellectual communities, from his own Midwestern university to Harvard and Yale, there were frequent and overheated arguments as to why he did this. Political despair at the emerging climate of the Fifties was one of the most popular theories, repressed homosexuality the other. A few quieter voices (wives) mentioned loneliness, isolation, the sheer fatigue of living.

The dean who had organized the seminar, and who so believed in its success, suddenly left the academic world altogether and went into real estate, where he made a fortune in the late Fifties and early Sixties.

The eminent professors, on the whole, went on to further eminence, except for one, the historian, who, as an enthusiastic adviser to President Johnson on the Vietnam War, an eager hawk, was generally (academically) considered to have disgraced himself.

The unreconstructed Austrian boy married the Fascist Italian girl, amid great pomp, in Venice.

Another marriage: the dark Spanish boy and the pretty blond Estonian girl were married, at her parents' home in Brittany.

Most of the people in the Jewish DP camp made it to Israel; only a few, very old and already sick, died on the way. There in Israel they were generally happy, although some of the youngest were killed in later wars. The classics professor from Munich lived on to have numerous grandchildren. The physicist, having enjoyed a distinguished career at the Hebrew University, was honored at several international conferences.

Stanley Morris did not have quite the career that anyone would have imagined for him. He married as planned, but instead of Harvard, as he had dreamed, he ended up in a large Southern university. A good school, but not Harvard. He was unfaithful to his wife with a succession of younger and younger girls, most of whom strongly resembled her; they were all dark and rich and graceful and intelligent, as she was. Stanley wrote one book—interestingly, on the theme of ambition in American literature—which did not do well. He was flabbergasted when, in early middle age, his wife left him for a much younger man.

Vittorio Garibaldi, who had taken a train to Rome, via Innsbruck, early on the morning after the dance, thus not seeing Diana again, enrolled that fall in law school in his native Padua. A few years after that he married a beautiful girl from Ferrara. He remained a Socialist, despite strong pressures from almost all other directions, and he had, increasingly, a reputation for kindness, intelligence and utter probity. He was at last appointed to a judgeship, a position in which he continued to be admired, sought after, loved. His wife and children loved him very much. He was truly a remarkable man; in his way, a hero of his times.

For a while Diana McBride did follow the wives-of-graduate-students pattern, rather than the grander plan of law school that she had announced to Vittorio, and sometimes she felt that as a broken pledge. She went to work in a law firm, thus helping to support the education of Braxton McBride; she was underpaid and condescended to, and she even had a miserable, punishing affair with one of the junior partners. But what she managed to learn of the law was extremely interesting to her, even exhilarating; she found the judicial system fascinating.

Sometimes she thought of Vittorio, and longingly she would imagine that she had run off with him and shared whatever life he made; remembering that he had not asked her to was painful. In fact, those hours with Vittorio, recalled, were bruising to her during her own worst years. What she had experienced as beautiful rebuked her; she had turned out to be unworthy after all. At other times she could barely believe that it had happened.

Braxton got his degree, and then he got a job, in another, smaller Midwestern university. At that point, to everyone's surprise (including her own, although she was sustained in part by a sense of having fulfilled a contract), Diana said no, she did not want to move to the smaller town with Braxton. She wanted to go to law school, and she wanted, almost incidentally, a divorce.

By this time William McBride had died and Braxton was rich. Diana asked for enough money to put herself through law school. She applied to and was accepted by Yale, her undergraduate record having been exceptional—a fact that over the years she had tended to forget.

Braxton eventually became the head of his department in his very small college. But he was a very big frog, and he liked it there.

Initially terrified, Diana worked her head off at Yale, and she did extremely well. And gradually she was able to calm down and to enjoy it, this first experience of competence, of gratifying work. She learned how to keep up superior grades with a somewhat more relaxed work schedule. And she was crazy about New England, exploring the countryside. During one gaudy fall she became involved with a

fellow student, another older overachiever named Jerry
Stein, from Worcester, Massachusetts. Jerry was a strong,
dark man, sturdily built. He was more easygoing, much more
relaxed than Diana was, warm and friendly, whereas she
tended to be diffident; they were good complements to each
other.

"I used to know a professor named Stein. He was famous, very distinguished. Howard Stein," Diana said one
morning to Jerry—an idle remark as from his bed she
watched him making breakfast; thin Diana, huddled in blan-
kets. It was early November, after one of their first nights of
staying together.

"*Well*. Howard Stein was my cousin, distantly. The Boston branch."

They smiled at each other, delighted at this new coincidence (the first had been of feeling), this new proof of the
logic of their love.

Then Jerry said, "He never liked me much. He thought I
was one more unnecessary little brat running around."

"Oh, really? He didn't like me either, not at all." And
slowly, but eagerly, over breakfast, the good coffee and
warm rolls and cheese, Diana told about the seminar that
summer: Howard Stein's opening speech, in the clearing,
among the statuary, and the dumb thing she said to him on
the truck ride home, about the look of the countryside.

"Well, that wasn't really so dumb. He must have heard
worse." Jerry laughed.

"I know, but he looked so mad. I felt awful. I hated
that summer." Saying this, Diana thought suddenly, sharply
of Vittorio, and to herself she added: I hated everything
about it but Vittorio—and even at that moment, newly in
love with Jerry, she had the most vivid sense of Vittorio. She
could hear his voice.

She never tried to tell Jerry about Vittorio, as much out

of a sense of impossibility as from delicacy: how to describe such a collision, and its long reverberations?

The involvement with Jerry, which Diana never thought of as an affair, and certainly not as a "relationship," continued over the winter and into an extraordinary New England spring. Diana felt herself to be another person; she hardly recognized this new, confident, loved woman—a thin woman, with gold-brown eyes. She and Jerry got married over a long weekend late in August, almost ten years after the seminar, after Vittorio and after Diana's time with him.

Out of law school, both Diana and Jerry managed to get federal jobs in Washington, and during the Sixties they were actively involved in civil rights, and then in the peace movement.

Toward the end of the Sixties, discouraged at the political scene in Washington, they moved back up to New England, to a small town in western Massachusetts, near the Berkshires, and also not far from Worcester, where Jerry had grown up, and where he had sometimes met his distinguished cousin Howard Stein at some family gathering. Jerry and Diana were very busy, both practicing law, and they remained, for the most part, quite happy with each other.

In the early Seventies, perhaps as an outcome of the growing women's movement, Diana was elected a district judge. She was tremendously proud of that office, and she worked extremely hard. And she, like Vittorio some five or six thousand miles away, acquired a reputation for fairness, for honesty and kindness—a coincidence all around, which neither of them could possibly have known about, and which, assuredly, no one could account for.

The Break-In

In a fairly new Porsche, on a Friday night early in June, two people—a young woman and an almost middle-aged man, Cynthia and Roger—are driving up from San Francisco, toward an exceptionally beautiful house in the mountains, near Lake Tahoe. A house that was broken into the night before. They have been talking, unhappily and disjointedly, about knowing versus not knowing about the break-in in advance of their arrival—as though there had been a choice. They have agreed that it is on the whole better to know, despite this present miserable anticipation.

The house belongs to Roger, but since they plan to marry in the fall it soon will be partly Cynthia's, and sometimes she sighs at the thought of such responsibility; she is unused to owning things, her instincts being somewhat nomadic. And the news of this break-in has deeply upset her; she feels an unaccustomed rage and an ugly desire for vengeance: whoever broke in should be punished, and this sentiment is out of character too, for Cynthia.

Once a couple of years ago, Roger, probably with another girl, arrived to find the house flooded, dirty water everywhere, stained upholstery. Another time he came up to find it severely burglarized, all the pewter and copper things tastefully selected and removed. He says that it is better to know.

Cynthia, who is in her late twenties, works as a reader for a local publishers' representative. In fact, just before meeting Roger, she had a rather silly affair with her employer, an erratic and on the whole irresponsible young man. Roger's stability as well as his age have seemed reassuring. She has never married, just had a lot of affairs, most of which in retrospect also look silly, if great fun at the time. Roger has been married three times, each ending in divorce; no children. But he is ready to try again; he really wants to marry Cynthia. They both think that it is time she married. They look well together: small, red-haired, brown-eyed and lively Cynthia, and large, just-graying Roger, who does not look ten years older than she, not really. He likes the commitment of marriage, an attitude new to Cynthia, who is used to more feckless younger men.

Cynthia means to marry Roger, but he has one habit that bothers her: he sometimes calls her by the names of his former wives: Charlotte, Caroline, Christine. "You see? I'm faithful to the letter C," he teases. But none of those names sound like Cynthia; can't he tell the difference?

Lately, before the rip-off, Cynthia has begun to wonder if the house doesn't figure, perhaps, too prominently in her marriage dreams: does she think of marrying Roger, and like the thought, partly because he has such an exceptional house? Roger inherited the house from his mother, a famous beauty in her day, and sometimes Cynthia thinks he cares too much about it, but by now so does she, and this break-in has sorely afflicted her spirits.

The phone call came that morning from an aging and lonely mountain neighbor, Mary Drake. She had no phone, and was calling from a gas station, in her oddly childish voice, among the other voices and sounds of cars and trucks and dogs. On her way to the Safeway that morning she had noticed that the draperies in Roger's house were drawn and a light was still on. Going bravely to look in a window, she saw, she told Roger, "all this broken glass and food spilled all over. Liquor bottles." From the Safeway she had called the sheriff, who, by the time she finished shopping, was at the house, and with him she went in. "I think someone got sick," she indistinctly, and horrifyingly, told Roger.

Still, Cynthia and Roger were glad to be forewarned, although they were powerless to do anything but race toward the house, both their minds full of appalling images.

"Free-floating" anxiety (Why free? she has wondered) is sometimes a problem for Cynthia; she dislikes vague problems like when to end a love affair, when to marry. She functions better when, as now, there is something concrete to deal with. She stares out the window at the speeding scenery, the lovely slopes of ground, live oaks, cows, and she tells herself that it is only a house. This works, and she achieves some degree of calm.

Roger, to whom it is not only a house; it is *his* house— Roger is less generally anxious than she is; he is more direct. In extreme situations, like this one, he copes by outstripping the stimulus, so to speak. He shouts and swears, he makes things even worse than they are; he keeps the small car racing up the highway.

"Let's face it," he says grimly. "This is a lot worse than those frozen pipes, and rusty muddy water all over the house." And Cynthia has to agree that yes, it is probably much worse. Food and waste are intimately revolting, totally so (not to mention the horror of "sick"). They are worse than rust, than any impersonal dirt.

And much worse than theft.

Twice in the past few years Cynthia has had minor but unpleasant surgery, for cysts that turned out to be benign, and she thinks of these operations now; she is reminded of their scheduled unpleasantness. Of feeling well, but knowing that at 7 a.m. she would be rolled onto a gurney and wheeled into a green operating room, from which she would later emerge and wake up feeling terrible. She now feels well, really, but knows that at about five-thirty they will arrive at the house, where they will open a familiar door, and see—something horrible.

She looks across at Roger, whose face is tense, and she decides not to tell him about this analogy. He feels bad enough already. Besides, he has never had an operation.

They have so often driven this exact route that it is possible to be blind to the racing views: the elaborate motel-restaurant clusters, the curious isolated bars that now advertise TOPLESS AND BOTTOMLESS. It is possible to ignore the strong homey smell of onions as they pass the packing plant at Vacaville.

Cynthia is, in fact, thinking about her first visit to that house, when the now familiar door first opened, and she saw that most beautiful room, that house.

It was nine months ago, a warm September day, air that held the barest hint of fall. Cynthia and Roger had only met in June, had been lovers ("in love") for almost that long, an enchanted summer of discovery. They moved back and forth between Cynthia's rambling, ferny Mission District flat, and Roger's trim Telegraph Hill apartment, which held no traces of former wives, or, indeed, little sense of Roger himself. He apologized for its austereness, saying that it wasn't really where he lived, and he showed her pictures of his true house: long, low-lying, shingled, with a slate roof and stone chimney, on the river. In some pictures there were banks of snow up to the level of the row of windows. Cynthia said yes, it was really beautiful. And still she was unprepared.

They drove across the narrow black bridge; they turned onto a white dirt road, through a meadow of tall grasses, between tall strict dark pines, toward the house. It looked like its pictures, only more beautiful. The shingles just turning silver, the leaves of a wild rosebush beside the steps just yellowing. Cynthia felt her face smile automatically, and at the same time she felt a queasy excitement, in some unspecified place.

They got out of the car, in the clean pine-smelling air, in the sounds of the rushing river, and walked up flagstone steps, across a stone porch, to a massive brassbound door. Which, first putting down their suitcases, Roger with difficulty unlocked. "It always sticks," he affectionately said; he might have been speaking of an unruly pet.

Then he held open the inner screen door, so that Cynthia had to go in first.

An enormous room. She looked dizzily from a maze of high silvered beams to a huge stone fireplace, to a long leather sofa, velvet chairs, a bearskin rug. Deerheads, mounted at intervals.

She turned, she hid her face against Roger. "It's too much, it's too beautiful."

Not knowing that she meant it, he laughed, and, moving away from her, he went about turning on lamps; he picked up their suitcases and took them into another room.

More beauty: a white room of rough painted wood, three windows that faced the river. A wide brass bed, white-and-yellow quilt. Could anyone sleep there? It turned out that Cynthia, at least that time, could not.

In fact, several of Cynthia's problems that weekend were physiological: the altitude, or something, took away her appetite; she was perpetually hungry, and unable to eat. A drink, on the rear terrace, overlooking the river, plus a glass of wine at dinner, made her unpleasantly dizzy, in the handsome long dining room that looked out to the verdant flowing meadow, in the deepening green evening light.

And that night she could hardly sleep.

The next day the sight of the lovely yellow poplars saddened her, a sign of fall. What could she and Roger do, after the end of summer? What they did was to continue more or less as they were; then, at Christmas (of course), they quarreled violently, and with no reason. They violently reconciled in January.

Aside from admitting to not feeling very well, Cynthia had not mentioned the non-success of that first weekend. Since later times at that house were generally so good, with wonderful weekends in the snow, it seemed unimportant, her first impression. But she allowed herself to realize that she had been much too aware of the house; she had been almost jealous. As though the house were Roger's mother? She rejected that as too simple, too "Freudian." As though the house would outlast her, not only in Roger's affections but on the earth? This was mysteriously closer to the truth.

Now, once past Sacramento and the dullness of those entwined and endless freeways, the acres of "mobile" homes and depressing, shoddy shopping centers, the worst of the drive is over. They could look forward to the lovely cool ascent into the mountains, the views of small lakes and ponds, the rivers. The distant still-snowcapped peaks, the Sierras, stretching to Nevada.

They could look forward to their desecrated house.

And now Roger says, "We might as well stop for a drink, don't you think?"

Gratefully: "Yes."

Somewhat dramatically he mutters, "It hardly matters what time we get there, does it."

"I suppose not."

They stop at a nondescript bar beyond Auburn, where often in more cheerful moods they have stopped before, where Roger has always stopped on his way up to his house. The bartender, a fake rural with handlebar mustaches, has lost a lot of weight. "Gave up drinking beer," he tells someone else, farther down the bar, as he mixes their gin-and-tonics. An unobservant man, he persists in believing that he has known Cynthia as well as Roger for a long time. Do all Roger's wives and girlfriends look alike? Cynthia wonders, but has not wanted to ask this question; she believes that it would sound jealous, even if she is not; just curious.

Now, in the half-light, Roger's eyes darken, and his voice is low and intense as he says to Cynthia, "Sometimes I feel like saying, Christ, come on and take it, it's yours, you know?"

She knows.

"But who would I say that to? We haven't even identified the criminals yet." A quick grin. "It's almost meaningless, these days. Owning anything."

"It is," says Cynthia.

The last third of the trip.

Seeing almost nothing, they pass lovely tree-lined canyons with lakes shimmering below, and vistas of distant bare gray Sierra rocks, and quiet ponds. Flowering orchards and fields of tiny multicolored flowers.

Their drinks have intensified rather than lightened their

moods. Cynthia is thinking of all the named and nameless threats that haunt everyone alive, in this time and place. Pollution in seas and rivers everywhere. Drought and famine. Rapes and knifings in ghettos and in well-lighted suburban streets. Cancer. Broken glass in Roger's house. Someone sick. She is also thinking that someone could have been murdered in the house. Killed and left there. Did the sheriff go over it all? Did Mary Drake?

Roger slows down; he signals, and they cross the highway, and turn down the steep road to the river. They go over the bridge, and turn onto the road through the meadow, the high green grass, between the tall dark trees. Beside the porch the lilacs are in full lavender bloom, and the wild rose has tiny tight pink buds.

Roger opens the door, and what they see is awful; but it is not quite as awful as what either of their imaginations had conjured. A game table in one corner of the room has been overturned, and its cast-stone base is smashed. Broken glasses everywhere, as though thrown violently to the floor. Shards of glass stick out from unidentifiable foodstuffs. In the kitchen, there is several inches' thickness of Cheerios, or whatever, on the floor. A large cast-iron pot on the stove holds burned popcorn.

Someone has been sick in the sink, but not very. Mary exaggerates.

The bedrooms and the bathrooms and the upstairs dormitory appear to be untouched.

As they are to say to each other from time to time that night and the rest of the days of the weekend, it could have been a great deal worse.

Roger continues to inspect and to remark: "Christ,

what's this red sticky stuff? Cranberries—Jesus!" Cynthia, with no clear plan but with a broom and a dustpan and cardboard box for rubbish, begins to clear up what she can of the surface mess. Roger goes into the kitchen and makes strong drinks for both of them, and he starts in too, with both more energy and more system than she applies.

Their combined efforts work out well, and by a little before midnight the house has a clean, bare look; it might have been washed over by a flood of clear water rather than violated by human beings.

They are by now exhausted, barely sustained by a series of drinks and some scrambled eggs. And, as they have been doing on and off all evening, they try to reconstruct what sort of people the breakers-in were. At first they both thought it must have been some passing fishermen; now Cynthia decides that it was probably some very young kids, boys, about twelve or thirteen. Getting drunk for the first time.

She says, "I can imagine one of them standing on the table, can't you? Saying, Wow, am I drunk, or something. Imitating grown-ups, television drunks." And as she speaks she notes that she has lost her thirst for vengeance.

Roger scowls. "I just don't think it was kids, somehow. More likely some of those lousy summer picnickers. They spend months casing the place."

The sheriff, who arrives the next morning as they are starting the floor-waxing chore, is red-faced, with a huge beer-swollen stomach carried tenderly in front of him. And, just as predictably, he is sure that it was hippies who broke in; he has never forgotten nor forgiven hippies. Cynthia and Roger thank him for his concern; after he goes they look at each other and sigh, and get back to work.

By the time Mary Drake arrives, at her usual hour, eleven-forty-five, her time to be offered a gin-and-tonic, the whole house shines. Only the table base is still in pieces. And poor Mary is almost visibly disappointed. "Well, I never would have believed—" is what she says.

Apologetically they explain that they've really been working. "Both of us," Cynthia emphasizes: lonely Mary tends to be hard on men.

The three of them with their drinks sit on the rear terrace and speculate further about who broke in. Mary has her own idea. "Lots of times the cops won't even come because they're afraid of finding their own kids there," she says. "Cops' kids are the worst of all." Mary has been a social worker.

Cynthia and Roger give this some thought; certainly it is possible. But Mary is such a sad woman, a reminder of old age and loneliness, like a cool fall wind, that they often have to force themselves to be nice, especially Roger, who over the years has grown tired of her evident relish for disaster. She is not glad that they were broken into, really; but she is glad that something has happened, something to animate their conversation and to create a momentary closeness between the three of them. Perceiving this, Cynthia finds it more sad than tiresome.

"I would never have believed that it could look like this again," Mary repeats, on leaving. And then, a little brighter, "Of course there's that table base. They really smashed that good, didn't they now."

As she frequently does, Cynthia has brought some work up with her: a stack of manuscripts, which, after lunch, she takes into the guest room, where by long-standing habit she usually works. She soon becomes absorbed in her manuscripts—or, rather, in a single manuscript, which strikes her as being exciting; so often she has a sense of lonely wasted effort, of words that are important to one person alone.

At some point in the afternoon she walks through the living room, and she sees that Roger, who is sitting on the floor beside the table that was wrecked, has accomplished a minor miracle: the broken pieces of stone have been fitted together so that the table base looks almost exactly as it did before, only perhaps somewhat older—now it is lined with age, and no less beautiful. Seeing this, how hard and skillfully he has worked, Cynthia is filled with affection for him. She is moved, as she has been before, by his love for his beautiful house. And at the same time, quite irrationally (she thinks), she is envious of the time he spends on it, his total devotion.

And so everything is almost done, and that Saturday night is spent as they often spend Saturday nights up there: good food and wine, some joints, and love, and a lot of sleep.

The next day is balmy, caressingly warm. In the meadow the tall green grasses bend to a slight breeze; chipmunks and tiny birds scamper across the outcroppings of rock, among clusters of trees. A day and a scene that would seem to deny the possibility of evil, of pollution, decay, corruption and misery.

They lunch on the rear terrace, above the noisily rushing river that is still too cold for swimming.

Then, out of nowhere, Roger says, "I'll bet it was those Mexicans."

At first Cynthia does not know what he is talking about, although a premonitory chill, like the onset of fall, informs her that this could be the start of one of their less fortunate conversations. False innocent (now she has remembered), she asks, "Mexicans?"

"You know, that noisy group having a picnic. They probably cased the place and then decided to come back. Mad because I ran them off."

Of course Cynthia remembers the Mexicans, picnicking on the riverbank, on Roger's property—in their bright clothes, making a lot of noise as they splashed their hands in the rushing cold river water, as they unwrapped and passed around their food. Still, Cynthia felt bad when Roger went over to tell them to leave; a coward, she hid in the house, not wanting to watch their departure. And of course it is possible that being sent off made those people mad, and they came back to desecrate the house. But Cynthia does not believe it.

After dinner Roger goes back to his table, the finishing touches.

Watching him, looking up from time to time as she fails to concentrate on her book, Cynthia has a sudden and curious perception, which is: Roger has actually enjoyed everything about this break-in—the dramatic suspense of the drive up, the speculations as to what they would find, wondering about who had perpetrated this misdeed. Even, looking back, she feels that he was slightly disappointed that it wasn't worse. He is the proud rescuer of his house, like a man who has restored his wife's honor.

A few minutes later this view seems somewhat unfair— or not entirely true. But as it retreats from her mind another, simpler thought enters, a single sentence: I cannot marry Roger, or his house.

. . .

And that is true: in the middle of the night Cynthia, unable to sleep, *knows* that she can't marry Roger, and for the moment that knowledge makes her feel lonesome, bereft of love, homeless.

And guilty: in her mind she begins to explain herself to the sleeping Roger, who lightly snores beside her. "It's not just your insisting that the Mexicans ripped you off," she says, "although I didn't like that. It's just that we are too different, and for us to get along I'd have to become more like you, more concerned with owning and taking care of things, better at cleaning up."

At that moment, as though in answer to another, as yet unspoken thought of Cynthia's, Roger murmurs, "Caroline."

Cynthia's musings take on another tone. "You really don't know who I am," she says. "You just keep getting married because you can't tell women apart; they are just adjuncts to you, and keepers of your house. Well, I'm sure you'll find another, a Clara, maybe, who will be a lot better at it than I am."

At last she falls asleep, and wakes to bright morning sunlight on her face. She has just been dreaming of her own flat, on Liberty Street, the ferns and the sunlight there, her cats, the mess. And as she vividly remembers her decision, or revelation of the night before, she wonders how it took her so long to come to; of course she can't marry Roger. And she wonders too how at first that knowledge could have made her feel lonely—homeless, even—when she has a perfectly good place of her own, good friends, great cats.

Roger is already up—not there. She looks at her watch: nine o'clock. She gets up and goes into the kitchen, where there is a note from Roger; he has gone to the hardware store, the plumber, the sheriff's office. Relieved (she is still not quite ready for the next conversation with Roger), Cynthia makes coffee, and then, as though with a plan, she begins to wander about the house, coffee cup in hand. Perhaps, in her way, she is saying goodbye to the house?

An instinct of some sort leads her to a small corner table, near the bookcases, and there she finds what it is amazing that she did not notice before: a black notebook that is embossed in gilt, "St. Christopher's School." Roger himself went to that expensive, ultraconservative school, in the hills of the East Bay, and at first Cynthia thinks, Oh, an old notebook of Roger's. But the book is new, and it must be twenty years since Roger left St. Christopher's.

Several realizations come to Cynthia at once, the first being that there is a train to San Francisco at ten-thirty; they have often talked about taking the train, she and Roger—how beautiful it would be, over mountains and valleys, as opposed to the dullness of the drive by car.

And so Cynthia writes a note, which she attaches to the incriminating notebook. "Dear R., Isn't this hard evidence for my theory about drunk kids? Rich drunk kids at that. I'm taking the train, I hope you won't mind. Let's talk in S.F. C."

Fifteen minutes later, small overnight bag in hand, and sack of manuscripts, she is up on the highway, walking fast toward town, toward the train and the beautiful trip, going home.

A Southern Spelling Bee

One afternoon in the late Thirties, in Washington, D.C., a blond and handsome man who was to become a World War II hero, a fighter pilot of exceptional daring—that man got so irritated at a little girl of six, his daughter's age, that he decided to get even with her by having a spelling bee. As he told this story over the years, which he often did, he forgot a lot that actually happened, including his own irritation which began it all, and how it ended. It became just a funny story about two little girls.

The man's name was Cameron Lyons, and he was from Charleston, South Carolina, and he always spoke in those soft and unusually slow accents. His wife, Lillian, was from North Carolina, but more and more she spoke as her husband did. He was from a better family, with a better Southern name. Their daughter was called Helen Jane, plump and pretty and blond, and dearly loved by both her parents. The irritating other child was Avery Todd, and she was a distant cousin, or child of cousins, from Cameron's side of the family; her father, Tom, was in a sanatorium in Virginia, drying out, and her mother was busy with Avery's younger brother, a delicate boy, and with her bookstore. And so Lillian had said that they would take Avery for a while. That was like Lillian; she was always taking people in, even in their narrow Georgetown house, even in the Depression, providing food and shelter for stray relatives. She had a strong sense of family.

Avery was a dark, sharply skinny child, with large melancholy eyes and a staggering vocabulary. She was physically awkward, not good at jump rope or hopscotch or roller-skating, but her mind was exceptional. She read all the time, read grown-up books from her mother's store—more than was good for her, in Lillian's opinion—and had been heard to describe *Gone With the Wind* as "boring." The two children got along fairly well, but that was probably because Helen Jane had an extremely peaceable disposition.

But Cam, who was unexpectedly intuitive, and open to vibrations, felt waves of pure hatred that flowed toward his cherished daughter from small Avery. And *why?*

His irritation at Avery began to reach a peak at lunch when innocent Helen Jane said, "Oooh, macaroni and cheese! I just love macaroni," and Avery said sternly, "Helen Jane, inanimate objects are not to be loved." Cam also repeated that remark over the years, but again, as something funny that little Avery had said.

And so, while Lillian and the colored girl were clearing up from lunch, Cam took the two children into the living room and announced that they were going to have a spelling bee.

Avery looked very pleased, but Helen Jane pouted and said, "Daddy, you know I can't spell anything."

"That's all right, honey, you'll be all right." He turned to Avery. "Mississippi."

"M-i-s-s-i-s-s-i-p-p-i."

To Helen Jane he said, "Helen."
"H-e-l-e-n."
To Avery, "Constantinople."
"C-o-n-s-t-a-n-t-i-n-o-p-l-e."
"Jane."
"J-a-n-e."
And so on, for quite a while.

("I ran upstairs crying, of course," said Avery, many years later, when asked what happened after that.)

In the Forties, while Cam was heroically in England and France, the two young girls continued in their divergent directions. Sexually as well as intellectually precocious, Avery had an early and violent adolescence; there was always some passionate involvement with a boy—her heart was often broken. Sheltered, passive Helen Jane never fell in love until she was eighteen, and then she fell in love with Stuart Claiborne, an exceptionally rich and handsome Southern boy, whom she married a year later, and to whom she bore four children, and whose secret ugly temper she endured until he was finally involved in a housing scandal during the Johnson administration.

In Avery's case there was a rumor of a very early (annulled) marriage to a colored trombone player, but—to Lillian and Cam—this was so monstrous a thought that they loyally discounted it as slander. But she did get married several times, although never in church or even in her own home so that silver could be chosen and presents sent, permanent addresses noted down. One husband (they believed) was a professor—a divorced man, a Jew. Another husband (they *thought*) was a poet.

Avery's mother died (she of the bookstore), and her father remarried.

They had had only the briefest glimpses of Avery over the years, but Lillian, with her strong sense of family, had kept her newest name and address in the book, and so, when they came to San Francisco, where Avery was living, they telephoned. Somewhat surprisingly ("I could hardly believe it—she was so—well—*gracious*—grown-*up*," Lillian reported to Cameron), Avery invited them to dinner. To meet her husband, Joseph. They were not sure what he did—some kind of a doctor? Although, given Avery, anything so sensible was unlikely.

Over the phone, Avery had said to Lillian, laughing in a new (to them), dry, grown-up way: "You'll see, he looks a little like Cam."

At first glance neither Cam nor anyone else would have noticed a resemblance between himself and Joseph. But what Lillian and Cam did continuously peer at Joseph to find out (they did not know they were doing this) was: what is wrong with this one? Why did she choose him? On the surface at least there was nothing wrong: he was blond, conventionally handsome and polite, if a little quiet. The apartment was attractive. And Avery in her own dark way looked quite beautiful.

But, being a Southern woman of a very definite kind, Lillian withheld compliments, and instead she launched into a recital of their day in San Francisco. Adventures on cable cars, exotic stores. "Well, I just want you to know I found the most lovely brocade in this little bitty store on Grant Avenue, but instead of Chinese there were these Jews. You know, I just love the Jews. I think they're absolutely marvelous. I don't care what anyone says."

Cam caught a startled glance exchanged between Avery and Joseph, but at least neither of them said anything. Years back, he knew, Avery would have lashed out at anything anyone said about Jews, even Lillian saying she *liked* them. But after all, Avery was Southern, and somewhere she knew what not to say.

Lillian had not stopped talking for a minute. "It's for Mary Lillian's wedding, in June," she said. "That's my oldest granddaughter. Not a speck of money but they're both real smart so I reckon they'll be okay."

Then Avery announced dinner, and the four of them went in to her pretty table. Lillian cried out, "Avery, isn't that your mother's silver? I recognize it, I always said you should be the one to have it, even if some people thought your brother would appreciate it more."

Cam had to admit to himself that Avery looked younger than Helen Jane did, probably because Avery was so thin. With her burning dark eyes and her long proud neck she had turned into quite a woman. Strange.

Lillian was telling about Helen Jane's recent remarriage. "The nicest man you'd ever want to meet. A widower, and he'd never had any children. Now, doesn't that tell you something about the kind of man he is? To take on four not his own? He works in Washington, of course. In the C.I.A."

Avery said, "The C.I.A.?"

"Oh yes, the grandest job. They come down to see us all the time and we have the best old time."

Cameron said, "Avery, this fish is delicious, just plain delicious. Whoever would have thought you'd grow up and learn to cook?"

"No one related to me, certainly," Avery said.

And Joseph, "Actually, she's a terrific cook."

Cam noticed that Joseph drank a lot, lots of vodka before dinner, and now he was really pouring down the wine.

To Cam this was an amiable and familiar weakness, more comprehensible than Jewishness or writing poetry, but for Avery, with all her father's trouble with the stuff, it seemed an odd choice; it was as though she had made some sort of circle.

"What is it that you do out here, Joseph?" Cam asked.

"I'm a psychiatrist. Mainly children."

"I married my doctor," said Avery, as though she were making a joke.

Consciously refraining from telling any of the psychiatrist jokes he knew, Cameron said, "Well, if you're interested in children you'll like this story about this little old gal here, your Avery." And he told the story about the spelling bee. And at the end in his gentle way he chuckled, and he said, "Helen Jane never did catch on, but of course Avery did."

"What did you do then?" Joseph asked Avery.

"I ran upstairs crying, of course," Avery said.

"Did you, old sweetheart?" old Cameron asked. "I didn't remember that."

By the middle of dessert, Joseph, who had indeed been drinking a lot, beginning with the vodka sneaked into his tomato juice, to cope with the hangover from the night before, slumped over in his seat. His unconscious face was no longer handsome, but swollen and coarse. "The ugliest old thing you'd ever want to see" is how Lillian later, with considerable exaggeration, described Joseph's passed-out face to Helen Jane and Ken, of the C.I.A.

But after one glance each of those Southern-trained people pretended that he was not there—what had happened had not happened—and none of them glanced a second time.

And after dinner Joseph was left snoring at the table; they all (those three Southern people) went into the living room, where Avery served coffee, and Lillian showed pictures of the grandchildren and of her daughter's marriage to Ken. And then Lillian and Cameron got up to go, and to make their prolonged Southern ritual of farewell.

At last that was over and Cameron had bundled Lillian into their rented Mercedes and he stood on the sidewalk with Avery, in the cold San Francisco summer night. Avery's arms were bare and she shivered, and at that moment Cameron was seized with an impulse toward her that was violent and obscure and inadmissibly sexual. He reached toward her— surely he had simply meant to kiss her good night?—but as he stepped forward everything went wrong and his heavy foot bore down on the uncovered instep of her high-arched foot, so that she cried out in pain.

"Oh, my darling, I'm so sorry!" breathed old Cam, drawing back.

"It's all right, I know you are," she said.

("But why did you ask them to dinner?" Joseph asked her sometime the next day.

"I don't know, I think just the sound of their voices over the phone. When I was little I thought Cam was the most marvelous, glamorous man alive," and she sighed. Then, "I thought they'd be nice!" she cried out. "God, don't they know? How I must have felt about a little girl who could just smile to get love and not have to spell Constantinople?")

"What took you so long? What on earth were you talk-ing about?" Lillian asked Cameron, in the heavy, purring car.

"I—uh—stepped on her foot. Didn't mean to, of course. Had to say I was sorry."

"My, you are the clumsiest old boy, now aren't you." And Lillian chuckled, quite satisfied with them both, and with the evening.

True Colors

Just a year ago, another balmy blue May, here in San Francisco, I was newly and madly in love with a man I had met a couple of weeks before. We were silly, like adolescents; love seemed to us our own unique invention—love meaning, of course, the most overwhelming, most intense and inexhaustible sensuality. We thought that no lovers had ever made love so frequently, or so violently as we. David, a just-divorced father of three, a lawyer. I am, and was then, a divorced mother of one, and an editor, part time.

We met, David and I, in the Washington Square Bar and Grill, where I had gone to dinner with a friend, Anna, an actress, who is talented but often unemployed; we see each other fairly often, more for lunches than for dinner, since she is usually involved with some man or other. I am usually not.

I had not been to that particular restaurant before, perhaps because I had heard almost too much about it; it is the sort of place mentioned in columns, locally. Anna goes there a lot; she lives in North Beach, she says it's her neighborhood pub. And the "singles" aspect of the bar, as we waited for a table, hemmed in by such a lively crowd, made me feel somewhat shy; Anna, dramatically blond, handles situations of that nature considerably better.

In any case, we were standing there in the crowd, hoping to get a table soon, I suppose looking somewhat helpless, when a smallish man with thick gray hair (obviously premature; he looked young) and sad brown eyes moved closer to us and asked if he couldn't buy us a drink. He had on a dark gray suit (with a vest!) but looked okay. I was the one he had addressed, oddly enough, but it was Anna who said yes, he sure could; we'd love some white wine. At that moment the most striking thing about him, aside from the gray hair, and that vest, was the fact that he had a big fistful of silver dollars, jiggling them in his hand. And when Anna said we'd like white wine he went off to the bar to pay for the drinks—with silver, probably. He came back with the glasses of wine at the same instant that the waiter said our table was ready, and so it seemed polite to ask him to come along— Anna asked him.

In that way we three sat down in a booth together, David seated across from Anna and me. Right off, after introducing himself, he explained about the silver dollars: he had spent the weekend in Las Vegas, and made a lot of money there. Anna and I laughed at the very idea of Las Vegas, of making money in that way, and he laughed too. The first real luck he'd had in several months, David said, since his divorce. Being single was okay, he guessed, but he missed his kids. Handsome David, with that thick surprising hair, slightly slanted brown eyes, a strong nose and rather delicate narrow mouth—from the start I was very aware of his mouth.

He told us that he was a lawyer, and I was struck, at that moment, by the odd fact that the only lawyers I know these days are young women—friends of about my own age, I mean. The men I know are in what could be loosely described as the arts, although you would have to stretch that to include journalism and some commercial art. Which, according to a rather conservative friend of mine, explains why I have so often been dumped: I tend to be drawn to "unreliable" artists, beginning with my husband, a painter, who cut out for New York when I was pregnant with Barbara, just leaving a note. (This was not as bad as it sounds; we were not getting along well at all, and it is probably harder to bring up a child with a husband you don't get along with than by yourself, or that's what I imagine. Besides, like so many good artists, my husband—my former husband—was much more successful in New York than out here, and sometimes sent money for Barbara.)

Anna asked David what kind of law he practiced, and he said that actually he was in investments. "I still find it exciting, sometimes," he said, and he laughed in an appealing way. "Basically I'm just a gambler."

I said that sounded like fun, which it suddenly did, and I got a beautiful smile from David. "Well, it is," he said.

How is it that certain things between people become so quickly clear? I don't know, no idea, but quite soon it was obvious that David and I were—relating? communicating?—were compellingly drawn to each other, would probably spend the rest of the evening together, and probably in bed. It was clear too that Anna didn't mind or feel left out; actually she seemed pleased at the situation, as though she had introduced us to each other, and I could feel her thinking, Oh, at last someone sensible for Maud, a lawyer in a three-piece suit. Also—the early luck of lovers—she was meeting the current man in her own life at the airport, coming up from L.A., later on. And so we all three talked and laughed, and David and I stared at each other with curiosity, sneaking smiles—and with an almost breathless anticipatory lust.

Then Anna went off to meet her Hollywood friend's plane, and David and I came back to my place, on Pixley Alley, where Barbara (ten, old enough to be left alone, I hope) was already asleep. And immediately, on my old brown corduroy sofa, we fell to kissing and touching, to falling in love.

Like Romeo, he left my house near dawn, a faint yellow light that seemed an enemy, so famished were we still for more of each other—although, by then, so utterly exhausted. But I am bringing up Barbara, or trying to, in a way that could be thought prim, old-fashioned; I do not force the fact of my lovers upon her attention; for the most part I keep them out of sight. And actually there haven't been so many; my experience with my husband scared me off men for a while, and I was very busy then with Barbara. But I have had a couple of long-term involvements that ended badly, by being dumped; I don't seem to know when to get out first.

In David's case, however, being so much in love, I asked him for dinner with me and Barbara, the very next night.

He and Barbara got along well. I had made a spicy pot roast that is one of her favorites (and also, I remembered at some time during dinner, the favorite of the last lover in my life before David came along), and David liked it too, and we all ate and laughed a lot together. Obviously used to meals with kids, David did not ask about school or her plans for being a grown-up; instead he mentioned a couple of movies that he'd seen, and he said that when his kids were little he used to take them to the small beach in the Marina, very near us—Barbara and I used to go there too, which she remembered.

And, aside from a few furtive but uncontrollable embraces when she was doing something in another room, we waited for Barbara to go to bed, to fall asleep. And then we rushed together, wild and insatiable. And tender. In love.

Two weeks later, that was how we still were, still wildly in love, and astounded at our luck in meeting, although a few problems of a practical nature had made themselves apparent; namely, money and children. About money problems David was very direct, which I liked. When I asked him for dinner again, he said, "It's really good of you to cook. I'm trying to stay out of restaurants until the next infusion of silver comes along," and he laughed, making it okay, not grim; and he always brought along the wine. The child problem was harder to get around, though; his three spent weekends with him, and if they met me just then, he thought, they would tell their mother and she would be even angrier, more demanding when they got to court, and it would not be fair to tell them not to tell her, too burdensome. And so the second weekend of knowing each other we were apart for two whole days, early (very early) Saturday morning until late Sunday night. Barbara was less of a problem, having met and liked David; still, she was why we didn't get to spend the night together.

But the weekend after that—it seemed a miracle—we got to go away together. His wife was taking the kids somewhere, to see her parents, I thought—and Anna offered to have Barbara stay with her; Barbara loves North Beach. And so—a weekend away. We were going to Las Vegas.

About Las Vegas, I was not entirely clear on why David thought that was such a good idea, other than his having had some good luck there, just before we met. But actually I didn't care, and in my fantasies Las Vegas was so awful that it was almost great: supremely tacky, high camp.

We were even going to stay at Caesar's Palace. I wondered about that—it sounded expensive—until David explained that at Caesar's Palace he was "on comp"—which, he
then further explained, meant that everything is complimen-
tary, the room and the food and drink. "I'll just have to roll a
few dice," he said, laughing. Actually I didn't much care
where we went, I was so reveling in the prospect of sleeping
and waking together.

Picking me up to go to the airport, David seemed a little
surprised by my suitcase, a striped canvas bag that I have
always liked. He eyed it, said, "What a curious bag."

"Well, it's very practical; you don't have to check it on
planes," I explained, and then overexplained, "You said not
to bring too much; no one dresses up, you said."

"Oh, baby, it's a terrific bag, don't fuss. It's just that it
looks sort of like a backpack."

Feeling criticized, and fighting that feeling, I then
began to think how surprised and pleased he would be to
find that I had brought mainly wonderful nightclothes. In
that way, with those thoughts, I succeeded in cheering up.

On the plane, drinking champagne (comp of the airline), we passed by the most glorious, fantastic clouds that
I had ever seen: white and mountainous, almost imper-
ceptibly shifting, like avalanches, and all that whiteness
gilded with the sun, in the California and then Nevada midafternoon, in late spring. They must have been omens of
some sort, those clouds, I thought; our weekend would be as
glorious as clouds.

. . .

We landed at the Las Vegas Airport, nothing remarkable. Perfectly all right. Why then did I experience a moment of panicked craziness, in which I imagined myself actively going mad, running amok? I saw myself crazily hitting someone (David?) or flinging myself on the bright green carpeting, in a child's tantrum. That passed quickly, however, a hallucination; I held David's arm and we pressed together sexily, walking along toward the Avis desk.

There were slot machines all around; well, of course there were, and only that fact made that airport different from any other where I had been. Taking my arm from David's for a moment, I reached into my bag for quarters; coming up with several, I told him that I would be right back.

But he restrained me. "No, don't do that now."

"Oh, why not?" I was really surprised, he looked so serious.

"Well, if you didn't get a jackpot right away I'd think we were jinxed. The whole weekend shot."

He laughed, but clearly he meant it; I guessed that he was superstitious over money. And then it was clear to me that he was serious, really serious about making money on that trip, and I thought, Oh, poor David, how foolish you are. (I was not in wonderful financial shape myself, at that time, having been demolished by the I.R.S., but I had seen no need to tell David about my money problems; why add to his.) I secretly planned to see that we spent most of our time in bed.

Falling in love with people you hardly know of course is in some ways a problem, it then occurred to me; you know the shape and taste of each tiny vein in their flesh, and all their secret smells, but maybe not how they feel about money, for example, or how they really like to spend their time when they are not making love.

. . .

By the time we got to the car, then, I was braced for heading straight for the tables, and hoping for the respite of a short siesta (I love siestas; the best time for love, I think) between gambling and our dinner. And so I was quite surprised when, in the rental air-conditioned Cougar, heading out of the airport, David said, "I really want you to see some of the land around here. The desert. We don't have to go as far as Hoover Dam, Lake Mead, but I'll head down in that direction. First."

Another problem of not knowing a person well: when he's making some sacrifice for you, you can't tell him that you don't really mind, it's perfectly okay to go on into town and start shooting craps, or whatever, right away.

However, thigh to thigh, in the cool new Cougar, speeding out on the wide white highway, at first it seemed wonderful, interesting: strange rock formations in the distance and, nearer to hand, all that sand and brush, like a set for a cowboy movie.

Out there on the desert it was terribly hot, I could see that, could almost see the heat in the shimmering blue air, but inside the car it was cold—too cold, but I hated to complain, and for all I knew it was comfortable to David.

And very soon it got monotonous, all that gray sage. And frightening: I began to think of missiles, ballistic ranges, nuclear tests. I wondered why there were no rabbits around, it had so much the look of rabbit country; and then, as quickly as I wondered, I thought that probably they had all been killed, war victims, dying of guns and cancer.

David could have been reading my mind, for at the moment that I had my sinister rabbit thoughts he said, "Well, actually it is a little grim, isn't it. Think we might as well head back?" And he turned off the air conditioner and rolled down a window. We were instantly warm—hot, really —but that seemed preferable to the unnatural cold, in the menacing gray desert. We turned around, and headed back toward Las Vegas—going much faster, I noticed, than when we were headed out.

Caesar's Palace: it must cover several city blocks. Acres of white filagreed concrete, rising in towers, in endless curved archways—much more Indian than Roman in appearance. In fact, in moonlight or a heavy dusk it could be miraculously mysterious. Close up, in the harsh sunlight of midafternoon, in spring, it was just violently tawdry, a monumental excrescence.

Which should have prepared me for the interior, but it did not. David and I walked into a series of enormous rooms that could have been subterranean, so dim and unreal was the light. And in those rooms were *a million slot machines*, at least a million; every space for walking was an aisle between those consummately garish, volcanic machines. Everywhere people feeding in money, jerking handles, scooping it up. Everywhere money, and smoke; everyone was smoking, and most of them drinking something. That afternoon could have been the middle of the night, been anywhere at all—the middle of hell.

I whispered to David, "It's unreal."

"Oh no, baby. It's real, all right."

David seemed to know where he was going, and I followed his not quite familiar shoulders; I behaved as though it were perfectly okay, the tacky-funky place of my imagination. I could not wait for us to be alone, to touch and kiss, familiarly. And a great fear seized me that he would want to start gambling right away; at any moment he could have put our bags down beside a machine, or one of the black tables where cards were being dealt, chips thrown out, along with dollars. He could have stopped there and smiled at me and said, "Well, how about it?" and I would have had to smile back and say okay—a good sport, a friendly lover. I could almost see and hear him saying that, but surprisingly he did not; he continued past another roomful of machines (that I could see was labeled "Salon di Slots") until we were at a check-in desk, and then a few minutes later, after a quick encounter with the computer, we were standing at a bank of elevators.

"We're in what's called the New Fantasy Tower," David said to me, and we smiled at each other in the private way of happy lovers.

The other people who went up with us in the car, to the fantasy tower, were large and pale, Midwestern-sounding. I paid very little attention to them; they seemed quintessential Las Vegas visitors.

We got out and went down a red-carpeted hall to our room, and David opened the door. At first glance it was a fantasy room, a very sexual fantasy. A round bed covered in pink velvet, with a round mirror on the ceiling, and not far from the bed, an elevated pink tiled bath, also round, and as large as the bed. *Well.* How super, is what I thought, at first. But right away quick second thoughts leapt forward. For one thing, new lovers, so far confined to sneaking around in the dark, David and I were not used to so much naked exposure to each other. Even the washbasin was out in full sight of the bed, no way to brush your teeth without the other person watching, much less to take a bath—and bathing together, at such an elevation, in the middle of the room, seemed somehow too forward a step for us, just then. It was a room for just sex, a man coming into a hooker's room, or she into his for an hour or so, and then leaving, no brushing teeth or washing faces. No breakfast together.

Looking at David, I thought I saw or felt the same conclusions on his face; he looked shy, slightly taken aback. And as I started to open my bag he said, "Well, I guess you'd like to wash up? This may be a good time for me to go downstairs and roll a few. Keep up my comp status."

He smiled and I smiled back, and we kissed in a friendly way as I thought how sensitive he was, how delicate his instincts. But then as he smiled again, and left the room, I thought, Dear God, he could stay down there for hours. I panicked; what would I do?

In fact, I was thinking two contradictory things at once: one, if I got into a bath, David would surely come back early, to find me looking a little silly in that tub. And, two, he would be down there for several hours. Weighing those possibilities, I pulled the draperies apart, more heavy pink velvet, and looked out into the still-bright late afternoon sunshine.

Close up, just outside the window, that filagreed concrete looked barely stuck together, and I had the San Franciscan's familiar thoughts of earthquakes. Beyond all that dangerous lace stretched miles of casinos, giant signs that advertised casinos, miles of jammed thoroughfares, people, cars.

I closed the draperies and started my bath. Of course the tub filled very slowly, such an enormous volume; after what seemed a long time there was only about half an inch of water on the bottom. I rushed through with washing, somehow, thinking that actually I should have lingered; I would look much less foolish if there were a lot of water (maybe David would join me in the tub?) and besides, I probably had a lot of time to kill.

But I didn't, no time at all: I was out of the tub and wrapped in a towel, deciding what to wear, when David burst into the room, grinning and exhilarated. "I knew it, you bring me luck!" he almost shouted, among welcoming swift kisses on my neck. "You're wonderful—I may have to keep you around."

Well, great. I would have liked to ask how much money he won, just out of interest, but I did not, and it didn't matter; I was so pleased that he felt lucky; he was lucky and attributed it to me. And mostly I was terrifically pleased that he had come back so soon. And I thought, maybe that would be enough? No more machines and tables?

David had gone over to the telephone; he was dialing and getting room service. I heard him order champagne and a plate of hot Chinese hors d'oeuvres. He said, "They're terrific here. I'm starving, aren't you?"

I smiled, but I thought that since we were expecting room service we could not, just then, make love. No siesta. Also, I wished that I had brought something to wear other than the pink sweater tidily folded up in my bag, since David was feeling so festive. However, I saw no point in regrets on either score, or not for long. I got dressed, as modestly as I could, and David said how clever I was to bring a sweater that matched our pink velvet room, and we both laughed—in love, having a good time together.

The champagne arrived, and the hot Chinese hors d'oeuvres, which somehow made us hungrier; we reminded each other of all the San Francisco jokes about being hungry after Chinese food. We decided to go on down to dinner, to something called the Bacchanal Room.

Our high mood continued through dinner, in that crazy room which almost exceeded my fantasies of camp, of tackiness. The waitresses had obviously been selected for the size of their breasts—huge breasts bursting from the tops of their miniskirted "Roman" tunics, as they bent down to pour out wine from great round green glass bottles. I finally saw a wine label on one of the jugs: Californian, fairly good and very cheap. David and I laughed at all that, amiably. I saw that we were having the fifty-dollar dinner, and I thought again how nice that everything was comp.

David said, "Do you realize that we're celebrating two weeks of knowing each other? Two weeks ago tonight."

I was very touched by his saying that; it was not something that many men would say, or even think of. I would have liked to tell him that I couldn't believe it had only been two weeks, but that seemed too trite to say.

We smiled, and leaned together in a kiss, and whispered words of love to each other. "I am crazy about you," I murmured to his ear, and at that moment I surely was.

All the wine, or simply the heady excitement of love, had made even the gaming room look better. Walking toward a roulette table, I felt a sense of possibility. Maybe we would go on being lucky, in dollars as well as love. Sometimes a few thousand can really improve your life, and it's silly to think otherwise.

Several turns of the wheel later on, maybe fifteen minutes later, I caught a very unhappy look from David, which I took as a cue that maybe I was not, just then, Lady Luck; maybe it was time to walk around on my own for a while. I went over and whispered to him that I'd be back soon, I wanted to explore. He nodded distractedly, with the smallest smile.

Walking through those rooms, I was suddenly in an underworld of weird lights and unfamiliar, discordant and disturbing sounds, of money and machines. And faces: pale and harried, anxious underwater faces, all frighteningly alike. And I remembered something strange: some years ago, having heard that mescaline was fun, lots of laughs and great sex, my then husband and I took some, and it wasn't fun at all, or sexy; I went off into a nightmare of plastic buttons, weird clothes, plastic, everything distorted and ugly, *wrong*. I didn't know the man I was with—my husband. Of course, at that moment in Las Vegas, I was not nearly as terrified as I was on mescaline, and at least I knew where I was, but I hated it, I was frightened.

I walked for as long as I could, trying, and failing, to find the wonderful tackiness that I had imagined. Also, I was afraid that David, losing money, would want to go on playing for most of the night. I was braced for that; I was perfectly ready to say, in a good-sport voice, that I didn't mind at all, and to go up alone to our crazy fantasy room.

However, when I came up to him, touching his arm in a fairly tentative way, although for a moment he looked unsure about who I was (well, by that time I was not too clear about him either), in the next moment he looked relieved. He nodded good night to the people just next to him; he took my arm and we headed toward the elevator.

On the way up he said, "Well, I guess you can't win every time."

"I guess not." I did not ask how much he lost, of course not.

Then at last we were in bed, finally making love. But even as we went through the familiar gestures, as we kissed and touched, as our rhythms meshed and accelerated, I had a crazy sense that we were not ourselves. We were any two people at all, tired people, straining for pleasure, in a room whose fantasy was not their own.

I had a thin sleep, disturbed by violent dreams that I could not remember in the morning. I looked over at David, already awake, just barely smiling, and saw how pale he

looked, how suddenly old. He must not have slept well either, and I hoped that was not a sign that we did not sleep
well together. More likely we were disturbed by the un-
familiarity of the place, and David was unhappy about however much money he lost. We did not make love; we got up
and dressed very hurriedly.

We had breakfast in a too bright cafeteria sort of place,
where everyone looked as anxious and unrested as we did.
On one wall there was a big flashing keno board, so that no
one would have to miss one minute of the thrill of gambling.
I asked David how keno was played, and he explained,
minutely, but I found it hard to listen, much less to understand what he was saying.

At last we left that depressing room and walked out into
the netherworld light that never changes, although it was
actually about nine-thirty in the morning. With a meager
smile David said, "Well, back to work," and sinkingly I
understood that he would probably be at the tables all day
("comp" doesn't come exactly free). I thought I could go out
and spend some time at the swimming pool; I wondered if he
would even come out for a swim.

Suddenly, then, we were standing in front of a mam-
moth, double-sized slot machine, a giant, and David was saying, "Do you have any singles, by chance? This baby really
pays, and you can put in up to three one-dollar bills."

I had three singles in my change purse (and five twenties in my billfold; I knew exactly how much money I had
which is how it is when you're more or less broke, I've found
—in flusher times I don't precisely know, and rich people
never know). I was getting my dollars out of my change
purse, obligingly; I was about to start putting them into the
maw of the machine when out of nowhere a tall gaunt

woman strode up to it. She was dark brown, sun-withered, with startling, ferocious bright blue eyes; she was wearing purple, with pounds of silver jewelry, an expensive old desert rat. With a challenging look at the huge machine she expertly slipped three dollar bills into its slot; with one heavily braceleted arm she reached for the lever and pulled it down. And a clanking cascade of silver fell into the trough.

Which would, of course, have been ours if I had got out my dollars a little sooner.

"Well, *Jesus*," David said to me. "Why didn't you— Oh Christ!" For at that moment she did it again, right in front of us: put in more paper money and pulled the lever and caused a deluge of silver dollars, all banging against each other.

David was so angry that for a moment I thought he was going to hit me. His face was pale and swollen, almost ugly, his eyes wildly large and dark; for a flicker of an instant I was reminded of his look in moments of sexual passion, but this was rage, pure fury.

Instead of hitting me (or maybe in order not to) he mumbled something: I'm sorry—I hate you—I'll see you later? I honestly do not know which of those things he said; he turned away and walked off, a small neat man, going fast, I had no idea where.

I stood there, I watched the woman in purple, the cause of our trouble, as she shoved in a couple of dollars more, which did not pay off. Then she scooped up all her loot into an old cracked brown leather bag. She turned and looked at me as though she, and not I, had been abandoned (well, perhaps she was, years back) and then she too was gone.

In a blind way I headed toward where I thought the pool was, but I found only more rooms full of machines, for which, at that moment, I had no stomach. In one of them the light was jarringly bright—in fact there were spotlights all over—and I saw huge cameras. It was a movie set; they were actually making a movie, at that very instant, in Caesar's Palace, Las Vegas. I recognized the star, in his canvas chair; it was Omar Sharif, anyone would have known him, with those big black sulky eyes. I had never liked him much, and it occurred to me then that he and David looked a little alike, although Sharif is larger and older than David, and I thought, in passing, how odd, to fall in love with a man who looks like a movie star you don't really like.

I did not find the swimming pool, and I walked faster until sheer luck or something landed me in front of the elevators. Nowhere to go but back up to the fantasy tower, where I realized that I rather expected David would be. Maybe to apologize, or maybe to say what an unlucky person I was for him; why didn't I leave?

I was answering that last accusation; in my mind I was saying to David, Well, what was I supposed to do, knock that woman down?—as I opened the door to an empty and unmade room.

Sunlight strained through a chink between the draperies, but I did not want to open them; I did not want to see (again—ever) that network of concrete filagree, so precariously stuck together, nor the acres of casinos just beyond. I did not want to see Las Vegas again, not ever.

That knowledge came over me with the force of cold water, a wave, and in the neutral temperature of that room I shivered for a moment, standing there perfectly still, and resolute. Then, suddenly galvanized, I rushed into motion. I pushed everything barely folded into my canvas bag (my "backpack"); for a moment I stared at my slightly awry image in the mirror, but decided to do nothing about how I looked, no effort at order.

I was thinking that David might come in at any moment, for whatever reason. Or someone might stop me, leaving the hotel with my suitcase. Or, worst, I might not have enough money for air fare. Right then I decided to go home by Greyhound; there was a chance that David could have been at the airport, but he would never go by bus; I could not say why but I was absolutely sure of that. I hoped I had enough money for the bus.

My heart had risen to the top of my chest and it beat there violently, so that it was hard to breathe. But I made it from the room to the elevator without meeting David in the hall, and he was not, of course, in the elevator, going down.

Despite trembling legs and a displaced heart I got across the lobby; probably, actually, I was not the first person to leave that place, in that condition. Also I guessed that my suitcase could have looked like an oversized handbag, if anyone wondered.

A bellboy handed me into a waiting taxi, and I had to say "Greyhound" twice before the driver understood; I was having trouble with my voice, and probably that is an uncommon destination from Caesar's Palace. As we flashed past those miles of casinos (the bus station was a long way off, worse luck) I thought, I *knew*, that I should have left a note for David, but I was really running scared, and besides, what could I have said, beyond something dumb about neither of us being quite the person the other one thought, which he had undoubtedly figured out on his own. What can you say to a person who really likes it in Las Vegas—who thinks it's real?

My first piece of luck: there was a bus just leaving for Reno, where I would have to change for San Francisco. The long way home. It was also more expensive than the more direct way, through Bakersfield, would be, and I had just enough money, in fact three dollars over (the three that I did not put into that machine, which must have meant something). I could have a hamburger in Reno. I bought my ticket and I got on, just in time.

The bus lurched into motion, out of the station, and onto a freeway where there were casinos all over the place. Again. But fairly soon we were past all that, and heading out into the desert.

I settled down for a fairly long trip, maybe boring, maybe in some ways a little frightening, so much desert. But from then on I was going to be all right, I thought.

At the Beach

The very old couple, of whom everyone at the beach is so highly aware, seem themselves to notice no one else at all. Tall and thin, she almost as tall as he, they are probably somewhere in their eighties. They walk rather slowly, and can be seen, from time to time, to stop and rest, staring out to sea, or to some private distance of their own. Their postures, always, are arrestingly, regally erect; it is this that catches so much attention, as well as their general air of distinction, and of what is either disdain or a total lack of interest in other people.

Their clothes are the whitest at the beach; in the ferocious Mexican sun of that resort they both wear large hats, hers lacy, his a classic panama.

They look like movie stars, or even royalty, and for all anyone knows they are, deposed monarchs from one of the smaller European countries, world-wanderers.

Because there is not much to do at that resort, almost nothing but walking and swimming, reading or whatever social activities one can devise, most people stay for fairly short periods of time. Also, it is relatively expensive. The Chicago people, who have come as a group, will be there for exactly ten days. The couple who have the room just next door to that of the distinguished old couple will be there for only a week—a week literally stolen, since he is married to someone else, in Santa Barbara, and is supposed to be at a sales conference, in Puerto Rico.

But the old people seem to have been there forever, and the others imagine that they will stay on and on, at least for the length of the winter.

And while everyone else can be seen, from time to time, to wonder what to do next—the Chicago people, apparently committed to unity of action, were heard arguing in the dining room over whether, or when, to rent a boat for deep-sea fishing—the two old people have a clear, unwavering schedule of their own. After breakfast, to which they come in quite late, as they do to all meals, they sit out on their small porch for a couple of hours. The girl in the room next door, who is named Amanda Evers, is passionately curious about them, and she tries to look through the filagree of concrete that separates the two porches. But she discovers nothing. (She is in fact too curious about too many people; her lover, Richard Paxton, has told her so. Curiosity contributes to the general confusion of her life.)

The old man reads his newspapers, a Mexico City *News* that he has delivered to his table each morning, at breakfast, and sometimes he seems to be writing letters—or perhaps he keeps a journal? The woman does not read the paper; she seems to be doing nothing at all—a thing that Amanda, who is restlessly energetic, cannot imagine. (Amanda manages a travel agency, in Santa Cruz, California; she often considers other careers.)

.　.　.

The arrival of the elderly couple, down at the beach, at almost precisely noon each day, is much noticed; it is when they look, perhaps, most splendid. In trim dark bathing suits, over which they both wear white shirts, in their hats and large dark glasses, advancing on their ancient legs, they are as elegant as tropical birds—and a striking contrast to everyone else on the beach, many of whom wear bright colors. One woman in the Chicago group has a pea-green caftan that literally hurts Amanda's eyes.

The old people sit each day under the same small thatched shelter, a little apart from the others, at the end of the line. After a while they will rise and begin one of their long, deliberate walks, the length of the beach and back. Then, returned to their shelter, in a slow and careful way they divest themselves of the shirts, the hats and glasses; they walk down to the edge of the water, and slowly, majestically, they enter the lapping small green waves. After a not quite total immersion they return to the shelter, to rest. Even in such apparent repose, however, they both have a look of great attentiveness. They seem highly conscious of each moment, and very likely they are.

They take lunch quite late, and always, of course, alone, at one of the small restaurants down the beach. They are seen to chatter away to each other, and to eat rather little. But no one can ever overhear what they are saying, nor would anyone dare address them. *Her* accent, however, is recognizably "foreign"; his is English, probably—giving further credence to the theory that they are royalty, deposed.

And that notion is not entirely incorrect: those people are named Carlotta and Travis Farquhar, and once, if not royal, they were famous: Carlotta, originally Polish, as an actress, and Travis, a Scot, as an astronomer; an asteroid has his name. They both, simultaneously, reached their heights of achievement about forty years ago; since then, not entirely by choice, they have eased themselves into retirement. In Travis's case, what was then called a nervous breakdown took two years from his life; coming out of it, he was, or felt himself to be, too far behind, in terms of research. He could still teach, of course, but he tired of that, fairly early on. And Carlotta, who took care of him during those years, had never been truly dedicated to the stage; later she was happy enough to yield her place to younger actresses, or so she said.

They never had children, always traveled a lot.

One ostensible reason for the high cost of this resort is its extraordinary natural beauty—a beauty that most people seem to take some note of on arrival, and then, curiously, to forget.

The hotel is built on the downward slope of a hill above the beach, from which one faces a very large cove of bright, often glassy-green water. Far out across that water, at the mouth of the cove, there are two widely spaced but rather similarly shaped promontories of land; both slope gently down to the water, like great dark obedient beasts. Delicately feathered trees are silhouetted out there, at sunsets, which are almost always brilliant and violent, or in the first pale light of early mornings.

The beach, a wide white ribbon, encircles the cove; above the sand is the powerful, encroaching, mysterious green jungle—impenetrable, probably dangerous. It marks the start of a mountain range that extends almost to Mexico City.

The skies are nearly always clear and blue and pale, and the air is warm—subtle, moist, insinuating. Getting off the plane, their first night, still in her northern California clothes,

Amanda gasped with pleasure at that tropical air and the smell of flowers that even at the airport hung in the slight evening breeze. "Oh, feel the air, it's so lovely," she cried out to Richard, by which she meant: Our time here will be lovely. But then she forgot about the air, or stopped thinking about it.

Richard is usually foremost in Amanda's mind and consciousness; he is a difficult lover (although she has reflected that all her lovers have been difficult, in one way or another). Her obsession with Richard is so anxiety-ridden that she cannot sort out those emotions; indeed, it is hard for her to imagine love without anxiety. Richard is not only married, in an explosive off-and-on way, but he is exceptionally handsome, a golden southern California boy; he is spoiled, rather moody and seemingly fond of his moods—he has put in some time at Esalen. He is five years younger than she, which is not supposed to matter, but somehow, sometimes it does.

At this resort, though, he seems exceptionally cheery and calm. Before breakfast he runs on the beach, two lengths, and he has announced that the sand is superior. Amanda, whose discovery this place has been, is more than relieved; she is delighted. They swim far out into the cove together, in the clear warm green water; sometimes, looking down, they can see small stray brightly colored fish. At lunch they drink the excellent Mexican beer, and eat fresh garlicky seafood. They shower and sleep, they make love. They swim again, and shower again, and head up to the bar, which is cantilevered out into the open, starry, flowery night; they drink margaritas, toasting each other and the lovely, perfect place.

And the next day they repeat the pattern.

Perhaps for that reason, Richard's relatively "good mood," Amanda's attention wanders from him more than usual, and she finds herself acutely aware of the elderly, possibly royal couple next door: how long have they been married, she wonders. And who *are* they?

"You could ask them for autographs," Richard suggests. "Then you'd know."

It is just past noon. From their beach chairs Amanda and Richard are watching as the Farquhars slowly rise and start out on their walk, watching the slow progress of those erect, high, narrow bodies, on their thin brown wrinkled legs.

Choosing to ignore Richard's facetiousness (he enjoys teasing her), Amanda asks him, "Will your hair be white, do you think?"

He frowns a little. "Not any time soon, I hope." And then, as though taking her earlier question seriously, he says, "Why don't you ask those people to have a drink with us, if you really want to know something about them?"

"Oh, well. I really don't think so." Amanda says this calmly, but inwardly she has quailed at the very idea; of course it would have to be the other way around, the older people would have to ask them for a drink, which of course they never will do—but oh! if they should. To be with those people, to know them at all, Amanda feels, would itself confer distinction; in their presence one would find peace.

And then, as she contemplates the two tall, erect figures that gradually grow smaller, walking down the very white beach, slowly, near the bright green-blue water, for a moment Amanda's consciousness blurs; from behind closed eyelids she has a sudden vision of herself without Richard, without the chaos of his presence in her life: she sees herself in some new and calmer phase, even released from her frenetic occupation. She is running a bookstore, perhaps. There is one for sale in Aptos, a town next door to Santa Cruz but smaller and quieter, by far.

Opening her eyes, as though she had been asleep, she shakes her head, and drowsily, rather impersonally, she speaks to Richard: "It's so restful here, isn't it."

"Well, that's one thing we came for, I thought. Leave our old problems behind?" He grins in a familiar, challenging way; they both know what "problems" he means, and her usual fondness for discussing them.

But this time she does not take him up. "It's so beautiful. I could stay here forever" is all she says.

If the Farquhars are objects of Amanda's admiring curiosity, the Chicago group inspires opposite emotions: she finds them noisy, obtrusive, in their too bright clothes. One of them, a heavily mustached young man, even smokes a cigar, *all the time*, which you can smell all over the beach. Their loud, quite unself-conscious voices dominate the dining room or the bar when they are present—as they seemingly always are, and always together. Amanda cannot imagine herself, with or without Richard, as a part of any group at all.

"Wouldn't it be great if they'd leave before we do," she whispers to Richard.

"They look pretty settled in," he observes.

"That's probably how they'd look anywhere. Do you realize that there're actually only six of them? I just counted. They seem more like ten or twelve people."

Richard laughs. Her ability to amuse him is a thing that Amanda counts on; it almost makes up, she feels, for being older and less beautiful than he is, although by most standards she is pretty enough (which she sometimes forgets), in a thin, rather original way, with her heavy dark hair, narrow face and large pale-gray eyes.

Another object of Amanda's wayward curiosity is the hotel's manager, or manageress: a large blond strong-looking woman, who is unfailingly cheerful. A big happy woman, she walks about in old soft white pants and a blue work shirt. She is called, by everyone, Lisa, and she seems to have neither a last name nor a history; her accent, in English, is vaguely Central European. She also speaks German and Spanish, fluently.

She and the Farquhars appear to know each other, and this too, of course, draws Amanda's attention. Lisa is, in fact, the only person to whom the Farquhars are ever seen to speak.

Amanda wonders how Lisa happened to come to Mexico, and if she has ever been married. Mainly, though, she would like to know the secret of such level cheerfulness: how can Lisa cope with the whole hotel, the guests and the help, and answer everyone's questions and still smile like that? Her own work has taught Amanda more than a little about the irritations of travel.

In fact, Amanda is wrong about the people from Chicago: there are seven of them, not six, although she may have counted when one of them was missing. And they are not quite as homogeneous as, to Amanda, they appear. At least one of them, a recent widow, Natalie Barnes, is quite out of sorts with the rest. It was good of them to ask her along, without Herbert, but they all make too much noise, and she knows them well enough by now to have tired of all their jokes and stories. Besides, her skin is getting too old for all this sun.

Natalie, like Amanda, like everyone there, is fascinated by the Farquhars—especially that woman's skin, which is remarkable, so fine and smooth and white. Natalie wishes she knew what kind of sun block that woman uses.

And she wonders about their marriage, the Farquhars': have they always been married to each other, and got along as well as they now apparently do? Natalie and Herbert were actually separated at the time that he died, a fact known to none of their traveling friends, so that Natalie has been cast, by them, in a role that does not precisely suit her, that of Herbert's beloved, bereaved wife. But she is just as glad that none of them knew about the girl.

Did those old people ever quarrel and get back together? Would Herbert have come back, had he lived? Would he have tired of that girl? Natalie sighs, afraid that she will never have an answer to anything.

The bougainvillea, in that place, blooms with a wild extravagance; there is every shade of pink, of red, even violet and purple. Vines cling to the steep hillside, from which the gaudy blossoms foam. Brilliant colors lurk between the low white plaster buildings of the hotel; everywhere there are sudden bursts of flowers—on the way to the dining room, or going up to the bar, and flowers bloom all around the porch-balconies of the rooms. Just beyond the porch that Amanda and Richard share with the Farquhars (except for the intervening filagree) there is a bush of yellow angel's trumpets, and beside the bush a strangely branched small tree, reddish blossoms among its crooked limbs. Hummingbirds are drawn to the tree's red flowers, while among the trumpet flowers there often appear small yellow butterflies, almost indistinguishable from the yellow petals.

By their fourth day Amanda is acutely aware of just that: four days gone, only three remain. Less than half their time. And the four days seem to have passed as one, she feels. Just as the years of her life race faster and faster. Soon she will be middle-aged, then irretrievably old. In a discouraged way she looks around the beach, at so much exposed and aging flesh, the sags and wrinkles that painstakingly acquired suntans do not conceal.

Richard, though, is simply a darker shade of gold. The small fine patch of hair on his chest and the hairs on his arms and legs are all bleached out, pale, almost invisible. No wrinkles, anywhere. Amanda sighs, thinking of what they— or, rather, she—will be going back to: at work, days on the phone or at the computer, people either impatient or angry with her, or both, and most nights spent alone, either not hearing from Richard or hearing, via a hurried call, that they cannot meet, after all, wherever they had planned to.

For reassurance, or perhaps to answer some unformed question, she turns toward the elderly couple, who are resting beneath their small thatched shelter. He is lying back in his chair, his eyes closed against the sun and his mouth slightly open. But she, her white skin shaded by the lace-brimmed hat, sits intently forward; she is looking, looking— but at what? Following the direction of her gaze, Amanda sees, in the foreground, a small outcropping of rocks, spattered with a little white moss. Then sand, and then the water, bright and clear and green, rippling out in the dancing, dazzling sunlight, as far as the horizon. And the hot flat blue endless sky.

Further sadness for Amanda: after four days she and

that couple, whose name she still does not know, are no closer to speaking or even nodding terms than they were on her arrival. They have never even seen her, Amanda believes.

That afternoon, after their siesta, Amanda goes up to the hotel desk to mail some postcards. Rounding a corner, she is confronted with a trailing vine, a cloud of peach-pink bougainvillea; she sees it against the soft blue midafternoon sky —she has never seen that particular color before.

Reaching the desk, she is surprised to find Lisa standing there, in a skirt and blouse, black pumps. Lisa looking older than usual, and tired. The change in her is so marked that Amanda assumes she is leaving for good, and she cries out, "Oh, Lisa, you're not going away?"—as though everything, lacking Lisa, would fall apart.

Lisa smiles, but her blue eyes remain worried. "I only go to Mexico City," she says. "Probably I return tomorrow. I go each other week."

"Oh. Well."

Several other people, Americans, come up to the desk just then, followed by two Mexican boys who carry the American luggage—unfortunately they are not the Chicago group, Amanda notes. The airport bus arrives, and they all get in, including Lisa.

Feeling abandoned, Amanda buys her stamps, and she sends off the cards to her friends; on all the cards she has written, "This is paradise!"

From the plane, on which Lisa and some of the former guests are flying to Mexico City, they can see, as it gains altitude, the whole great horseshoe cove: the white curve of beach, abrupt green jungle at the edge of the sand and even the clearing where the hotel is. Then the plane veers and heads directly inland, up over the huge sharp jungle-green mountains that are sometimes briefly, darkly shadowed with clouds.

Lisa is simply going to Mexico City on hotel business, but the prospect always unbalances her a little. Never married, a childless but strongly maternal Polish woman (nationality being her common bond with Carlotta Farquhar), she loves her work, finds it deeply satisfying.

She is genuinely concerned about the well-being of all the guests, and especially that of the Farquhars: she grew up on the romantic legend of Carlotta, who left the stage so relatively young. And she has worked it out that despite appearances the Farquhars do not have a great deal of money. She daringly hopes, on this trip, to persuade the owner of the hotel to give them a special rate, as long-term guests. In the meantime, she reminds herself to do their errands: a scientific magazine, in German, for Mr. Farquhar; for her a French cosmetic.

The next night, which is Amanda's and Richard's fifth, they decide to return to the bar for after-dinner drinks; once there, they are dismayed to find the Chicago people, who obviously have had the same impulse. But, feeling that they have not much choice, there being not much else to do, really, at nine-thirty, Amanda and Richard sit down anyway.

Early in the afternoon Richard spent a long time on the phone with his wife, or so Amanda believes; he only said that he had to go up to the desk. Unable to read, she lay waiting for him, all that time not doing anything—not knowing, wondering, what they could be saying to each other. For all she knew Richard could be telling his wife that he is bored at his "sales conference" and can't wait to see her again. It is harrowing to her, Amanda, not to know, and she feels that it is forbidden to ask; she would sound suspicious. When at last he came back to the room Richard looked cross, but that could have meant anything at all. At dinner he was pleasantly noncommittal: his usual self. But Amanda still feels anxious, vaguely apprehensive.

At the bar she is seated next to a woman whom she had not seen in that group: a surprisingly pleasant-looking woman, with short gray hair and a pretty dress. Amanda wonders why she has not noticed her before.

Natalie Barnes.

The two women exchange faint smiles of mutual approval.

Although the night is as clear and dazzlingly starred as all the nights have been, there are also, tonight, a few small drifting gray-white clouds, mysterious rags. Tattered ghosts.

Natalie, who will be at the resort with that group for another five days, has hitherto felt that since they invited her along, in spite of her widowed status, she was in some sense their guest. But just now, perhaps fortified by dinner, and some wine, she recognizes the untruth, even the unfairness of this theory: she is not their guest; she pays her own way. And she further thinks, Luther does not have to leave a cigar burning in the ashtray, constantly. Bracing herself, and trying for a pleasant voice, she says, "Luther, couldn't you please put those damn things out when you're not smoking them?"

They all stare at her; as a group they are not self-critical, but usually supportive, all the way. However, they are also dedicated to going along with each other's whims, all whims, and so Luther says, "Well, Nat, of course, I'll put it right out. Why didn't you tell me before, if they bothered you?" Everyone stares reproachfully at formerly good old Nat, who was so brave when Herbert died.

Turning away from them all, for a moment, Natalie finds the dark girl with the very handsome husband (or lover?), who is smiling and saying, or, rather, whispering: "Terrific. That smell has been driving me crazy."

Natalie whispers back, "I didn't sound too mean?"

"Heavens no."

Richard joins in, smiling charmingly. "Amanda has a thing about cigars."

Still whispering, Natalie admits, "Actually, so do I."

"Well: we were just going to have another drink. May I get you one?"

Natalie argues, and then accepts, and they introduce each other: Natalie, Amanda and Richard. The darkness and the loose, informal arrangement of the chairs at that bar make such regroupings easy. As Natalie glances back for a moment at her former companions, she even sees smiles of approval on several of their faces: good old Nat is out there making new friends; all *right*.

At some distance from everyone else, as usual, the Farquhars are seated, she in something long and pale and supple, dimly shining, he in an open white shirt, a dark ascot knotted at his throat. Their postures, as always, are perfectly erect. Her head moves slowly on her long and slender neck as she turns toward her husband.

"Do you think she could have been a dancer?" whispers Natalie to Amanda.

Richard answers, "That's a really good guess. I'll bet you're right."

Amanda suggests, "Or maybe an actress?"

"But what was he?" asks Natalie. She is thinking of Herbert, who was in business, but not on the scale that he originally intended.

"He could have been an actor," offers Richard, who has often heard that remark made of himself. On the whole, though, he is glad not to be an actor; he likes the challenge of investments, at which he is very good. And most actors burn out young, their looks gone.

"Somehow I don't think he was an actor," Amanda muses. "He looks more like an elder statesman. Or some Nobel Prize-winning scientist."

Just at that moment, though, Mrs. Farquhar is seen and heard, by those three observing her so closely, to cry out, in evident pain. With both hands she grasps her side, at her waist, and she says something short and urgent to her husband. They both stand up, she with what is obviously great difficulty; they leave the bar, presumably going toward their room.

Amanda feels cold waves of panic in her veins, in the warm tropical night—and so irrationally: she doesn't even know those people. "What can we do?" she asks of Richard and Natalie, and she hears a quaver in her own voice.

Richard, who thrives on emergencies (it is daily life that bores him), stands up. "I'll go down and ask," he says, and he is gone before the wisdom of his course can be questioned.

"Do you think it could be an appendix?" Amanda asks Natalie; she has somehow assumed that Natalie, being older than herself, would have more medical information.

Natalie does not, actually, but she makes a guess. "It looked a little high for an appendix, where she was clutching. But I don't know."

Richard, apparently, has done the right thing: within minutes he is back at the bar, with an errand. "I'm going up to the desk to get Lisa and phone for a doctor."

Amanda cries out, "But Lisa's in Mexico City."

"She's back." And, over his shoulder as he hurries off, "Their name is Farquhar." And he is gone.

In a helpless way Natalie and Amanda turn to each other.

And just then, behind Natalie, the other Chicago people begin to get up, making sounds of departure. Luther, without his cigar, is the one who says, "Well, good night, Nat," with only the slightest querulousness in his voice. "See you in the morning," says someone else.

She turns to say, "Yes, see you then."

And they are gone.

"At their age, almost any pain must be frightening" is the first thing that Amanda finds to say. It is understood that she refers to the Farquhars.

"Or maybe not? They must have had a lot of pains by now." As she says this, Natalie is rather surprised by what sounds like wisdom.

In a fairly short time Richard reappears, with Lisa— Lisa once again in her old pants and shirt; comfortable, competent Lisa, who says to Amanda, "The doctor comes. You could wait here? She knows where is the bar but not the room of the Farquhars. You could show her the way?"

"Oh, of course."

Lisa sighs vastly, and to all three of them she says, "Oh, how bad that she should be sick now. I come back from Mexico City with some good news," and she sighs again. "She come soon. The doctor. She is a friend to me."

And then she and Richard are gone, in the direction of the Farquhars' room, as well as of Richard's and Amanda's.

"A woman doctor?" Natalie asks Amanda.

"I guess. But how will we know her, or she us?" Amanda says.

She, the doctor, is immediately recognizable: a brisk young woman with a classic black doctor's satchel, who hurries down the steps toward Amanda and Natalie. She smiles, in a shy, quick way. "It is you who will direct me to the lady not feeling well?"

"Yes, it's this way." And the three women, Amanda leading the doctor and Natalie, make their way down from the bar, down the series of dimly lit steps, past all the soft shapes of flowers, the colors now blotted out in the general dark. They reach the row of rooms, and go on to the room at the end, where Richard stands just outside the opened door.

As they arrive, through the door in one bright instant Amanda sees: two single beds, on one of which Mrs. Farquhar is stretched, immobile, her head back, chin raised, as on a bier. And beside her, bent toward her, is her husband. Lisa stands beside him.

Richard gestures the doctor inside, at which Lisa comes out, and the door is closed.

The four of them stand there, in the flowery darkness, Amanda and Richard, Lisa, Natalie.

"It is perhaps not something terrible," Lisa tells them all. "She kept saying she only wanted a shot. She said she could sleep off the pain."

Richard: "She looked awfully white."

"She's always white," Natalie tells him. And in a subdued way she laughs. "I only wish I knew her brand of sun block."

"I can tell you. I just bring it from Mexico," Lisa tells her, and she names the French cream.

"Well, thank you," Natalie murmurs, in surprise. And then, a few minutes later, she says, "Well, I think I'll go on up. After all, I don't really know them," and she says good night, and she leaves.

As though it would insure her safety, they all watch her as she walks slowly up the barely lit stairs.

Turning to Lisa, Amanda repeats what she had earlier

said to Natalie, but as a question: "At their age almost any pain is frightening, isn't it?"

Clearly thinking of something else, or possibly a little frightened herself, Lisa is slightly brusque. "At any age—no pain is good." And then, "You two should go in. There is no need for you also to wait. I know them a long time."

Dismissed, Amanda and Richard go into their room next door, from which they can hear nothing. Nevertheless they continue to address each other in whispers.

"Another drink? Some brandy?"

"Oh, thanks. I could use some."

"Here. It's a little full."

Later they hear the subdued sounds of the doctor coming out of the room adjacent, some murmurs of conversation, the door softly closed. Nothing more.

Later still they undress, and wash; they get into bed and make love. They are comforting to each other.

But, lying there in the hot unmoving night, Amanda is terrified. The beautiful, old and almost totally unknown Mrs. Farquhar could die, and that possibility is intolerable to Amanda.

In the morning, Carlotta Farquhar is perfectly well; the shot administered by the young doctor put her out for about nine hours, as she, Carlotta, knew that it would. Sitting out on the porch, propped against a small pillow, she breathes deeply, feeling only slightly sluggish from the morphine. Needing air.

Travis has made the tea; they always travel with a small kit. He hands her the cup, and he says, "Drink up. You look half asleep."

Carlotta smiles. "But, darling, I am." And then she says, "How kind of Señor Blumenthal. Our new rate."

"Oh yes, that." He frowns, just slightly embarrassed. And then he lowers his voice as he says to her, "The young couple next door, they were most kind, do you know? He went up to get Lisa, and to phone. They showed such concern, when they don't even know us. Don't you think— suppose we invite them for a drink?"

"Oh, darling, absolutely yes. We'll speak to them after breakfast. Or I'll write a note."

But just then Carlotta, who has been looking out to the early morning sea, and the bright pale sky, when she has not been turned to Travis, leans suddenly forward: there on the yellow bush at the edge of their terrace is the largest, the loveliest white butterfly that she has ever seen. She gasps with pleasure. There is nothing in her mind but the butterfly, on its flower.

Truth or Consequences

This morning, when I read in a gossip column that a man named Carstairs Jones had married a famous former movie star, I was startled, thunderstruck, for I knew that he must certainly be the person whom I knew as a child, one extraordinary spring, as "Car Jones." He was a dangerous and disreputable boy, one of what were then called the "truck children," with whom I had a most curious, brief and frightening connection. Still, I noted that in a way I was pleased at such good fortune; I was "happy for him," so to speak, perhaps as a result of sheer distance, so many years. And before I could imagine Car as he might be now, Carstairs Jones, in Hollywood clothes, I suddenly saw, with the most terrific accuracy and bright sharpness of detail, the schoolyard of all those years ago, hard and bare, neglected. And I relived the fatal day, on the middle level of that schoolyard, when we were playing truth or consequences, and I said that I would rather kiss Car Jones than be eaten alive by ants.

Our school building then was three stories high, a formidable brick square. In front a lawn had been attempted, some years back; graveled walks led up to the broad, forbidding entranceway, and behind the school were the playing fields, the playground. This area was on three levels: on the upper level, nearest the school, were the huge polished steel frames for the creaking swings, the big green splintery wooden seesaws, the rickety slides—all for the youngest children. On the middle level older girls played hopscotch, various games, or jumped rope—or just talked and giggled. And out on the lowest level, the field, the boys practiced football, or baseball, in the spring.

To one side of the school was a parking space, usually filled with the bulging yellow trucks that brought children from out in the country in to town: truck children, country children. Sometimes they would go back to the trucks at lunchtime to eat their sandwiches, whatever; almost always there were several overgrown children, spilling out from the trucks. Or Car Jones, expelled from some class, for some new acts of rebelliousness. That area was always littered with trash, wrappings from sandwiches, orange peel, Coke bottles.

Beyond the parking space was an empty lot, overgrown with weeds, in the midst of which stood an abandoned trellis, perhaps once the support of wisteria; now wild honeysuckle almost covered it over.

The town was called Hilton, the seat of a distinguished university, in the middle South. My widowed mother, Charlotte Ames, had moved there the previous fall (with me, Emily, her only child). I am still not sure why she chose Hilton; she never much liked it there, nor did she really like the brother-in-law, a professor, into whose proximity the move had placed us.

An interesting thing about Hilton, at that time, was that there were three, and only three, distinct social classes.

(Negroes could possibly make four, but they were so separate, even from the poorest whites, as not to seem part of the social system at all; they were in effect invisible.) At the scale's top were professors and their families. Next were the townspeople, storekeepers, bankers, doctors and dentists, none of whom had the prestige nor the money they were later to acquire. Country people were the bottom group, families living out on the farms that surrounded the town, people who sent their children in to school on the yellow trucks.

The professors' children of course had a terrific advantage, academically, coming from houses full of books, from parental respect for learning; many of those kids read precociously and had large vocabularies. It was not so hard on most of the town children; many of their families shared qualities with the faculty people; they too had a lot of books around. But the truck children had a hard and very unfair time of it. Not only were many of their parents near-illiterates, but often the children were kept at home to help with chores, and sometimes, particularly during the coldest, wettest months of winter, weather prevented the trucks' passage over the slithery red clay roads of that countryside, that era. A child could miss out on a whole new skill, like long division, and fail tests, and be kept back. Consequently many of the truck children were overage, oversized for the grades they were in.

In the seventh grade, when I was eleven, a year ahead of myself, having been tested for and skipped the sixth (attesting to the superiority of Northern schools, my mother thought, and probably she was right), dangerous Car Jones, in the same class, was fourteen, and taller than anyone.

There was some overlapping, or crossing, among those three social groups; there were hybrids, as it were. In fact, I was such a crossbreed myself: literally my mother and I were town people—my dead father had been a banker, but since his brother was a professor we too were considered faculty people. Also my mother had a lot of money, making us further élite. To me, being known as rich was just embarrassing, more freakish than advantageous, and I made my mother stop ordering my clothes from Best's; I wanted dresses from the local stores, like everyone else's.

Car Jones too was a hybrid child, although his case was less visible than mine: his country family were distant cousins of the prominent and prosperous dean of the medical school, Dean Willoughby Jones. (They seem to have gone in for fancy names, in all the branches of that family.) I don't think his cousins spoke to him.

In any case, being richer and younger than the others in my class made me socially very insecure, and I always approached the playground with a sort of excited dread: would I be asked to join in a game, and if it were dodge ball (the game I most hated) would I be the first person hit with the ball, and thus eliminated? Or, if the girls were just standing around and talking, would I get all the jokes, and know which boys they were talking about?

Then, one pale-blue balmy April day, some of the older girls asked me if I wanted to play truth or consequences with them. I wasn't sure how the game went, but anything was better than dodge ball, and, as always, I was pleased at being asked.

"It's easy," said Jean, a popular leader, with curly red hair; her father was a dean of the law school. "You just answer the questions we ask you, or you take the consequences."

I wasn't at all sure what consequences were, but I didn't like to ask.

They began with simple questions. How old are you? What's your middle name?

This led to more complicated (and crueler) ones.

"How much money does your mother have?"

"I don't know." I didn't, of course, and I doubt that she did either, that poor vague lady, too young to be a widow, too old for motherhood. "I think maybe a thousand dollars," I hazarded.

At this they all frowned, that group of older, wiser girls, whether in disbelief or disappointment, I couldn't tell. They moved a little away from me and whispered together.

It was close to the end of recess. Down on the playing field below us one of the boys threw the baseball and someone batted it out in a long arc, out to the farthest grassy edges of the field, and several other boys ran to retrieve it. On the level above us, a rutted terrace up, the little children stood in line for turns on the slide, or pumped with furious small legs on the giant swings.

The girls came back to me. "Okay, Emily," said Jean. "Just tell the truth. Would you rather be covered with honey and eaten alive by ants, in the hot Saraha Desert—or kiss Car Jones?"

Then, as now, I had a somewhat literal mind: I thought of honey, and ants, and hot sand, and quite simply I said I'd rather kiss Car Jones.

Well. Pandemonium: Did you hear what she said? Emily would kiss Car Jones! *Car Jones.* The truth—Emily would like to kiss Car Jones! Oh, Emily, if your mother only knew! Emily and Car! Emily is going to kiss Car Jones! Emily said she would! Oh, Emily!

The boys, just then coming up from the baseball field, cast bored and pitying looks at the sources of so much noise; they had always known girls were silly. But Harry McGinnis, a glowing, golden boy, looked over at us and laughed aloud. I had been watching Harry timidly for months; that day I thought his laugh was friendly.

Recess being over, we all went back into the schoolroom, and continued with the civics lesson. I caught a few ambiguous smiles in my direction, which left me both embarrassed and confused.

That afternoon, as I walked home from school, two of the girls who passed me on their bikes called back to me, "Car Jones!" and in an automatic but for me new way I squealed out, "Oh no!" They laughed, and repeated, from their distance, "Car Jones!"

The next day I continued to be teased. Somehow the boys had got wind of what I had said, and they joined in with remarks about Yankee girls being fast, how you couldn't tell about quiet girls, that sort of wit. Some of the teasing sounded mean; I felt that Jean, for example, was really out to discomfit me, but most of it was high-spirited friendliness. I was suddenly discovered, as though hitherto I had been invisible. And I continued to respond with that exaggerated, phony squeal of embarrassment that seemed to go over so well. Harry McGinnis addressed me as Emily Jones, and the others took that up. (I wonder if Harry had ever seen me before.)

Curiously, in all this new excitement, the person I thought of least was the source of it all: Car Jones. Or, rather, when I saw the actual Car, hulking over the water fountain or lounging near the steps of a truck, I did not consciously connect him with what felt like social success, new popularity. (I didn't know about consequences.)

Therefore, when the first note from Car appeared on my desk, it felt like blackmail, although the message was innocent, was even kind. "You mustn't mind that they tease you. You are the prettiest one of the girls. C. Jones." I easily recognized his handwriting, those recklessly forward-slanting strokes, from the day when he had had to write on the blackboard, "I will not disturb the other children during Music." Twenty-five times. The note was real, all right.

Helplessly I turned around to stare at the back of the room, where the tallest boys sprawled in their too small desks. Truck children, all of them, bored and uncomfortable. There was Car, the tallest of all, the most bored, the least contained. Our eyes met, and even at that distance I saw that his were not black, as I had thought, but a dark slate blue; stormy eyes, even when, as he rarely did, Car smiled. I turned away quickly, and I managed to forget him for a while.

Having never witnessed a Southern spring before, I was astounded by its bursting opulence, that soft fullness of petal and bloom, everywhere the profusion of flowering shrubs and trees, the riotous flower beds. Walking home from school, I was enchanted with the yards of the stately houses (homes of professors) that I passed, the lush lawns, the rows of brilliant iris, the flowering quince and dogwood trees, crepe myrtle, wisteria vines. I would squint my eyes to see the tiniest pale-green leaves against the sky.

My mother didn't like the spring. It gave her hay fever, and she spent most of her time languidly indoors, behind heavily lined, drawn draperies. "I'm simply too old for such exuberance," she said.

"Happy" is perhaps not the word to describe my own state of mind, but I was tremendously excited, continuously. The season seemed to me so extraordinary in itself, the colors, the enchanting smells, and it coincided with my own altered awareness of myself: I could command attention, I was pretty (Car Jones was the first person ever to say that I was, after my mother's long-ago murmurings to a late-arriving baby).

Now everyone knew my name, and called it out as I walked onto the playground. Last fall, as an envious, unknown new girl, I had heard other names, other greetings and teasing-insulting nicknames. "Hey, Red," Harry McGinnis used to shout, in the direction of popular Jean.

The next note from Car Jones said, "I'll bet you hate it down here. This is a cruddy town, but don't let it bother you. Your hair is beautiful. I hope you never cut it. C. Jones."

This scared me a little: the night before I had been arguing with my mother on just that point, my hair, which was long and straight. Why couldn't I cut and curl it, like the other girls? How had Car Jones known what I wanted to do? I forced myself not to look at him; I pretended that there was no Car Jones; it was just a name that certain people had made up.

I felt—I was sure—that Car Jones was an "abnormal" person. (I'm afraid "different" would have been the word I used, back then.) He represented forces that were dark and strange, whereas I myself had just come out into the light. I had joined the world of the normal. (My "normality" later included three marriages to increasingly "rich and prominent" men; my current husband is a surgeon. Three children, and as many abortions. I hate the symmetry, but there you are. I haven't counted lovers. It comes to a normal life, for a woman of my age.) For years, at the time of our coming to Hilton, I had felt a little strange, isolated by my father's death, my older-than-most-parents mother, by money. By being younger than other children, and new in town. I could clearly afford nothing to do with Car, and at the same time my literal mind acknowledged a certain obligation.

Therefore, when a note came from Car telling me to meet him on a Saturday morning in the vacant lot next to the school, it didn't occur to me that I didn't have to go. I made excuses to my mother, and to some of the girls who were getting together for Cokes at someone's house. I'd be a little late, I told the girls. I had to do an errand for my mother.

It was one of the palest, softest, loveliest days of that spring. In the vacant lot weeds bloomed like the rarest of flowers; as I walked toward the abandoned trellis I felt myself to be a sort of princess, on her way to grant an audience to a courtier.

Car, lounging just inside the trellis, immediately brought me up short. "You're several minutes late," he said, and I noticed that his teeth were stained (from tobacco?) and his hands were dirty: couldn't he have washed his hands, to come and meet me? He asked, "Just who do you think you are, the Queen of Sheba?"

I am not sure what I had imagined would happen between us, but this was wrong; I was not prepared for surliness, this scolding. Weakly I said that I was sorry I was late.

Car did not acknowledge my apology; he just stared at me, stormily, with what looked like infinite scorn.

Why had he insisted that I come to meet him? And now that I was here, was I less than pretty, seen close up?

A difficult minute passed, and then I moved a little away. I managed to say that I had to go; I had to meet some girls, I said.

At that Car reached and grasped my arm. "No, first we have to do it."

Do it? I was scared.

"You know what you said, as good as I do. You said kiss Car Jones, now didn't you?"

I began to cry.

Car reached for my hair and pulled me toward him; he bent down to my face and for an instant our mouths were mashed together. (Christ, my first kiss!) Then, so suddenly that I almost fell backward, Car let go of me. With a last look of pure rage he was out of the trellis and striding across the field, toward town, away from the school.

For a few minutes I stayed there in the trellis; I was no longer crying (that had been for Car's benefit, I now think) but melodramatically I wondered if Car might come back and do something else to me—beat me up, maybe. Then a stronger fear took over: someone might find out, might have seen us, even. At that I got out of the trellis fast, out of the vacant lot. (I was learning conformity fast, practicing up for the rest of my life.)

I think, really, that my most serious problem was my utter puzzlement: what did it mean, that kiss? Car was mad, no doubt about that, but did he really hate me? In that case, why a kiss? (Much later in life I once was raped, by someone to whom I was married, but I still think that counts; in any case, I didn't know what he meant either.)

Not sure what else to do, and still in the grip of a monumental confusion, I went over to the school building, which was open on Saturdays for something called Story Hours, for little children. I went into the front entrance and up to the library where, to the surprise of the librarian, who may have thought me retarded, I listened for several hours to tales of the Dutch Twins, and Peter and Polly in Scotland. Actually it was very soothing, that long pasteurized drone, hard even to think about Car while listening to pap like that.

When I got home I found my mother for some reason in a livelier, more talkative mood than usual. She told me that a boy had called while I was out, three times. Even before my heart had time to drop—to think that it might be Car, she babbled on, "Terribly polite. Really, these *bien élevé* Southern boys." (No, not Car.) "Harry something. He said he'd call again. But, darling, where were you, all this time?"

I was beginning to murmur about the library, homework, when the phone rang. I answered, and it was Harry McGinnis, asking me to go to the movies with him the following Saturday afternoon. I said of course, I'd love to, and I giggled in a silly new way. But my giggle was one of relief; I was saved, I was normal, after all. I belonged in the world of light, of lightheartedness. Car Jones had not really touched me.

I spent the next day, Sunday, in alternating states of agitation and anticipation.

On Monday, on my way to school, I felt afraid of seeing Car, at the same time that I was both excited and shy at the prospect of Harry McGinnis—a combination of emotions that was almost too much for me, that dazzling, golden first of May, and that I have not dealt with too successfully in later life.

Harry paid even less attention to me than he had before; it was a while before I realized that he was conspicuously not looking in my direction, not teasing me, and that that in itself was a form of attention, as well as being soothing to my shyness.

I realized too, after a furtive scanning of the back row, that Car Jones was *not at school* that day. Relief flooded through my blood like oxygen, like spring air.

Absences among the truck children were so unremarkable, and due to so many possible causes, that any explanation at all for his was plausible. Of course it occurred to me, among other imaginings, that he had stayed home out of shame for what he did to me. Maybe he had run away to sea, had joined the Navy or the Marines? Coldheartedly, I hoped so. In any case, there was no way for me to ask.

Later that week the truth about Car Jones did come out—at first as a drifting rumor, then confirmed, and much more remarkable than joining the Navy: Car Jones had gone to the principal's office, a week or so back, and had demanded to be tested for entrance (immediate) into high school, a request so unprecedented (usually only pushy academic parents would ask for such a change) and so dumbfounding that it was acceded to. Car took the test and was put into the sophomore high-school class, on the other side of town, where he by age and size—and intellect, as things turned out; he tested high—most rightfully belonged.

I went to a lot of Saturday movies with Harry McGinnis, where we clammily held hands, and for the rest of that spring, and into summer, I was teased about Harry. No one seemed to remember having teased me about Car Jones.

Considering the size of Hilton at that time, it seems surprising that I almost never saw Car again, but I did not, except for a couple of tiny glimpses, during the summer that I was still going to the movies with Harry. On both those occasions, seen from across the street, or on the other side of a dim movie house, Car was with an older girl, a high-school girl, with curled hair, and lipstick, all that. I was sure that his hands and teeth were clean.

By the time I had entered high school, along with all those others who were by now my familiar friends, Car was a freshman in the local university, and his family had moved into town. Then his name again was bruited about among us, but this time as an underground rumor: Car Jones was reputed to have "gone all the way"—to have "done it" with a pretty and most popular senior in our high school. (It must be remembered that this was more unusual among the young then than now.) The general (whispered) theory was that Car's status as a college boy had won the girl; traditionally, in Hilton, the senior high-school girls began to date the freshmen in the university, as many and as often as possible. But this was not necessarily true; maybe the girl was simply drawn to Car, his height and his shoulders, his stormy eyes. Or maybe they didn't do it after all.

The next thing I heard about Car, who was by then an authentic town person, a graduate student in the university, was that he had written a play which was to be produced by the campus dramatic society. (Maybe that is how he finally met his movie star, as a playwright? The column didn't say.) I think I read this item in the local paper, probably in a clipping forwarded to me by my mother; her letters were always thick with clippings, thin with messages of a personal nature.

My next news of Car came from my uncle, the French professor, a violent, enthusiastic partisan in university affairs, especially in their more traditional aspects. In scandalized tones, one family Thanksgiving, he recounted to me and my mother, that a certain young man, a graduate student in English, named Carstairs Jones, had been offered a special sort of membership in D.K.E., his own beloved fraternity, and "Jones had *turned it down*." My mother and I laughed later and privately over this; we were united in thinking my uncle a fool, and I am sure that I added, Well, good for him. But I did not, at that time, reconsider the whole story of Car Jones, that most unregenerate and wicked of the truck children.

But now, with this fresh news of Carstairs Jones, and his wife the movie star, it occurs to me that we two, who at a certain time and place were truly misfits, although quite differently—we both have made it: what could be more American dream-y, more normal, than marriage to a lovely movie star? Or, in my case, marriage to the successful surgeon?

And now maybe I can reconstruct a little of that time; specifically, can try to see how it really was for Car, back then. Maybe I can even understand that kiss.

Let us suppose that he lived in a somewhat better than usual farmhouse; later events make this plausible—his family's move to town, his years at the university. Also, I wish him well. I will give him a dignified white house with a broad front porch, set back among pines and oaks, in the red clay countryside. The stability and size of his house, then, would have set Car apart from his neighbors, the other farm families, other truck children. Perhaps his parents too were somewhat "different," but my imagination fails at them; I can easily imagine and clearly see the house, but not its population. Brothers? sisters? Probably, but I don't know.

Car would go to school, coming out of his house at the honk of the stained and bulging, ugly yellow bus, which was crowded with his supposed peers, toward whom he felt both contempt and an irritation close to rage. Arrived at school, as one of the truck children, he would be greeted with a total lack of interest; he might as well have been invisible, or been black, *unless* he misbehaved in an outright, conspicuous way. And so he did: Car yawned noisily during history class, he hummed during study hall and after recess he dawdled around the playground and came in late. And for these and other assaults on the school's decorum he was punished in one way or another, and then, when all else failed to curb his ways, he would be *held back*, forced to repeat an already insufferably boring year of school.

One fall there was a minor novelty in school: a new girl (me), a Yankee, who didn't look much like the other girls, with long straight hair, instead of curled, and Yankee clothes, wool skirts and sweaters, instead of flowery cotton dresses worn all year round. A funny accent, a Yankee name: Emily Ames. I imagine that Car registered those facts about me, and possibly the additional information that I was almost as invisible as he, but without much interest.

Until the day of truth or consequences. I don't think Car was around on the playground while the game was going on; one of the girls would have seen him, and squealed out, "Oooh, there's Car, there *he is!*" I rather believe that some skinny little kid, an unnoticed truck child, overheard it all, and then ran over to where Car was lounging in one of the school buses, maybe peeling an orange and throwing the peel, in spirals, out the window. "Say, Car, that little Yankee girl, she says she'd like to kiss you."

"Aw, go on."

He is still not very interested; the little Yankee girl is as dumb as the others are.

And then he hears me being teased, everywhere, and teased with his name. "Emily would kiss Car Jones—Emily Jones!" Did he feel the slightest pleasure at such notoriety? I think he must have; a man who would marry a movie star must have at least a small taste for publicity. Well, at that point he began to write me those notes: "You are the prettiest one of the girls" (which I was not). I think he was casting us both in ill-fitting roles, me as the prettiest, defenseless girl, and himself as my defender.

He must have soon seen that it wasn't working out that way. I didn't need a defender, I didn't need him. I was having a wonderful time, at his expense, if you think about it, and I am pretty sure Car did think about it.

Interestingly, at the same time he had his perception of my triviality, Car must have got his remarkable inspiration in regard to his own life: there was a way out of those miserably boring classes, the insufferable children who surrounded him. He would demand a test, he would leave this place for the high school.

Our trellis meeting must have occurred after Car had taken the test, and had known that he did well. When he kissed me he was doing his last "bad" thing in that school, was kissing it off, so to speak. He was also insuring that I, at least, would remember him; he counted on its being my first kiss. And he may have thought that I was even sillier than I was, and that I would tell, so that what had happened would get around the school, waves of scandal in his wake.

For some reason, I would also imagine that Car is one of those persons who never look back; once kissed, I was readily dismissed from his mind, and probably for good. He could concentrate on high school, new status, new friends. Just as, now married to his movie star, he does not ever think of having been a truck child, one of the deprived, the disappointed. In his mind there are no ugly groaning trucks, no hopeless littered playground, no squat menacing school building.

But of course I could be quite wrong about Car Jones. He could be another sort of person altogether; he could be as haunted as I am by everything that ever happened in his life.

Teresa

Some time ago, on the west coast of Mexico, there was a cluster of thatched huts around a lovely horseshoe cove, a tiny town to which no tourists ever came; the tourists went rather to Acapulco, a couple of hundred kilometers to the south, or to Ixtapanejo, perhaps thirty kilometers north. Back from the cove and the beach, and its huts, green jungle-covered mountains rose up steeply, a range that continued inland almost all the way to Mexico City.

At that time, in that small town, there was a young girl named Teresa, about sixteen. Teresa was not beautiful, nor even pretty, but something about her made more than one boy stare at her in a spellbound, desirous way. Her small face was dark and fierce, with its high-bridged nose and burning black eyes, her thin purposeful mouth and black, black hair. Her body too was small and dark, and neatly made, and strong. She had an odd way of walking: perhaps through shyness she tended to skip, like a bird. Several of the boys, and some older men too, stared at Teresa in an improper way, but especially a boy named Ernesto often looked at her;

and since Ernesto's glance was briefer, more respectful, than the others she sometimes returned it with a quick look of her own, although neither of them smiled.

Teresa at that time was excessively shy, perhaps partly because nothing that she saw of her own face pleased her, in the broken mirror beside the crucifix in her mother's hut. (Her father had left for somewhere, Guerrero, maybe, after the birth of her youngest brother.) She saw no reason why anyone should stare, least of all Ernesto Fuentes, who, although rather small, was straight-backed and almost handsome, very serious, with thunderous dark eyes and a curious sun-bleached streak in his heavy dark hair.

Teresa was an inward, thoughtful girl; she thought much more than she spoke: about Ernesto, of course, and about the coconut plantations where Ernesto and most of the men and boys of the village worked. She thought about Señor Krupp, the blond, mustached plantation owner, who drank beer or tequila all day and who was rumored to have an evil temper. And she thought about Ixtapanejo, and the incomprehensible tourists who came there, pale Northern people who tried to blacken their bodies on the beach. (She did not think about Acapulco, having never been there and having heard very little about it.) And, what must have also contributed to her shyness, she found much in her surroundings to fear: the staring men, and Señor Krupp, and even the Ixtapanejo tourists, who spoke so loudly in their own tongues and even more loudly and incorrectly in Spanish.

The person of whom Teresa was least afraid, with whom she talked as easily as she did with anyone, was Aurelia, an older cousin of hers. Aurelia was already married, to Francisco, a bad man who beat her when he drank and who did not work, but Aurelia had no fear of Francisco nor of anyone. She had established a thatched-roof restaurant in Ixtapanejo, on the beach, where she served the tourists fresh oysters and clams, and red snapper that she cooked in a special way, and quantities of beer. She did not even own the land where her restaurant squatted, there on the beach overlooking the green-glass sea, but Aurelia had explained to Teresa that what she did was not truly illegal; there was something in the laws of Mexico that favored the rights of Indian-blooded people. "And anyone can see that we have much Indian blood," said Aurelia, with one of her big laughs.

Aurelia very much liked her tourists, especially the North Americans; and she liked Teresa, often worrying about her shyness, and her fears. She had tried to persuade Teresa to come to work at the restaurant, speaking of large gratuities and sometimes presents. But Teresa could not bring herself even to think of taking orders and remembering and counting beers and asking for money and making the change correctly. Once, on an errand, she had gone to the restaurant, and the very look and the sound and the oil-sweet smell of those people had weakened her legs and tightened her breath, so that she was barely able to speak to Aurelia.

The town where Teresa lived at that time was so small that there was not a proper cantina, just a hut like the others in which beer was sold, and ice-cream bars. But there was a large, bright-colored machine for playing records, North American music, mostly: fast hard band music for dancing, and some slower Spanish songs. The boys of the village often gathered there at night, some of them buying beer, and on many nights several girls, in small groups, would walk past, in a slow, indifferent way. Two boys, or more, might saunter toward the girls, and invite them to dance, and maybe the girls would say yes. The ground around the hut was as hard and smooth and bare as any floor, and most of the boys and many of the girls danced barefoot, in the light warm breeze from the sea, in the flowery darkness.

On a certain night, one especially hot November, the season of rains, Aurelia, visiting from Ixtapanejo, persuaded Teresa to take a walk past the dancing place. Normally, Teresa stayed at home with the younger children; she would work on some small jars that the village potter had commissioned her to paint, to be sold in Ixtapanejo. Her shyness kept her at home, and a feeling that she was too clumsy for dancing. But Aurelia was very persuasive; with her, Teresa would be absolutely safe, she reasoned. No one would ask a married woman to dance, and thus it would be impolite for anyone to invite Teresa.

Fat and bright-eyed, darker even than Teresa, Aurelia was in an especially good mood that night. She was rich, she said; some North Americans who were returning that day to New York had given her a great many pesos. She bought them both ice-cream bars, as the music machine played Beatles songs. Teresa saw Ernesto standing outside with a group of boys, their white shirts silver in the dark, but she did not look at him, not really.

Aurelia and Teresa were on the point of unwrapping their ice cream, standing inside the hut, when they heard a thundering commotion. Teresa thought, An earthquake! Many years ago she had felt such a thing and had been told what it was, that trembling of the world beneath her feet, and naturally she had not forgotten. But this shaking was not an earthquake; it came from huge horses, a group of them just arrived, galloping up outside, and some shouting men.

The first man to enter the hut was tall and fat and blond, with a big yellow mustache; he looked like a North American but he spoke in Spanish, and before anyone had said his name Teresa knew that he was Señor Krupp, Carlos Krupp, the owner of many plantations. Even in the heat he wore leather clothes, and his face was red, perspiring. Other big blond men, very likely his brothers, followed him in, and they all opened their cold dripping bottles of beer, and drank from them, with a noisy rude gulping.

Then suddenly, and with no warning—she had no idea that he had seen her—Señor Krupp turned on Teresa, and with his huge blond-haired hand he grasped her chin; she closed her eyes as she heard him say, "And this lovely young girl, whose is she?"

Almost fainting (although a part of her that she had not known existed wanted to spit in his hand), Teresa heard Aurelia begin to speak: "It's Teresa, sir, my cousin—"

And then another voice, a young boy's, but stern and confident: Ernesto, of course. "Teresa Valdez is my friend, sir."

Startled, Teresa opened her eyes to see the look that then passed between the two men: Ernesto, at her side, and Señor Krupp, who was leaning sideways against the big music machine, which had unaccountably stopped playing. She saw that both men had forgotten her; in their look was violence, and murder, purely male and somehow familiar.

But nothing happened then. Perhaps Señor Krupp was too tired, or knew himself to be drunk, for he said, "Well, in that case my congratulations—Fuentes, I think your name is?" However, his eyes and his voice were stone cold, Northern, unforgetting and unforgiving.

Teresa and Aurelia, with Ernesto following, were able then to slip outside and into the clearing, where at one edge of the open space the great pawing, sweating horses were tied, and the other boys had gathered, staring at the horses. As Teresa and Aurelia moved away, toward the darkness that hid the rest of the huts, Teresa turned back to Ernesto, and for an instant they smiled at each other. Of course she wanted to thank him, but she could not say it.

The following night it rained, and Teresa stayed at home. She was very nervous, agitated.

The night after that was miraculously clear, millions of stars in the vast black sky, above the darker sea. It seemed right, then, for Teresa to walk past the hut with some other girls, and to say yes to Ernesto, coming up to ask her to dance.

That was the beginning of an unusual time in Teresa's life. Despite some trembling in her blood, and new bodily heats, she was unafraid; to be with Ernesto very soon seemed natural to her. She even found that she could dance with him. For the first time she felt herself to be a girl exactly as other girls; when she was not with Ernesto she spent time with girlfriends, laughing, discussing eye makeup. And when Ernesto drew her away from the clearing, into darkness, and then stopped and turned to her, holding their mouths together, that seemed natural too, nothing to fear. Even later when, farther away, in a hidden grove of vines, the heat of both their bodies forced them to lie down in the cool silver sand—even then, Teresa was not afraid; it did not seem a sin. She trusted Ernesto. She thought, but did not say, Love, you are my love.

After a few months spent in this way, months that included some long white beach afternoons with Ernesto, splashing at the edge of the waves, and a trip to Ixtapanejo, slowly some of Teresa's fears and forebodings began to return, including, of course, a new one, that she should be with child. She was not, and then she began to fear that Ernesto would leave her, as her father had left her mother. They talked so little, Teresa and Ernesto, and she did not know what was in his mind.

"He will want to marry you, he is a very serious boy," said Aurelia.

"That is possible," Teresa agreed, although she blushed. And then she tried to tell her cousin, her friend, what was in her heart. "But when I think of the future, the years ahead of me, I see darkness, shadows. Sometimes something worse, some disaster, perhaps a giant earthquake. And when I see these things I think that I should not marry Ernesto."

Aurelia frowned. "You are as superstitious as a grandmother. You should learn to read fortunes in the sand."

However, Teresa could feel that Aurelia took her fears seriously; it was as though Aurelia was able to see Teresa's visions of evil. And that was frightening to Teresa, a confirmation of her fears.

Still frowning slightly, Aurelia changed the direction of their talk. She said, "You really should come to work for me. Ernesto could find some work in Ixtapanejo."

"No, I don't think so," said Teresa, vaguely.

It was that very night, however, that Ernesto told Teresa that he had almost finished building his own hut on the plantation, Señor Krupp's plantation, where he worked. Where Señor Krupp permitted such building, for his workers. Then they should marry, Ernesto said. "You are so good, I want you always in my life."

They were married in January, just after the New Year —a day of the new moon, which Teresa had chosen, for luck. (The earthquake, years back, had taken place at a time of the full moon.)

And indeed, a long time of happiness and luck did succeed their marriage, so that Teresa became greatly less fearful, almost forgetting her former black forebodings.

In the month after the wedding she discovered that she was pregnant, and, unlike most of her cousins and friends, she experienced at that time extraordinary good health, well-being. At first the pregnancy scarcely showed, but many people remarked on how pretty she had suddenly become. Even Ernesto, who was generally kind to her without many words, murmured that she was beautiful, and on the next market day, a Saturday, he bought her a necklace of bright black beads—like her eyes, he said.

Teresa decided that her old superstitiousness had been a part of her girlhood, now outgrown, along with certain pains, and bumps on her face. The important thing was the child she carried; from its movements she was sure that he was a boy, and that he would be remarkable.

Felipe, who was born on the night of the first new moon in September, was a strong handsome baby, but difficult from the start: always willful, never eating or sleeping at proper times but seemingly moved by some interior plan of his own. However, Teresa and Ernesto were vastly proud of this boy, this small strong dark child who had, already, his father's thunderous dark eyes.

During her pregnancy and then in the early years of Felipe's life, Teresa continued with the painting of the potter's jars. It was fairly easy work for her to do, and she enjoyed it, and the potter said kind things about her efforts. He stopped telling her what he wanted in the way of decoration, so that Teresa could make her own patterns, trailing leaves, or sometimes bright bold stripes, in colors of her choosing.

Thus occupied with her baby and her pottery work, the cooking, and the cleaning of the hut, and all the laundry (to be washed in the plantation workers' communal tub, then spread on rocks to dry), Teresa paid not much attention to her husband, to Ernesto. He left early in the mornings, while she and the baby still slept, and he came home late, silent and exhausted. Neither he nor Teresa had the habit of exchanging words about their separate days, describing things to each other, perhaps because their activities were so divergent. Teresa could not, in her mind, see the smashing of coconut shells, the extraction of the meat. And often both she and Ernesto were too exhausted for speech. Sometimes in the night Teresa would wake, aware of the warm breathing body beside her, and then she would think how little she knew him, Ernesto, who had chosen her from among all the other girls. Who had given her their son Felipe. Who sometimes in the night made love to her, quickly and silently.

Within the next ten years Teresa had four more children, all girls, the last of whom died of a fever one week after her birth. Leaving Felipe, and his three younger sisters.

As Felipe approached his young manhood, at eleven, then twelve, thirteen, he was still quite small, with protuberant shoulder blades and eyes that seemed always full of thunder, like his father's. And like Ernesto he stood very erect, straight-backed, his head proud; he seemed eager to have done with being a child, to become a man. Watching the two of them together, her husband and her son, Teresa sighed: how dark and mysterious they both were, and how distant from her. She felt closer to the little girls, all of whom were rather quiet children, and much easier to care for than Felipe had been.

On an afternoon in September—a day of the full moon, and shortly after the fifteenth birthday of Felipe—the little girls were out playing in the clearing, near the communal washing tub, and Teresa was inside the hut working on the decoration of two large matching jars. Felipe had gone off to work with his father, as many of the boys of his age often did; the boys would watch the men, and sometimes they would help, pretending to be men themselves, although Señor Krupp and the overseers never offered to give them any money.

Suddenly, Teresa, sitting on the bare dirt floor of her hut, felt a terrific trembling beneath her, shaking her bones, and before she could stop them the two jars had crashed into each other, breaking open. An earthquake: Teresa ran outside screaming for her children, although the tremors had stopped almost as soon as they began. The little girls ran over to her instantly; they were perfectly unharmed, of course, and had not even noticed an unusual event—although, at the sight of the broken jars, and of their mother's evident terror, they began to cry, and to cling to her. The four of them lay down together, Teresa and her small daughters, and they remained there for the whole afternoon. And, at the same time that she was attempting to soothe her children, Teresa experienced again the worst of her old visions. The earthquake was an omen, she knew, and worse, much worse, would follow. She could scarcely wait for the return of Ernesto and Felipe, so terrified was she that some disaster had befallen them.

At the first sight of their faces, as they came through the door that night, Teresa thought, Oh, I was right. Her husband's face was pale and stormy, his mouth tight shut, and her son Felipe was paler still. On both their faces she read great rage, and a violent fear.

It was a while before Teresa could understand what had happened, but slowly it came out: that morning, a little before noon, there had been a ferocious quarrel between Señor Krupp and Luis Sender, a worker, a friend of Ernesto's. Because Luis was late for work (his mother was sick) and because Señor Krupp had been drinking beer all morning, he shouted and yelled terrible threats at Luis. And that afternoon the body of Luis had been found, face down in an irrigation ditch, bloody and battered and swollen. As Ernesto described the dead Luis to Teresa, she saw the face of her son go paler yet, until he was greenish yellow, and then she saw him rush out the front door, and she heard the sounds of his retching.

The days that followed the day of the earthquake and of the murder of Luis Sender were rainy and drenched with gloom and fear, for everyone: for Teresa and Ernesto, for Felipe, for all the men who worked on the coconut plantation. What everyone knew was that Señor Krupp had killed Luis Sender and that nothing had been done to Señor Krupp; he had got away with it. He could get away with anything, probably.

Teresa began to feel a perpetual weak aching in her bones, a trembling that seemed to originate within her breast. She even thought of running away, of trying to escape the next calamity, which she was sure would come very soon. Maybe she would run to Aurelia, to Ixtapanejo, on the beach. But actually she could not run away; truly, there was no escape.

No visions or forebodings, though, had prepared her for the rainy afternoon, late in November (a time of the full moon, of course), when Felipe ran home, ran into the hut and stood there before her, his face the color of ashes, tears running from his eyes. *Ernesto.* She screamed out the name even before Felipe told her, and she went on screaming, wailing even as he spoke: Ernesto had argued with Señor Krupp, had complained about money withheld from men who had sickness, about no raises, ever—and Señor Krupp had knocked him down, and then hit him again. Ernesto's head had been bashed into a rock. Dead, murdered. A small child, unseen by Señor Krupp, had witnessed all this and reported it to Felipe, and to the other men. "Then I looked for him everywhere but he could not be found," Felipe told her, in a terrible new voice. "I would have killed him with my hands. Carlos Krupp is a murderer."

Later some men brought Ernesto home, on an improvised stretcher, through the rain. Teresa by now was totally numb, although she still wept, and wept; numbly she washed off the blood and changed the muddy clothes of Ernesto; she put on the clean white shirt and light pants that she had prepared for market day, in Ixtapanejo. And the next day the same men came with a coffin, into which they lifted Ernesto. They carried him in the coffin to the church, with Teresa and Felipe and the little girls all following behind, in rusty black clothes that the women of the plantation had found for them.

Throughout the next days, weeks, months, Teresa was like a person who is automatically propelled into motion; she performed all her duties; habits of industry pushed her through the hours, but within herself she felt a vast black emptiness. Grief, and fear.

Felipe, although he was so young, and still not very tall, was allowed to do the work that his father had done, and for almost the same pay; on the day after Ernesto's funeral one of the overseers had come around to tell them that. And so now every night Felipe came home as pale and exhausted as his father had been, and he spoke as little as Ernesto had, although his eyes said a great deal. What she saw in Felipe's eyes was terrifying to Teresa.

One night he came home shouting, in a terrible rage that frightened his little sisters. "That man, he dared to speak to me! All these months he has avoided my sight, as he should, and then today he comes over and speaks; he asks if the work is too hard for me. Too hard! I should have spat at him. Oh, why did I not?"

It was of course Señor Krupp of whom he spoke, his father's murderer, who had dared to address Felipe.

In a pacifying voice Teresa said, "Our cousin Aurelia was here for a visit today, and she always asks, don't we want to come and work for her? You could be in the restaurant, and perhaps I could get some work in the large hotel."

"You would like to be a maid, and all of us sleep on the floor of the restaurant, like Aurelia and her family?"

What he said was true: Aurelia and Francisco and their children did sleep on the floor of their restaurant, a small space already crowded with tables and chairs; and in truth Teresa had not much wanted to be a maid in the big hotel for tourists, mostly foreigners, or rich Mexicans from Mexico City.

"It is necessary that I stay here," said Felipe.

On some market days, just as she used to with Ernesto, Teresa, still in black, would go off to the market at Ixtapanejo, with Felipe and her daughters, the five of them packed into the back of a neighbor's truck, or sometimes, much more slowly, in the potter's cart, along with the plates and jugs. Arrived in town, they would wander through all the booths of the market, almost never buying anything, and then, a small procession, they would cross the town, with its new bricked-in streets, its stores full of ridiculous hats and bright bathing costumes, cameras and all manner of sweet-smelling oils for the tourists' skin. They would walk across to the beach, past the large white city hall, with the small jail in back, and they would stand at the edge of the water, near the men who were busy repairing nets. There they could observe the arrivals and departures of the fishing boats, and sometimes out in the harbor there would be an enormous white ship, from which North Americans, in smaller boats, would cross the harbor water and arrive at the dock, in their light bright clothes, to walk about in the town and to buy an incredible number of things, huge baskets and satchels of objects, all in an hour or so.

On some afternoons Teresa and her children would then walk all around the sandy cove, the harbor of Ixtapanejo, climbing over the large rocks where seabirds perched and flapped away at their approach, all the way to where the grand hotels were situated, up a hill and back from the beach. There the tourists spread themselves out on towels, almost naked in the sun, or else they sat in large chairs, beneath small thatched shelters, drinking beer or another thing which was sucked through straws from a coconut shell. At the bottom of the small steps that led up to Aurelia's restaurant Teresa would stop, and she would send one of the girls up to seek out Aurelia. After a few minutes, there Aurelia would be, laughing and wiping her hands on her apron, offering them something, anything to eat or drink. Which they never accepted, but soon went on their way, back to the main road that led out to the miles and miles of coconut palms, with their high dry rattling fronds: the plantations, Señor Krupp's plantations.

Because in many ways she found him increasingly disturbing, with his silences and angry eyes, Teresa paid less and less attention to her son. She was able to be with her daughters, to take care of them and even to enjoy them, hardly thinking at all. Whenever she did think, in a serious way, the pain and emptiness that had followed Ernesto's death would return and almost overwhelm her, like an enormous and darkly threatening storm cloud. And Felipe seemed to personify her fears, to remind her of everything of which she did not wish to think. Once she even caught herself thinking that without Felipe she would be just another young widow, with three young daughters, herself almost a girl among girls again. But Felipe was nearly a man, the son of a murdered father, and she was twice the age of her son.

Once, on a Sunday afternoon, when there was no work being done on the plantation, their day of rest, Teresa heard a series of explosions, loud and irregular, like the sound of war scenes in a motion picture. She asked Felipe, and he said yes, there were guns. But she was not to worry; a couple of the other boys had .38s, that was all. No, he did not know where they got them. They took turns practicing, using coconuts thrown up into the air for targets. Teresa started to say that he should not, guns were dangerous, but then she sighed and said nothing. She saw no way to try to direct the life of Felipe.

Felipe shot and killed Señor Krupp, Carlos Krupp, on a rainy night in November, almost exactly a year after the killing of his father, Ernesto.

Teresa heard the shots, muffled but resounding through the rain, and she thought it strange, shooting at coconuts on such a night, in the greenish darkness, in the rain. Somehow, sinkingly, she knew that they were not shooting at such targets, and when, a few minutes later, Felipe ran in through the door, blood flowing from a wound in one leg, she knew what must have happened before he spoke.

His face shining and fierce and pure white, he said, "I have killed him. Finally there has been justice. I do not care what happens, after this."

As she had washed off Ernesto's blood, Teresa now bathed Felipe's leg. She felt that in some way Felipe too was now dead; certainly he had passed into a new and unreachable place, he was lost to her. He was no more a child, nor a young boy. He was a man who had killed, who had murdered the murderer of his father.

Soon after that, an hour or so, when Felipe's leg had barely stopped bleeding, two policemen came to take him away. They were men whom Teresa had known from her village; they spoke gruffly but with an apology in their manner. "You know, Teresa, that we must do this. The boy has shot Señor Krupp; the man is dead, and people saw him do it. We must take him to the jail, in Ixtapanejo."

That was the beginning of a terrible time in Teresa's life, perhaps the worst. She had seen the white exterior of the jail at Ixtapanejo, but she had no idea how it was inside, nor what was done to people there. A few times, boys from her village were arrested for drunkenness, on market days, and they spent some time, a weekend, in that jail. Teresa remembered a black look of fear in their eyes when they spoke of it, although of course they swaggered and pretended that it was nothing. But Felipe had shot and killed a man: would they keep him in jail forever? Would they hang or shoot him? Or would anyone, possibly, understand that it was the murderer of his father whom he had killed—an evil man—and understand that he was very young? She knew the answers to none of these questions; they raged back and forth in her mind, like waves in a storm, and she could think of nothing else.

Aurelia arrived in a large American car recently purchased by Francisco. ("He will never pay for it," Aurelia muttered. "We will all go to jail.") She brought a large pot of fish soup and some tortillas, a basket of tomatoes and a large bunch of bananas. And she offered to drive Teresa to the jail.

At the jail's front door there was a thin young soldier with a very large gun held across his chest. At first he did not seem to understand whom they wanted to see, but then when they explained he said, "Oh, the young boy," and with some large keys he opened a heavy door. "You can go in there," he said, and once they were inside he closed the door behind them.

In the middle of that room, on the floor, sat a very old man with no legs, on a tattered blanket; he grinned and stared at Teresa in an evil way, so that she shuddered and held to the arm of Aurelia. And the room was so crowded with persons, mostly men, but also some young women, one of them holding a baby, that at first Teresa and Aurelia could not find Felipe. Also it was so dark, no windows at all and one single light bulb, very dim, that hung from the ceiling.

They found him in a small room just off the main one. He had been sitting on the floor, but he got up as they came in—still really a boy, not very tall. He embraced his mother, who despite herself was crying, and then his cousin, who also wept.

Then for the three of them, standing in that place, there was not much to say. Teresa asked how he was, and he said that he was all right; his leg did not hurt much. But even in that bad light she could see how pale he was. Fortunately, Aurelia found more things to say; she asked about food, what they could bring to him. She asked if they were ever taken out for air, and she told Felipe what of course he already knew: that the beach and the ocean were only a few yards away from where they all at that moment were standing. How unfortunate that there was not at least a small window so that they could have more air, and could see the beautiful waves, and the clouds and the sun.

Teresa listened gratefully to all this chatter of Aurelia's. She felt that everyone in the room was staring at them, at her: the legless man and other men with pale, pale faces and crazy eyes. And she had the terrible thought that they too might have to stay there, she and Aurelia; some confusion might occur, making it impossible to explain that they were in the jail as visitors.

And, looking at Felipe, she noticed what she had never seen before: how very much he resembled herself. Always she had thought him so like Ernesto, but now, pale and isolated, she saw her own frightened eyes staring back at her. However, the way he stood, so straight, his neck a little stiff, was the way Ernesto had always held himself.

After that first visit, and then a second, a third—visits that differed from each other only in the composition of the other prisoners, who came and went—Teresa began to feel that a part of herself had indeed been kept on in the jail; all night, every night, she thought of that terrible room, the terrible men and women who inhabited it, along with Felipe. She thought of the unspeakable dangers to which her son was always exposed.

Aurelia tried to get in to see the Comandante, in his office across from the jail, but he was very busy, smoking his fat cigar, and very unpleasant. At one time a guard, a nice-looking boy, told Teresa that really she had nothing to fear; Felipe would soon be sent to a special place for young boys, he would not even have to stand trial. But Teresa was not truly comforted; the guard himself was so young, he could have been wrong. Besides, where was this special jail for boys? Was it in a place where she could ever find Felipe?

And, no matter where Felipe was sent, she knew, more

surely than any other knowledge, that eventually, finally, the brothers or cousins or friends of Señor Krupp would find him: a boy with no money, the son of a plantation worker, could not kill a rich and powerful man, and live.

Felipe was in fact killed in what was described as a prison fight, although the police could not say how it had started nor who else was involved. Felipe had never before got into fights. When one of the same policemen who had taken Felipe away arrived at Teresa's house and told her of this, she began to scream, and to cry out to God, as would the mother of any murdered son. Her daughters and some neighboring women gathered around to comfort her; among themselves they were saying, Aie, poor Teresa, she has had more to stand in her life than any human woman would be able to stand. Aie, poor Teresa.

And what they said was the truth; Teresa had withstood more than was possible for her. Perhaps for that reason, even as she wept and made much noise, in another part of her mind new words were beginning to form, new ideas and sentences; she began to think, Now I have no more to fear; now everything has befallen me that possibly could, and for the rest of my days I am safe. I can go to sleep without fear, I could even walk among North Americans, fearing nothing. Now it will be possible for me to work in the great hotel, maybe even to work for Aurelia, in her restaurant. With my daughters I will find a small beach hut to live in, away from these coconut palms that rattle so fiercely in the windy nights. We will live there together, by the sea, and grow old and be safe forever.

At First Sight

Two people, just meeting, do not necessarily react in identical or even in similar ways to each other: a long time ago, in the early Forties, war years, a little boy was introduced to a small blond woman, a new grown-up, at one of his parents' parties, in their spectacular lakeshore house—and that boy's whole heart rushed out to the older woman. He wished that he were grown and could marry her, or, he wished that she were his mother. Much later in life, during some bad times, he felt that he was being punished for those wishes, the second of which had in a sense come true; by then she was his stepmother. Posey, originally from Dallas.

In any case, at that first moment, what young Walker Conway saw was a woman not a great deal taller than himself, with curly short fair hair, a light-blue dress that shone like glass, like her light-blue excited eyes. Almost all the other women in the room wore black dresses, and they all seemed much larger and darker than this Posey, Mrs. McElroy—especially his mother, Althea, a pianist, who was larger and darker than anyone.

"And this is my son Walker. Walker, this is Mrs. Mc-Elroy," big John Conway had just said. An architect, he was the designer of this innovative (for the Midwest, at that time) and impossibly uncomfortable house, in one of whose curiously tight corners (the room was trapezoidal) the three of them were standing.

Taking everything in, perhaps especially this gorgeous "modern" house, and her host, so big and blond, with a beard, like someone in a story—and the little boy, still in short pants, for which he was too tall, with those skinny knees—Mrs. McElroy said, in her soft but penetrating voice, "Most everybody calls me Posey."

Although he had not been addressed, Walker asked, "How do you spell Posey, with an 'i-e' or 'e-y'?" Just beginning school, and already the best speller, he was proud of new skills.

"Well, if you aren't the smartest little thing! I'll bet you can spell lots longer words than my silly old name." And Posey laughed, looking up into the child's father's face. Her teeth were very small, and shiningly white.

Having taken her at her word, a habit that he was slow to break, in life, Walker glowed. "Well, actually I can. Last week I learned to spell 'Massachusetts' and 'committee.' "

"Well, those two are going to come in mighty handy. What a lucky boy!"

At that instant the tiniest doubt as to her intentions may have stung at Walker's love-swollen heart, but, like most children, he denied ambiguity; things were what they seemed, and a beautiful lady who said he was smart and lucky meant just that, and he was. "But how do you spell Posey," he insisted, believing that they were having a conversation.

"P-o-s-e-y. And I'll bet I can spell your name without you even telling me how to do."

"W-a-l—"

But his father had cut in. "Now, Walker. Mrs. McElroy didn't come to our party for a spelling bee. Why don't you go and ask your mother if you can't do something to help? You be the butler." He turned to Posey McElroy. "You wouldn't believe the help problem around here since the war began."

"Oh, would I not! Why, down home every darkie in town has got a de-fense job."

Wounded, frightened and angry—for Walker, a familiar constellation of emotions—the boy turned and made his way between the tall thick clumps of people, their legs firmly planted, arms and hands in motion. A few women caught at him and asked how he was; they seemed pleased at remembering his name, although several of them got it wrong and called him Walter.

His mother was near the corner window, with two much older ladies. "Dad said to ask if I should pass something, or do anything," said Walker.

"Oh, no, darling. I don't think so, not now. Mmm—did you meet Mrs. McElroy?"

"Her name is Posey. P-o-s-e-y. But that can't be a real name, can it?"

Beyond the window the lake was ruffled with waves, frilly whitecaps on the dark bright blue. A few sailboats were out, faraway sails as small as handkerchiefs, against the black opposite shore, another state. It was a brilliant October afternoon, an hour or so before sunset.

Althea sighed. "Posey. Well, I suppose it must be a nickname. They're Southern, although I know some people don't consider Texas the South. Her husband is that young Army captain over by the bar." And luckily John doesn't like very small women, thought Althea, hopelessly, and mistakenly. Distrust of her husband had made her give up what had been a promising career, but she still practiced all day, on most days, always intending to take it up again—and to lose some weight.

From another corner of that inconveniently shaped room, another woman also had her eye on John Conway, who was still talking to Posey. Lucienne Malaquais, a widow (her husband was rumored to have been in some way a French hero, in the Resistance), she had recently (inexplicably) settled in that small suburb of a great Midwestern city, on the lake. "It's the perfect climate for a rose garden," she said, but no one believed her. Lucienne wore, that afternoon, an old Balenciaga, whose extreme chic no one in the room could recognize; they thought her rather plain, with her short gray hair, that brown dress, no jewelry to speak of. Earlier that afternoon, as she put on the dress, which was her favorite, Lucienne had caught herself thinking of John, who was powerfully attractive to her. Surely, on seeing her, he would make some gesture? But there had been nothing in his eyes as he greeted her, as they talked for a moment or two. Neighborly, he had been.

And, watching John's face as he listened to Posey, even from that smoky distance, what Lucienne saw written there forced her to several conclusions, the first addressed to herself, an admonition: Don't be a fool. And secondly, more gently, she thought: Ah, poor Althea. She must have witnessed such a scene quite often, in her time. Lastly she thought, And that sad little boy, that funny tall Walker.

The house in which the party was taking place, the splendid house that Posey had already fallen in love with, was relatively new, completed the year before. John's detractors said that he imitated Frank Lloyd Wright, or Saarinen; others, a smaller but noisy group, spoke of the house's originality. Built on a huge outcropping of rock, on the lakeshore, it jutted into and over the water, with cantilevered balconies, a lot of steel and plate glass; inside, there were giant fireplaces of massive, indigenous stone. But somehow the construction had not quite worked out. In the high narrow passageways between those eccentric rooms, the floorboards creaked, and everywhere the cold Midwestern winter winds leaked in. What was a wonderful house for parties was also, for three isolated people, quite miserably uncomfortable: cold, damp and wretchedly lonely, with so much space. John traveled a lot, was often away. Off in her wing, Althea practiced furiously, relentlessly, although she complained that the damp was wrecking the strings of her piano. And Walker, in his narrow, built-in bed, in his long ship's galley of a room, told himself long interwoven stories. In his favorites he was the son of some very plain but substantial Midwestern people, who lived in a big plain square house that was warm.

It was never clear to anyone who observed them at what point John and Posey became lovers in actual fact—not to Althea, nor to Walker, nor to Lucienne Malaquais, who remained an interested friend. But that historical date hardly mattered. What was important, for many years, was the lively friendship between the two couples, a friendship animated, of course, by the strong attraction between Posey and John. For a long time the others felt themselves to be included in that liveliness, that excitement. They all had fun together.

Captain Jamie McElroy, a rather prissy young man, seemed as pleased by John's attentions as Posey was—big flamboyant John, with his store of dirty limericks and his hard-core Midwestern isolationist opinions, although now that the war was on of course he was all for it: let's slaughter those Japs. Too bad a punctured eardrum had kept him out of the Army, Jamie often remarked to his wife; what a fine general he could have been. Posey agreed.

Also, Jamie cared a lot about music, in a knowledgeable way, which gave him a bond with Althea. Usually unfriendly Althea liked Jamie, and she chose to take John's word for what he felt about Posey, that she was a helluva lot of fun, a nice gal. Her private view was that Posey was exceptionally stupid, which of course her brilliant, talented John could perceive without any comment from her, couldn't he?

Young Walker, brought along on visits to the McElroys, at various Army bases, had a pretty good time. He enjoyed the comfort of Posey's overheated houses, and he liked the piles of bright cushions that she moved from Fort Benning to Fort Bragg, Biloxi to Sill. He still thought Posey was the prettiest grown-up woman he had ever seen, and her unfailing effusiveness (a contrast to his somber mother) beguiled him, as it beguiled his father, and soothed an innately suspicious nature. For quite a while, he thought she liked him. She served him wine at dinner, like an adult, and strange sweet after-dinner drinks, even arguing with his parents: "Now, Althea honey, you know a couple of little sips of that crème de menthe is not going to hurt a boy."

Sometimes what Posey said to him was puzzling, even vaguely troubling, as, "I think it's absolutely wonderful, the way you've always got that cute big old nose of yours stuck in some book," or, "Such a tall boy you're getting to be, a person'd think twice 'fore calling you a sissy." Eager for love, Walker chose not to understand. Also, like many exceptionally intelligent people, he was slow to perceive exceptional stupidity. And, perhaps worse, an awareness of his own deficiencies in physical charm—knobby knees had persisted, along with a nearsighted, narrow-shouldered stoop, and a non-cute big nose—made him overvalue grace and beauty in others. Surely such a perfect physical specimen as Posey must also be good?

Lucienne Malaquais, in quite another way from Posey's, became and continued to be a good friend of that family; more precisely, she was a friend of each of theirs, seeing them individually rather than as a group. With each of them she had a separate topic of conversation: with John it was architecture, and painting, about which she was highly educated; with Althea music and with Walker books. Novels, poetry—she urged him to read Mann's stories, Proust, Elizabeth Bowen, Virginia Woolf. She was a woman of extraordinary modesty, a remarkable listener who almost never spoke of herself. And her vast charm somehow summoned from everyone his or her best qualities; even troubled, difficult people, the three Conways, were at their best and quietly happiest with Lucienne, in her small memento-crowded house that smelled of roses.

She seemed not to age. Vaguely middle-aged when she first came to their town, Lucienne remained ageless, perhaps in part because she so seldom spoke of herself and thus seemed to have no history. She spoke with the slightest accent, with an odd attractive huskiness in her voice. Only much later, when Walker felt that he had known her all his life, would she occasionally allow him some glimpse of her past, dealt out like some small present, and he would learn that her husband had been a painter, which had been her own girlhood ambition. Which had somehow not worked out.

She had been right, though, about a climate for roses: her rose garden flourished extravagantly, an incredible profusion and variety of color, of scent.

Walker, as an adolescent, during the strictured Fifties, had no idea what to do with himself, with his unruly, brilliant mind nor his ungainly body. It was not a time for eccentrics. His grades were terrible, despite those big I.Q.

scores. He was secretly in love with James Dean, but afraid of motorcycles. What he liked to do best, he early discovered (perhaps at Posey's), was to get drunk, and by the time he was fifteen he had worked out a technique for staying drunk all day, an undetectable buzz from a dose of wine here, a shot of brandy there, at carefully timed intervals. Usually he drank alone, but occasionally he would have a friend, sometimes a girl, who also liked to drink, and that was always the crucial thing between them, drinking. He was a lonely mess, and he knew he was.

But somehow he got into a small New England college (actually pull from Althea; it was in her hometown) and for a while his life considerably improved. For one thing there was an extraordinary teacher, a young man just out of the Harvard program in American Civilization. Timothy Stern: his black eyes were wild and his mouth had a slightly delinquent twist; he spoke passionately of Hawthorne, Melville, Emerson and Henry James—and what had been greedy but desultory reading on Walker's part came into focus. He drank considerably less, and he too became a passionate student of the American Renaissance.

During the fall of his junior year at college, Althea wrote to her son that Jamie McElroy had died—"quite suddenly"—and that Posey would spend part of her Christmas vacation with them. Not having been especially fond of Jamie, and still, to some degree, well disposed toward Posey, Walker's general reaction to both those pieces of news was neutral. But any guest in that chilling house raised its temperature a little, and protected that family from each other. Mainly, as on all vacations, he looked forward to conversations with Lucienne, and to drinking by himself at the local inn.

"But what did Jamie McElroy die of?" Walker, for no

clear reason, asked Lucienne, on one of their first afternoons together. "No one's said."

A small pause, and then Lucienne's almost harsh, quiet voice: "I believe that he committed suicide."

"Oh, really?" Somehow that seemed surprising, an act so extreme from passive Jamie. "Does anyone know why?"

"Well, certainly I do not. Some anger, some despair. But middle age can be cruel to people who have not had much satisfaction in their lives," she told him. Walker wondered if, possibly, she could refer to her own life, and concluded that she did not; she was not given to even such veiled references to herself, nor to self-pity, and besides, she had always such a look of contentment, of calm.

And then, on the last night of his vacation, which was, coincidentally, the first of Posey's visit, Althea went to bed early ("I've got to get some sleep; these new pills had better work") and Walker went to the inn, alone, for brandy. He came back less drunk than he sometimes was, and fairly early. In that creaking, moaning house it was quite possible to enter and leave without being heard, and thus, from the corridor outside the living room, Walker caught the following brief but illuminating conversation:

Posey: "But, darlin', if you told her I'll bet she could just move back to New England and be near that boy of hers. They have so much in common, really. Honestly, it's always been hard for me to believe he's really your son—"

And John: "Look, I'll tell her when I'm ready. Don't push me, baby doll. And don't think she's just going to move out for our convenience, even if the house is actually mine."

"Oh, darlin', please don't sound so cross. I don't care about Althea or Walker, or even the house, just you—"

Walker continued on to the kitchen, where he found a bottle of brandy. He finished that off in his room, the old ship's galley, before going to sleep. Fortunately, perhaps, on the trip back to school, the next day, his state of shock was somewhat mitigated by a severe hangover. Later he thought of that vacation as the last time he ever saw his mother, with whom, despite Posey's stated view, he had not had much in common.

It was Lucienne who telephoned, several months later, in the spring, to say that his mother had died: like Jamie McElroy, a suicide, an overdose of pills. Walker had never asked how Jamie killed himself; curiously, he did so now, just after hearing the news of Althea.

Lucienne seemed not to think it an odd question, under the circumstances, and only said, "He shot himself."

"Oh. Well, that makes it really neat for them, doesn't it. Jamie and my mother just clearing out, conveniently. They must be in absolute heaven." Knowing himself to be hysterical, Walker knew too that as long as he went on ranting he could not break down, although, with Lucienne, even that would have been all right. He said, "They're murderers. I will never speak to either of them again."

Lucienne, as she always had, chose to take him seriously. "Perhaps you are right; almost certainly you are right not to see them for a while, and I have never believed in the foolishness of funerals. I will tell John. But you know, she has succeeded in punishing them quite a lot. They will feel it."

Walker thought she was probably right—they would feel Althea's punishment, but at that time, and for years to come, he was absorbed in his own violent hatred for those two people. He hated them with the intensity reserved for former loves—for surely in some dim unremembered time he had loved his father, and he could remember the moment of falling in love with Posey, with humiliation, rage.

Obsessively, he thought of killing them. Easy enough: in

some disguise or other he could travel to his town, that now-burgeoning suburb on the lake, and, as he often had, he could sneak into that house, unheard. Confront them, with a gun. Talk for as long as possible and terrify them, absolutely, before shooting them both. This was not, however, a very satisfying fantasy—remaining, as it did, implausible.

His only real comfort and source of support in what were truly months of agony, so powerful and pervasive was his anger, aside from letters to and from Lucienne, was Timothy Stern, his former instructor who had now become a friend, a drinking buddy. Timothy's mother too had died relatively young, although not a suicide, and his father had remarried with indecent haste, as Timothy saw it. Someone awful. Timothy's father had died soon after that, leaving everything to the stepmother—"of course!" And so Timothy, brilliant and somewhat older, could easily understand.

From drinking and talking companions Timothy and Walker became, not too surprisingly, lovers. Walker, who had had no previous experience of that nature, although very little experience with girlfriends either, at first was deeply shocked, but quite soon it all seemed perfectly right, seemed logical, even. He felt at home with Timothy in a sense that he had never felt at home with any person, nor in any place. Except possibly with Lucienne, in her small cluttered house, or walking in her garden—and something about Timothy even reminded him of Lucienne. If only he and Lucienne had been the same age, he thought; she was the only woman he could have loved.

Thus, what had begun as an exchange of angry confidences, revelations of familial agony, became a source of warmth, of friendship and perfect confidence. When Timothy went on from the New England college to a better job in New York, Walker went along. Together they took an apartment in the East Village, and Walker, who had a little money from his mother, worked at various bookish jobs, articles, reviewing, at the beginning of the more permissive Sixties.

Walker had adhered to his principle of noncommunication, ever, with his father and Posey, who of course in due time had got married, as Walker was informed by letter from Lucienne. Nor had he ever, of course, returned to his town, to that house.

A couple of years after his marriage to Posey, John died, of a heart attack, which Lucienne called Walker to report. What Walker first said was, "Well, now Posey can have the house. She's getting what she always wanted most."

"It is quite possible that you are right. Still, she is not as young as you remember her. It may not be the most comfortable place for a woman who ages."

"Christ! It was never comfortable for anyone. It's a terrible house, except from the outside. You know that, Lucienne."

"Well, I have to confess to some admiration for it. And you know I always had a great feeling of friendship for your father. I will miss him."

Again, as when his mother had died, Walker experienced more anger than grief. Though he could hardly have expected his father to have left him the house, or any part of it, still he hated the thought of Posey in residence.

"Couldn't we go there?" asked Timothy. "Disguise ourselves in fright wigs, or sneak in when Posey's out? Doesn't she ever go back to Texas for visits? My stepmother went tearing back up to West Newton as soon as the old man died. After first selling his apartment, of course. But I'd love to see your house. I have such a sense of it."

Despite their continued rapport, in some areas, however, Timothy and Walker by this time were less lovers than generally amiable, sometimes quarreling comrades. For each of them there had been "other people," then guilt, recriminations and at last a somewhat uneasy acceptance of each other, as less than perfect friends.

To Walker's considerable surprise, a year or so after his father died, Posey did sell the house ("You see?" said Timothy) and she moved back to Texas. ("I believe there was an old beau somewhere in the offing," wrote Lucienne.)

Walker wrote and asked if she knew the people who had bought the house; strangely, that was important for him to know. But Lucienne answered that she did not know them. People named Engstrom.

The notion of totally unknown, unimaginable people in that house was, curiously, deeply disturbing to Walker. Although he had for the most part hated and been miserable in that house, he had also been proud of its splendor—from the outside, or at a party. At least with his father and Posey living there, or even Posey alone, he could perfectly imagine the house, and thus in a way retain it; but now, with strange people (it occurred to him that he did not even know how many people: a family? little children?), he felt a severe deprivation.

His father's death had been in November, and the news of Posey's selling the house in February. And then in May, although he had not tried to describe his feelings to her, Lucienne responded as though he had.

In a more imperative tone than he had ever heard from her before, she wrote that he must now come for a visit. "I have met the people who live in your house, and they are quite nice. A middle-aged couple, and a son who sometimes visits. I have spoken to them of you, and they have said they would always be pleased to see you there. And so, my dear Walker, I urge you to come. Of course I would wish you to stay with me, but perhaps at the inn you would be more private and comfortable. But do come. I think that to see the house would kill off some of the ghosts in your mind."

A strange letter, and one by which Walker found himself strangely, deeply excited. He made plans to leave the following weekend, which would be the first in June. He chose to go alone, Timothy being "involved" with one of his students, or so Walker believed. He would stay at the inn.

And so at last, after so many years, once more Walker sits in Lucienne's small memento- and photo-crowded living room, in the heavy June scent of roses, and earth. They are a mile or so from the lake, from his house. "I will give you a cup of tea on your way there," Lucienne had said. "But I think you should go out alone, don't you?"

Violently agitated, Walker agreed. Now, seated across from her in that warm familiar room, he is exhilarated, even, with a sense of some extraordinary event quite close at hand.

Lucienne has at last left middle age, he notes; she is old. Her fine skin is finely wrinkled, her hair quite white, and soft. She moves a little stiffly, pouring out the tea, going back into the kitchen for something forgotten—as always, refusing his help. But her voice is exactly the same: slightly accented, a little hoarse, and low, and beautiful.

She is talking about the Engstroms, who now live in what she tactfully persists in calling "his" house. Mr. Engstrom is an engineer; Mrs. Engstrom teaches in the local public school, and is politically involved, somehow. The son is mentioned again: a graduate student, at Madison, in literature. "Quite handsome," remarks Lucienne—and in his overcharged, susceptible state, for one wild instant Walker wonders: is Lucienne trying to "fix him up"? They have never in an explicit way discussed his "tastes," but of course she must know. But the very idea is crazy, and he dismisses it.

And then it is time for him to start out. Four-forty-five. He is due at the house for drinks at five; taking his time, over that familiar mile (an inner, imperative voice has insisted that he walk), he will make it by five-fifteen. Just right.

"You won't be too hot?" cautions Lucienne, seeing him off. She has offered to drive him, or to lend her car.

"Oh no." They kiss in their customary way, brushing each cheek, and then Walker starts off, in the early June warm bright dusk.

Lucienne's house is on a ridge of land from which one cannot see the lake, at first, so thickly wooded is that area. The wide white highway winds down and down; on one side, where there used to be the deepest, thickest woods, of oak and beech and poplar, now there are newish houses: expensive, very conventional, set widely apart from each other. Across the highway there is an upraised, still-unpaved sidewalk, where Walker makes his way toward his house. His clothes are indeed too hot for the day—old tweed blazer, gray flannels—and he feels, as he walks, a painful weight of apprehension, somewhere in his chest. The combination of the blood-familiar landscape with the unfamiliar new houses superimposed is radically jarring.

Then, before him, there is the lake. All his life it has been unexpected, a sudden violent glimpse of the deepest, sharpest possible blue. And enormous, miles and miles of lake, lake water.

Hurrying now, his heart risen, Walker can see his house, and he experiences a soaring pride in its splendid outline: the wide high spread of roof, and all the bright reflecting glass, in which, as he draws closer, he can see the wind-driven lake.

Someone has put in flower beds where there used to be a

severe graveled area, Walker notes as he approaches the actual house: beds of multicolored primroses, giant pansies and thriving yellow cowslips.

He knocks, and almost immediately is confronted with a big round-faced smiling woman, who greets him enthusiastically. "Oh, Mr. Conway, I'm so very glad you could come. Such an amazing coincidence: I've been reading and admiring your reviews for years, and now it turns out that this is your family's house!"

Quite unused to being greeted in that way—book reviewers do not gather a lot of fans, Walker has learned—he tries to readjust his normally diffident manner, but it comes out stiffly as he says, "You're too kind."

Undeterred, Mrs. Engstrom smiles yet more warmly as she says, "Oh yes, you seem to have such a different feeling for what you read. Most reviewers—they're so—smallminded."

Walker murmurs in what he hopes is a helpful, assenting way, but she needs, apparently, no help.

With a small frown she tells him next, "I'm so glad you're here, but I have been worried. How you'd feel about how we've changed your house." And she begins to lead him down the hall, which is now lined, he notes, with blown-up cartoons by an artist that he himself very much likes.

He is not prepared, however, for the turnabout of the living room: all the stark built-in furniture—those bleak narrow banquettes, ceiling-high bookcases and the trapezoidal central coffee table—has been taken out, and replaced with much more ordinary things: a big overstuffed, faded, flowered sofa, some cracked leather club chairs and low bookcases that overflow with old and a few new books, and some magazines—including, Walker observes, the one for which he most frequently writes (and, out of his old suspicious nature, there comes the pleased thought: Oh, she wasn't lying. She does read my reviews).

But he has hardly time to react to all this, for there, coming toward him, is a man who must be Mr. Engstrom. He bears, in fact, a striking resemblance to his wife, both being large and fair and square in shape—a phenomenon that Walker has noted with certain very compatible couples. (He and Timothy do not look in the least alike.)

Mr. Engstrom, in a deeper voice, says almost exactly what his wife has just said. "So glad you're here, but we have worried how you'd feel about the ways we've changed your house. Well, what can I get you to drink?"

Knowing himself to be already too stimulated for drink, Walker opts for club soda, which is produced, and the three of them settle down to small talk—surprisingly easy, for Walker, with these strangers.

Most of his mind, however, and his vision are absorbed in taking in that familiarly shaped and vastly changed room, a change that he would not have believed possible: if it has become a little dowdy, it also has been made—Christ! the impossible—*comfortable*.

Not sure that he will be believed, he tries to say as much to the Engstroms. "Actually," he says, "I quite like what you've done. It was always so cold."

As they are responding, in a pleased, accepting way ("Well yes, it was a little chilly, those lake winds"), a fantastic thought comes to Walker, suddenly, which is: these are the people, the parents, he dreamed of and longed for, as a cold child, in this house, in his galley bedroom, all those years ago. It is as though once more Lucienne has responded to an unspoken dream, or wish, and he is flooded with gratitude for the magic and the kindness of her intuition.

Somewhere in the house, even, there is music playing—

not Althea's despairing, brilliantly unresolved chords, but what must be a record, or an FM station: a Mozart quintet. The music stops, and at that moment steps are heard in the hallway.

"Our son Paul." Mrs. Engstrom beams as a tall, somewhat stooped but good-looking, bearded blond young man comes in.

Weak-kneed, Walker rises to be introduced. Smiling, Paul Engstrom says, "I guess I'm sleeping in the room that used to be yours? A sort of ship's galley?"

In a diffident New York way, Walker shakes Paul's hand, and he smiles and says, "Well, actually I guess you are," as, for the second time in his life, in that same room, his whole silly trusting heart rushes out, toward Paul, with love.

To See You Again

Like so many acutely dreaded moments, this one arrived
and passed in an unanticipated fashion: the moment after
which I would not again see my most brilliant and beautiful
student, Seth. I looked up from the group of girl students—
ironically, the ones I had least liked—who were asking me
silly questions; I looked toward his seat, and was confronted
with his absence, his absolute loss.

Considerably older than these kids, and especially, cruelly, older than Seth, I had envisioned quite another scene: I
had imagined and feared a moment at which the students
would recognize, collectively, that it was over, that this was
my last class, the end of my temporary and quite accidental
presence in their lives. They would never see me again, any
of them. At that instant of recognition, I thought, I would
have to smile and say something like "Well, it's been very
nice knowing all of you. I've enjoyed this time at Cornford."

(Of course I would look at Seth as I spoke, but could I
do it with no break in my voice, no catch?)

And what would they all do, my students, including
Seth, I had wondered: would they smile back and maybe

clap? What sort of expression would Seth wear, on that most entrancing face?

But that is not how it went at all. The class—it was in freshman composition—simply ended as it had every day of my time there. Across the campus some clear bells chimed; in the classroom books were gathered from the floor; slowly the kids began to get up and move toward the door. And some of the silliest, noisiest girls gathered at my desk, not to say goodbye or anything so formal, just to be told again what they already knew: that their final papers were to be collected from the English office. And then I looked up to the total absence of Seth.

One of the things I first thought was: If I ever see him again he'll be older. Still handsome, probably, but he won't look quite like *that*.

Seth: red-gold curls, a wild never-combed tangle, curls that shadowed remarkably white unfreckled skin. Narrow green eyes; a small childish nose; and a wide, somehow unformed mouth—a young mouth. And an incongruous, scruffy reddish beard. Just a messy red-haired kid was how someone else might have seen him. Whereas to me: perfect poignant beauty. And what he wrote was extraordinary—weird wild flashes of poetry, flaming through the dullest assignments. At times I considered the possibility that he was in some way crazy, at others the possibility of genius. But how can you tell with anyone so young? He might be, or might become, anything at all. Anything, in his case, except ugly or ordinary.

Not quite anguished—I had had worse losses in my life (I have them still)—but considerably worse than "let down" was how I felt as I began the drive from Cornford west to

San Francisco. To my house, and Gerald, my sad fat husband, a distinguished architect—and my most precariously balanced, laboriously achieved "good life."

Cornford is about forty miles east of San Francisco, near Vallejo, in the tawny, oak-shadowed foothills. It is on Interstate 80, the main east-west thoroughfare; after Vallejo and Cornford, the highway continues past Sacramento to Tahoe, Reno, Salt Lake City, the East. Going anywhere in that direction, and Gerald and I often spend time at Tahoe, we will pass right by Cornford, again and again. Next fall Seth will be there, after a summer of hitchhiking in Spain. How will it feel, I wonder, to drive right past where Seth is, in the fall and following winter?

Or suppose he should move to San Francisco. Kids do, all the time. Just what would I do with him? What, really, do I want of him? I have asked myself that question, repeatedly, at terrible sleepless predawn hours, and have come up with no answer. The obvious ones do not apply.

Meaning that it is nowhere near as simple as sex (Christ! as if sex were ever simple). If my strong feelings in his direction do have an object, it is not the act of love—I find the very idea both terrifying and embarrassing, and oh! how horrified he would be if he knew that I had even, ever, considered that. How old I must seem to him! Revolting, really, although I am in very good shape "for my age." But to him revolting—as I sometimes am to myself; as often I feel that I am to Gerald.

I reread *Death in Venice*, and, with all due respect, I do not think that Aschenbach knew what he wanted of Tadzio, either.

In an earnest way I have tried to see Seth as objectively as possible—to catalogue him, as it were. I began, for whatever reason, with his voice, and right away I was balked. I could not decide whether the sound was high or deep, and I concluded that it is simply young, a little rough. Some softness in the lines of his face might suggest a plump body, but the actual body that I saw in his daily, worn, taut jeans is thin, a thin boy's body; maybe in middle age he will be heavy? I wistfully considered that. His facial expressions, too, are elusive, escaping definition—a shade of defiance, sometimes a slow smile; he is far less ready than the rest of the class to show amusement. A wary, waiting look, perhaps—is that it?

And so I was left with nothing clear, no definitions, only the weight of my own meticulous observations. And his face in my heart.

Spring and summer at Cornford, so near the Sacramento Valley, are hot and dry—a heat and dryness inversely proportional to the cold gray wet San Francisco fog, one set of weather pushing out the other. And the transition from one climate to another struck me as symbolic as I drove back and forth, in May and then in June, between the two areas. The heat of Cornford was like an adolescent summer—urgent, flushed—and San Francisco's cold like middle age. Resignation. Disappointment. Grief.

Approaching the hill where the fog always began, on my last drive home from Cornford, when everything was over, I shivered, thinking of my own, known, familiar life: Gerald, our cold clean flat. And no Seth. Ridiculously, I thought, I can't live without seeing him—what shall I do?

Gerald and I know an older man—considerably older than ourselves, that is: Larry Montgomery. As I crested that hill, for no reason that I could immediately understand Larry came into my mind. And in the next instant I saw that he had arrived there for a very clear reason: Larry is exactly as much older than I am as I am older than Seth. He has what Gerald describes as a crush on me. Larry looks at least ten years younger than he is, trim and tan, with lively blue eyes and fine silver-white hair. A Forties dandy, he hums snatches from Gershwin, Rodgers and Hart, Cole Porter; he wears gold-buttoned navy blazers. His blue eyes widen and deepen, always, when I come into a room. He makes excuses to stand very near me; sometimes he touches me, but in a serious, respectful way.

Once, though, finding ourselves alone at a party, instead of beginning a romantic or even an affectionate conversation, we got into a silly argument—or, rather, he led me into it, baiting me, really. Which, as I thought back to times when I was curt with Seth, almost pushing him out of my office, I now understood: Larry was terrified that whatever he felt would show.

Once I even asked Gerald, though very idly, "What do you think Larry would do if I propositioned him?"

Surprisingly—I had supposed he would laugh—Gerald gave me a serious, considered answer. He said, "I think he would be scared to death, but very polite about how he put you off." I thought Gerald was right; whatever Larry wanted was not an affair with me; a stray motel afternoon with Larry was as unimaginable as it would be with Seth. Larry just likes to see me, to be near me, sometimes—and very likely that is what I feel for Seth, pretty much?

The accident of my teaching at Cornford came about because my friend Amy, who teaches there regularly, was suddenly, between terms, summoned to the side of her ailing mother, in New Hampshire.

"But, Amy, I've never taught," I said.

"It's easy, there're just a few tricks to it. I'll teach you."

"But credentials—"

"Private junior colleges don't much care. They'll be so impressed that you've got a master's—"

"But that was just to stay on in Cambridge another year." To stay on and be with Gerald, as Amy already knew.

"How would they know that? And you got it, didn't you? Besides, Laura, it'll be a good change for you. You need . . ." For a moment Amy faltered at prescribing for my needs, then finished, lamely, "You need to get out more."

However, getting out more was surely among the things that I did need, and partly for that reason I began the twice-a-week drive, back and forth to Cornford College. I began to teach, and there was Seth, in the second row, nearest the door. Red curls, green eyes.

At first, despite the handsomeness that I noted in passing, Seth was simply one among fifteen surprisingly nice, clean young California kids—much nicer and more civil, all of them, than the Cornford faculty, none of whom ever bothered to speak to me, the substitute teacher. However, I had been warned by Amy that this might be the case. "They're incredibly rude," she had said, knowing how thin-skinned I tended to be. I managed not to mind; I told myself that I wouldn't be there for long, and that the kids were what mattered.

The first assignment I gave was a physical description of something encountered outdoors. "You want very simple, specific assignments," Amy had cautioned. "Anything else only confuses them." The papers ranged from the outrageously illiterate to the adequate; they were mostly misspelled descriptions of lakes and mountains, mountain streams and sunsets. But Seth wrote about an abandoned truck, come upon, surprisingly, in a small eucalyptus grove: the heavily stained windshield, the drifts of leaves all over, and their smell. Rotted tires, rust. A dead truck. His style was flat, specific, and yet the total effect was haunting. I, who have almost no feeling for cars, and surely none for trucks, was haunted by this mechanical death, this abandonment. I began to look closely, even wonderingly, at Seth. And I saw that he was more beautiful than I had seen at first, as well as possibly, probably, brilliant.

In fact, as my short time at Cornford passed, my feelings in regard to all my students polarized—as I might have known they would, given my propensity for extremes of feeling. Some fairly silly girls who at first I thought were just that, fairly silly, after three weeks and then four I found intolerably fatuous—the very ones who were to block out my last view of Seth. About one student other than Seth I became enthusiastic: a dark shy girl, who seemed to have read everything, discerningly, with real intelligence. And always there was Seth, about whom my feelings were strongest— were inexplicable, and impossible.

But when I was midway across the Bay Bridge, suddenly the perfect solution to those unruly feelings came to me; in effect I would domesticate them, just as, years back, I had tamed my wild mania for Gerald. Quite simply, I would make him a friend of our family: I will write him a note next fall, inviting him for dinner. With some other friends, of course, maybe people with kids of Seth's own age. In that setting, my own home ground, Seth will seem a kid like any other, perhaps slightly handsomer, a touch more brilliant, but not noticeably so to anyone else, and surely not remarkable to Gerald, my sad, successful husband. And Gerald and I will present one of our best, our most convincing surfaces to the group at large, and especially to Seth: we will portray a very adult couple, stringently amusing: Gerald and generous-to-guests Laura. I'll cook something wonderful. The two of us mildly, fondly bantering with each other.

And after dinner Gerald will say, a little chillingly, "Well, my dear Laura, I do congratulate you on your springtime of patience with the young." And then, "When would you imagine that boy last combed his hair—care to place a bet?"

And slowly, gradually, Seth will disappear from my mind—or Seth as the author of violent feelings will go, to be replaced by the messy kid I first saw, of whom I will never think.

In that good mood, having even begun to plan the menu, I drove into the city and arrived at our house on Edgewood, Gerald's and mine. And I saw Gerald's car parked in front of the house, although it was much too early for him to be at home.

My stomach and heart seemed simultaneously to clench tight. Not out of fear. I did not wonder what was wrong; I knew. One and only one condition would have brought Gerald home so early—a new depression. His depressions are as severe and as invariably recurrent as they are apparently incurable. "My sweet old Melancholia, my maiden aunt, my child, my baby Melancholia," I once heard him say, babbling his way out of the shock treatment that didn't help.

I knew what was wrong, but not why, never why, or why now—and one problem about living with someone who is depressed is that inevitably you think it has to do with you, your fault, although you are told that it is not. And I knew exactly what I would find on entering the house: heavy Gerald immobilized, immobile, on the wicker settee in the entrance hall, unable to go comfortably into the living room, or upstairs to bed. Unable to leave the house, or the marriage, as I have thought that he must, sometimes, want to do.

He has explained to me how he feels, depressed. "As heavy as boulders," he has said. "I can't open my mouth, it's so heavy. Much less move." I can feel what Gerald feels— and can do nothing about it.

And there he was, slumped down, gray-faced, barely looking up as I opened the door and then closed it behind me. I went over and placed a light kiss on his forehead—the lightest kiss—but he flinched, a little.

"I'll call," I told him.

Something crossed his face; some shadow of relief, perhaps. Not hope.

The phone is in the kitchen. As I dialed, I thought, How immaculate it is, this room. How sterile. Could I paint it red? Would that help?

"Dr. Abrams, please," I said to the voice on the other end. "Right now, if I can." And then, "Hi, Ed. It's Laura. I'm bringing him over, okay?"

Passing Gerald in the hall, I prevented myself from touching his shoulder.

Upstairs, I packed his small bag: pajamas, toiletries, a sweater, one change of clothes.

I got him up and through the front door, and out to my car. I drove north this time, toward the Golden Gate Bridge. Marin. The small hospital in Larkspur. Yellow fog lights lined the approach to the bridge, and it was fogged in already—summer fog, gray and billowing between the dim masses of the headlands, and swirling below the bridge, obscuring the dangerous black water. Beside me, as far from me as possible, Gerald sat, heavy as cement and as un-moving.

I turned off the highway, past developments, shopping centers, schools, playing fields, jogging courses and a few small untouched areas of land—rough, with scattered small shabby houses.

Larkspur. The hospital is one-story, white, ranch style. It could be a motel, and there is even a swimming pool in back, for the more mobile, less desperate patients.

And there was Dr. Abrams, Ed, waiting, having recognized our car. Kind Ed, kind enough not to be hearty, or to pretend that this was a social occasion. He knows, too, not to touch Gerald. Gerald allowed me to help him from the car, and then for an instant Ed touched my hair; he must know that I love touching, any gesture of affection.

Although, driving over, I had not been aware of it, had not thought of weather, I now noticed that the day was still clear in Larkspur, a blue summer day, just fading.

The checking-in process was of course familiar, and minimal. We left Gerald in his room, and Ed Abrams and I walked toward my car, and although in a way we like each other, and surely wish each other well, we had little to say.

"Well, let's hope it won't be for very long this time," he said.

"Yes."

Then, remembering some prior conversation, he asked, "How was the teaching? You liked it okay?"

"It went pretty well. A couple of the students were ter-rific."

"Oh, good. Well, all done with that now?"

"Yes. Done. Today was my last day."

"Well, good."

I backed out of the driveway and headed back toward the almost invisible bridge, and the darkened, fog-shrouded city.

In Cambridge, a long time ago, I thought Gerald was so beautiful, so dark and thin, so elegant, so elusive that I used to trail him around the Yard: me, a silly undergraduate with a crush on a future architect who was studying at the School of Design. We had met a couple of times—I had seen to that, quizzing everyone I knew who might know him, and finally coming up with a girl with a brother who knew Gerald. But Gerald hardly had time to speak to me.

But there I always was, in St. Clair's, out of breath from following him on my bike but saying hello; and in Hayes-Bickford, or the Wursthaus. Late one afternoon I found him alone, on the steps of Widener, and with my heart in my mouth I asked him to a dance at Whitman Hall, where I lived. He came late, stayed a very short time and left, with an abstracted frown. But the next time he saw me, standing in his way, again on the steps of Widener, he asked me up for tea, in his room, at Dunster House, and instead of tea we drank a lot of gin, and fell into bed together—for me, the consummation of a major passion; for Gerald, the onset of a habit. I stayed on in Cambridge for a master's in English literature while Gerald finished his degree, and we married; we moved out to San Francisco and we bought and remodeled the house near Twin Peaks, and we had no children. Gerald began to be a considerable success. And sometimes to be sad, then seriously depressed. Recurrently. Ed Abrams says that with age the cycle may well lengthen, and the severity of each attack will decrease. A sort of flattening out of the curve. But age could take forever; I'm not sure I have that much time.

Driving back to the city, across the bridge, I did not think in symbolic terms about my re-entry into dark and fog; I hardly had to, having made that trip from Marin so many times before. I thought about supper, a glass of wine and getting into bed to watch TV, which I don't do with Gerald at home. And in a cautious way I wondered how long it would be this time.

As always, I made it home perfectly all right. But once I was inside, the idea of cooking anything in the impeccable kitchen was so discouraging that I just nibbled on a piece of cheese—a halfhearted graying mouse.

I even thought, in a lonely way, of calling Larry Montgomery, for a friendly conversation, God knows, not meaning to proposition him. But I am not really sure that we are friends.

I washed and got into bed. I turned on the TV, and I watched one foolish thing after another—until, at about ten, a play was announced, with an actress I liked, and so I propped myself up for that.

And then, Seth, there you were. A great deal older, of course, even older than I am now, curls all gone gray but the same narrow, unmistakable green eyes. It was absolutely extraordinary. In the play, Seth, you were a workman, a sort of handyman, which I suppose is one of the things you could become. The actress, funnily enough, was a schoolteacher. After a tremendous, wrenching love affair, you gave each other up, you and she, because you were married, and responsible. But, Seth, the resemblance was so striking that I thought, Oh, so that is how he will look: gray, slightly overweight but *strong*, with a brilliant smile, and those eyes.

I waited for the credits at the end of the play; for all I knew, your father could be an actor, that actor—I know so little about you—but he had another name, and besides, he looked more like you than like a possible father.

In any case, that sight of you was strangely cheering to me. I turned off the TV and contented myself with visions of my own.

I imagined a time when you will really be as old as that man, and as gray—when, much older still than you, I can say to you, "Ah, Seth, at last you begin to lose your looks. Now you are merely handsome, whereas before you were so beautiful that I could hardly look at you." We both will laugh.

And at that time, your prime and our old age, Gerald's and mine, Gerald will be completely well, the cycle flat, no more sequences of pain. And maybe thin again. And interested, and content.

It's almost worth waiting for.

A NOTE ON THE TYPE

This book was set on the Linotype in Janson, a recutting made directly from type cast from matrices long thought to have been made by the Dutchman Anton Janson, who was a practicing type founder in Leipzig during the years 1668–87. However, it has been conclusively demonstrated that these types are actually the work of Nicholas Kis (1650–1702), a Hungarian, who most probably learned his trade from the master Dutch type founder Dirk Voskens. The type is an excellent example of the influential and sturdy Dutch types that prevailed in England up to the time William Caslon developed his own incomparable designs from them.

The book was composed by The Maryland Linotype Co., Inc., Baltimore, Maryland, and printed and bound by The Haddon Craftsmen, Inc., Scranton, Pennsylvania.